MW00964157

Devil in the Details

GEG

BookLocker

Trenton, Georgia

Copyright © 2023 GEG

Print ISBN: 978-1-958878-14-9
Ebook ISBN: 979-8-88531-375-9

All rights reserved. No part of this publication may be reproduced, stored in a retrieval system, or transmitted in any form or by any means, electronic, mechanical, recording, or otherwise, without the prior written permission of the author.

Published by BookLocker.com, Inc., Trenton, Georgia.

Printed on acid-free paper.

The characters and events in this book are fictitious. Any similarity to real persons, living or dead, is coincidental and not intended by the author.

BookLocker.com, Inc.
2023

First Edition

Library of Congress Cataloguing in Publication Data
GEG
Devil in the Details by GEG
Library of Congress Control Number: 2022922158

Sexually Explicit Material

Dedication

This book is dedicated to my boys.
Continue to inspire each other, and
take flight and control of your path.

Chapter 1

The Bayou is a mysterious place, with many myths. Native Americans, over the years, told stories, handed down over generations. Stories that included the Devil.

The Choctaw Indians described one such myth: "The Girl and the Devil." The story goes, he called the girl, and she was unable to resist him, so she pushed the boat toward the spot where he stood. "Come nearer," said the Devil, "so that I can step into your boat." The girl said she could not do so, but she rested one end of her paddle on the side of the boat and the other end on the shore, telling the Devil to walk on the bridge thus made. He started to do so, but just as he reached the middle the girl jerked the paddle and the Devil fell into the water. He sank straight to the bottom of the bayou and never came up. The myth goes that the Devil would later trick women and claim their souls, thus getting his revenge.

June 2010:

The music playing: Marvin Gaye's "Sexual Healing." Dancing erotically, Kennedy felt hands underneath her mid-thigh dress, caressing the inside of her thighs and working up to her firm ass. The soft touch of lips, as they worked in between her legs. The pleasure was intense, Kennedy's mind and body lost. Her lover's hands worked their way up, sliding off the dress and licking her nipples. The lovemaking exquisite. This would be her last night on earth.

The killer brought Kennedy's body to an abandon cemetery. With a shovel in hand, the grave would be like all the others, a resting place for their latest victim. Her parents and friends would never know where she had been laid to rest.

Established before the Civil War, the cemetery included a few Civil War soldiers among its occupants. Called The Sanctuary, abandoned since the 1930s, except for the recent additions over a ten-year period.

The headstones showed their wear from years of weather, numerous hurricanes, or plain neglect. Tucked away ten miles off Highway 61, the nearest main road. You needed to take a two-lane dirt road before reaching the cemetery. Some sixty-five miles from New Orleans, the killer's hideaway, where they visited often, interacting with the young women buried there.

The newest member of the graveyard, a twenty-two-year-old brunette who had been held captive for the last three weeks. Kennedy had started her career as a real estate professional after graduating from the University of Tennessee. A vibrant young woman who explored her sexuality, which ultimately ended her life.

Dressed in an outfit she would have worn on a night out with friends. The headstone only read "Kennedy" with 1988-2010, the year of her birth and death. The kidnapping took place in Nashville, after she had met up with her date. Her friends, at a loss after she disappeared. The only clues: friends believed her date was a college professor.

The numbers and text messages on her cell phone didn't reveal much, except a number from a disposable cell phone, untraceable.

As the killer finished digging the grave, they took the casket from the van and placed it in the grave. Some two hours later the job was done. The sun would come up in a couple of hours, and another young woman would join the killer's graveyard, now numbering sixteen. The van pulled away from the desolate cemetery, with the killer eyeing their next victim.

Jordan Matthews became a homicide detective for the New Orleans police department after graduating from LSU. The youngest homicide detective in the department's history.

Character had become part of Jordan's DNA. A leader both on and off the field. At first glance a rough gruff look not unlike a cowboy from the late 1800's. After Hurricane Katrina, the department struggled recruiting younger officers. He came right out of college, attended the academy, and was hired by the department.

He played football at LSU and became their number one tight end during his playing career. During the later parts of the bowl game in his senior year, he tore his Achilles. The injury ended any opportunity for a pro career. He decided to start pursuing a career in law enforcement, hoping one day to be the commissioner of the department. His house, decorated with LSU gear including the jersey he wore during the national championship game they won in 2003. He scored once, with five receptions for eighty-four yards.

Jordan's father was a longtime detective for the Baton Rouge police department. His uncle and grandfather also worked in the department. The reason he didn't start Baton Rouge was that New Orleans needed help, and he wanted to blaze his own path.

He walked into the office on Broad Street. "Good morning, pup," said one of the detectives sitting at a desk. A nickname the older detectives had given Jordan, referring to his age, all in good fun.

"Did you get your nine hours in?" As the men began to snicker, trying to get a reaction.

"Don't mind them—they are jealous because you are good-looking and talented." Words of encouragement coming from one of the secretaries as she entered the office area.

"Capn wanted me to show you the email from the FBI office in New Orleans. He said it's something you should look at, since you don't have a case." Monic spoke in a distinguished southern voice, one the Northerners made fun of but the locals understood. A lady with a large personality who befriended everyone.

"What is it regarding?"

"The FBI thinks they may have a serial killer or serial kidnapper. Girls from the South only. No one sees anything, no leads from computers or cell phones, just girls disappearing." She continued, "There is a case from 2004 with similarities to some of the others," as Monic discussed the contents of the email.

"Remember the case of the young college student from LSU, who disappeared?" Monic paused, adding, "Her name, Angelica, I think?"

Puzzled for a moment, he thought back to his days at LSU. "I do remember. I met her a couple of times. My roommate's girlfriend knew her well." Jordan grabbed a bottle of vitamin water from the fridge before heading to his desk. The detective's area similar to those of other stations, cubicles with computers and phones.

His mind began to wander, trying to recall the information, the news in the papers and on the internet. Some blamed a voodoo priest, after a couple of sororities teased a priest during a night of partying. Her disappearance, a complete mystery, an unsolved mystery.

As he sat at his desk, he read the email. He thought to himself, *A girl disappears and never seen again.* Did she find her fate that night, was she a sex slave, or did someone kill her accidentally and hide the body?

The FBI requested the detective's assistance; he needed to respond to the email. First, he wanted to research the case by getting some background information. He summoned Monic back into his office.

She would find everything including contact information for the officers who handled the case.

"Hey, LSU." Another nickname used to refer to Jordan.

"We caught a case, gear up," said the thirty-year veteran Markus Jacobs. Markus's nickname, Sarg. He lived his entire life in the Deep South. Having dealt with the KKK, murders, and the changing times, his career soon would end. A Marine vet, from the Vietnam War. No one believed him until he pulled out a picture of himself in Saigon from 1973.

After coming back from the war, Sarg received his degree from Southern University in Criminology. He had been the lead detective for the NOPD for the last twenty years. He endured life's ups and downs. With retirement around the corner, he looked forward to spending time with his wife, kids, and grandkids. They planned on moving to the Panhandle in Florida, closer to the kids. A place where he could wake up late, drink on his back deck, and fish whenever he wanted. He didn't want to move, but with his two children living in Florida, it made sense. The Bayou, however, would always be home.

The two gentlemen grabbed their gear and headed to the car, something Sarg did too many times over the years. Hopefully this would be his last case in 2010, and soon retirement.

Chapter 2

Driving to the scene, Jordan reminisced about what the seasoned homicide detective taught him over the last two years. He encouraged the young detective to be his own man, his own detective.

One valuable lesson Sarg preached: "Sometimes the answer is right in front of you, but you don't want to believe it."

"Heh, Pops, are you ready for retirement?" asked Jordan, looking for conversation on the ride. This would be Jordan's thirtieth homicide case since being promoted to homicide detective.

"Yeah, I'm ready. I've had enough; my time is done," Sarg answered with a sullen voice. His mind and body, ready for retirement.

They rolled up to the area known as District 2, Dumaine Street, the familiar lights, taped-off areas, and onlookers surrounding the area. From the distance the detectives could see two bodies lying on the ground, covered by white sheets.

"What do you have?" questioned Sarg, taking the lead for what he hoped would be the last homicide case.

"Two deceased subjects, one male and one female." The officer continued, "Male subject ID says Jaron Lewis, twenty-one. Female subject's ID says Latonya Jenkins, age eighteen. So far no one has come forward to give us any details."

"Looks like a drive-by. Male, two wounds; female, one, through her head. It's not pretty, Sarg." The officer's voice lowered in tone with each word spoken. Sarg asked the officer to speak louder. After a few more moments, Jordan went to the bodies and uncovered the sheets.

LaTonya's wound went through her cheekbone, taking off a chunk of her skull in the back. The male subject, with two visible wounds, both in the chest.

"What a waste, so young. Why and for what reason?" said Jordan.

"Okay, ladies, and gentlemen, make the rounds, try to find out what you can, interview everyone," barked Sarg, as though he were leading troops back in the day.

A collective "Yes, sir" rang out, and the officers dispersed looking for clues.

In the distance, an older lady came running down the street crying and wailing, in uncontrolled delirium.

Jaron's mother, and for Sarg, an occurrence he had experienced far too often.

"Ma'am, please. Ma'am, help me out here." Sarg paused before continuing, "I am Detective Jacobs. Can you please tell me if you think you know someone here?"

"My son Jaron, I've been told he was shot," said the woman, barely getting the words out her mouth, losing her breath with every word.

"Ma'am, is your son's name Jaron Lewis?" quizzed Sarg, knowing full well the answer.

"Yes," she muttered.

"I am sorry to inform you, your son is deceased," words Sarg spoke too many times over the years.

Jaron's mother lost all control, crying as she collapsed, causing Sarg to catch her before she caused damage to herself. He held her tight, feeling the life leaving her body. The young girl next to her held tight too, trying to console her.

"May I ask your name, and how you are connected to Jaron?" asked Sarg.

"Jaron is my cousin. I'm Destiny," answered the young-looking lady.

"I am sorry about your loss," Sarg added. "Would you mind going with one of my detectives, and answer some questions?"

"Yeah, I'll do that," answered Destiny.

"Don't worry, I will take care of your aunt; she will be in good hands," trying to ease the young lady's mind.

The seasoned detective motioned for Jordan to come over and take Destiny to their squad car to ask her questions. Sarg and Jaron's mother would go someplace a little more secluded.

Both investigators would come to find out that this might be a case of mistaken identity. Jaron, a student at LSU, Latonya, a recent graduate from high school, would be attending Alabama A&M. The day would be long, but necessary to gather information pertinent to the case and solve the murder.

The detectives learned that a black Ford Crown Victoria had rolled up, with one male subject getting out. He unloaded on Jaron and Latonya before getting back into the car. An unimaginable way for two young lives to end.

The next morning Sarg came in a tad later, with Jordan already in the office.

Going over information the officers had gathered yesterday, sitting at his desk, the bewildered young detective said, "Sarg, there's something not right about this case."

"What's on your mind, kid?"

"Talking to the cousin last night, she says some guy confronted Jaron over his girlfriend. But mom says he has been dating his girlfriend for a couple of years, and there is no beef."

"Well, LSU, let's start there. Mom may not know everything going on."

A standard procedure: separate family members when questioning them. One of the reasons they may offer conflicting stories.

"Why don't we go interview the cousin again. Let's dig—we need to solve this case. I don't need this screwin' up my retirement," demanded Sarg.

With his sometimes-soft voice, not indicative of his challenging persona, you knew who was in charge. Jordan made the call, and they headed off to interview the cousin and mom again.

As Jordan and Sarg approached the porch, a large gentleman with a scowl on his face opened the door. "What the f--- yous doing here?"

Without missing a beat, "I'm Officer Jacobs. Unless you got some business here, step aside, son." The rigid tone let the discontented young man know who the boss was.

"I don't give a damn who you—" Before he finished his sentence, a young lady stepped on the porch. "Br'jon, back off."

Br'jon stepped off the porch while mumbling toward the detectives.

"I'm sorry, he is on edge with what happened yesterday."

"I understand, but bro needs to understand I'll put his ass down," sneered Sarg.

"How can I help you?" questioned the younger-looking lady at the door.

"We need to speak to Destiny and Julie. We called earlier." The young lady disappeared for a few moments and returned with Destiny and Julie.

"Again, ma'am, my partner and I would like to extend our condolences," said Sarg with sincerity.

Sarg took Julie, and Jordan questioned Destiny. After forty-five minutes both detectives came together and offered their deep-felt sorrow.

Getting back in the car. "Something is off. She contradicted herself again. I think she is involved somehow," Jordan said, pressing his eyes with his fingers, searching for plausible answers.

Jordan added, "She says her cousin wanted to score some weed, asking her the day before if she knew where he could buy some."

"What's the matter?" questioned Sarg.

"I don't believe her on the weed thing," he continued. "This kid is clean to me."

"From chatting with his mother, she tells me he aspired to become a doctor, volunteered at the hospital. I agree, clean-cut to me," as Sarg acknowledged Jordan's beliefs.

They drove back to the station, without all the facts or truths. Too many questions, with no answers.

Chapter 3

The afternoon dragged on, Jordan reading the additional statements. The revelations between the aunt and niece, contradictory.

His partner walked in and questioned him. "Who do you think is telling the truth?"

"Only Destiny believes he smoked," offered Jordan. "This kid has goals, he's focused, a vision. Drugs aren't in his DNA."

"Who did you interview," queried Sarg.

"His brother and sister both said he was a straight shooter."

"Got a motive?" said a puzzled Sarg, needing more information besides a college student with goals.

"Current GPA 3.8, 1450 on SAT going into pre-med First year at LSU, a 3.9. His brother says Destiny became jealous of Jaron's girlfriend. Not sure it means anything, but something we should investigate."

"I don't know, kid, a little fragile to me."

"I'll keep digging," said Jordan as Sarg left the room for a moment.

Monic came in needing an answer to her question. "Did you read the email?" giving the third degree. "The agent in charge called again."

The agent in charge, Koi Blackthorn. She grew up in New Orleans, her mom and dad, Choctaw and African American. Her name Koi— means panther. She attended the Academy of Our Lady and became an excellent student. An outstanding volleyball player as well. She received a scholarship to attend Georgetown University.

Her upbringing, one of education and sports. Showing her competitive nature from a young age, her career blossomed in the FBI, after graduating from Georgetown. She later received a master's degree from the University of Virginia.

Muscular and exotic looks brought legions of commits and proposals, which she deflected and demanded respect with the threat of violence if you didn't acquiesce. She did not tolerate misogynistic men.

"She is going to call back after 1. You need to answer the call—I'm tired of taking messages you don't answer," demanded Monic.

"Patch her through if I'm here." Before he spoke another word, Monic interrupted, "You will be here, you will take the call, and you will answer her questions."

"Having a bad day?"

"No, not at all. Need some of you detectives to answer your messages."

"I will. I'm involved in this case," adding, "I'm a little stumped. Things aren't adding up."

Sarg entered the room with a wondering expression on his face. Slow and methodical, which made him an outstanding detective. Over the years he instituted rules in his detecting. When he didn't follow the rules, chaos happened.

"Got a call from an informant. Our young Ms. Destiny is a drug dealer. She spent a little time in juvie. My informant tells me she is a player in the dope game."

"I understand what you are saying, but that is not a motive for murder," rang out a voice from behind the partitioned desks.

"No, but she demanded Jaron push for her at LSU. Also, showed dislike for his girlfriend," added Sarg.

Processing the information, Jordan leaned back in his chair. He needed to access Destiny's arrest record. He took a sip of coffee before he typed away on his computer, searching for the records.

In a matter of moments the info came on the screen. Only twenty-two, Destiny, with a sizable rap sheet. Twice pleaded No Contest for transporting with intent to distribute marijuana. *Why kill her cousin? It doesn't pass the smell test. There is another connection.*

"What did you come up with?" quizzed Sarg.

"She's a player. We might need to bring her in," said Jordan.

"There is something else, besides saying no to pushing."

"You think your CI can help us fill in the blanks?"

"Maybe—we are meeting later," said Sarg, finishing the conversation.

The phone at Jordan's desk rang as he came in from lunch. On the other end of the line, the FBI. "Detective Matthews?" said the voice on the other end.

"Yes, this is Detective Matthews."

"This is Special Agent Blackthorn. Did you read my email regarding the disappearance of Angelica Lawrence?"

The agent in charge of the case worked inside the BAU unit, which began investigating numerous disappearances over a ten-year period, with similar evidence.

Jordan answered, "I have briefly read the email."

"We have some leads on a serial kidnapper, possibly serial killer. I'm looking for information on Angelica Lawrence. I heard you attended LSU at the same time she did?"

"I didn't know her personally. We meet a couple of times, but my roommate's girlfriend and her were friends. I'll talk with her. Anything in particular you want me to ask?"

"Basic info would be great—friends, hangouts, etc. I appreciate this. Can we meet on Wednesday around 10 a.m.?"

"I don't see why not." They both hung up. Their lives would be linked forever.

Reading the email, the detective unlocked the files that Agent Blackthorn had sent over. The disappearance of Angelica baffled friends and family, along with the police. Jordan remembered the posters as well as the vigils held in her honor.

One week turned into two, then a month, and before he knew it, students would mention the disappearance from time to time.

He reached out to his old roommate, Dylan Patterson. "Dylan, this is Jordan. How have you been, bro?"

"Jordan, long time. How are things in the Bayou?" Dylan had been drafted by the San Diego Chargers and became an All-Pro DE. The two men stayed in touch only by email recently.

"Things are good. Did you hear about my promotion?"

"Yes, congratulations."

"How is the year looking?" said Jordan, asking about the upcoming season.

They talked for a couple more minutes about the season, before Jordan asked, "Can I ask you a question? Does Brittni stay in touch with Angelica's family, and can I ask her a couple of questions?"

"She does stay in touch with the family, and if you call back around three our time you can speak to her," answered a befuddled Dylan. "What's this about?"

"The FBI is looking into the disappearance, and I am gathering information for them, with the chance the local police missed something." The two men soon hung up.

Thinking about days gone by, Jordan walked over to the window, thinking about how the parents handled the disappearance of their daughter over the years. Had they given up? What about her friends? Did anyone think of her as she became a footnote in history? Jordan had never thought about Angelica since the time of her disappearance.

Chapter 4

The year 1966 brought about changes for blacks in America, but not quick enough for those who had just graduated high school. Sarg enlisted in the Marines in 1966, knowing full well he would be drafted. His family couldn't afford college, and the best way to afford it was through the GI bill, of course. His first task, survive Vietnam.

After being promoted to sergeant in the fall of '67, before the Tet Offensive in 1968, his platoon shipped out to Hue, the Imperial capital of Vietnam. Vietnam had been fighting a civil war since the '50s, first with French involvement and then the Americans. This was his first command, but not first deployment.

"Do you think we will see any combat?" a kid questioned him, a private from Jefferson City, Missouri. Young and green, like most of the combat soldiers sent to Vietnam. They were typically poor and uneducated. Sarg needed to deal with the youthfulness.

"Kid, don't wish for action. It's not like the movies," answered Sarg.

"I want a chance at getting into combat," said the kid, showing his excitement.

"Stay focused on the job at hand. I don't need to be sending your mom and dad a letter after you've been killed," said Sarg, getting angry with every word.

At 4 a.m., with Sarg sleeping in his bunk, calls from headquarters came in. The VC was attacking Hue. The Marines mounted up and headed into Hue, not knowing what they might be walking into. From a distance they heard gunfire. As his group entered the city, they came across four dead civilians, pieces of their bodies all across the road, a gruesome sight.

Barking out orders, calm and collected, like an experienced officer might, Sarg shouted, "Bowers, get the .50 caliber on the other side of the road to protect our flank."

"Roger, Sarg," answered Bowers.

"Henderson, keep a lookout across the street. Lewis, Gullock, and Jones, I want you guys to run across the street. We will cover your side, and you cover ours."

"Give us some covering fire," answered Jones.

"Ready, go." The men opened fire, which allowed the men to run across the street.

A machine gun placement, perched on a rooftop, kept the Marines pinned down. They would need to knock it out before advancing. With HUE city officials not allowing the Marines to use heavy armor, this fight would be street to street, hand to hand.

"Knock out the machine gun with grenades," yelled Sarg.

He watched as Jones performed admirably, getting shot once in the left arm, before getting within striking distance of the machine gun. Jones tossed the grenade right in the middle of the machine gun bunker, killing all three NVA. Retreating, a sniper killed Jones, shooting him in the head, his body falling in slow motion to the ground. Sarg ran to him and pulled him behind the wall with the others. The first man he lost, but not his last.

Gullock received a devastating wound not long after, taking his last breath. "Tell my wife I love her."

Before the fighting finished, three of Sarg's men lay dead. The fighting continued long into the night, until reinforcements arrived. The streets were littered with dead bodies, or pieces of bodies, both civilian and military. The VC on this day suffered an enormous number of casualties.

During the Tet Offensive, his platoon lost six men with twelve wounded. The one that depressed Sarg the most, the kid from Missouri; he had gotten separated from the unit. They found his body two days later, half of him gone, his face unrecognizable. He would never forget the kid. His whole life in front of him snuffed out on the streets in a foreign city. The war itself did not make much sense to Sarg. A civil war—let the Vietnamese fight it. Young men dying in combat took a toll on those who survived. The waste of men and resources would be hard to explain when writing letters to the next of kin.

Sarg arrived back in Saigon in 1972, a dangerous place for American soldiers with the war clearly lost. The sergeant's current mission, conducting covert operations by gathering information on insurgent activity. Although not an officer, his superiors wanted him to be a part of the intelligence teams. His talent and abilities proved vital to the Marines and the success of their operations.

Even though the United States stopped military ground operations, they still performed other duties inside and outside the country. Sarg was detailed with the duty of gathering intelligence, and turning the intelligence over to the South Vietnamese army.

Meeting with a lieutenant in the ARVN, South Vietnam's Army, Sarg spoke in Vietnamese, "How are the weapons coming in?"

"The VC built an underground system. They bring the weapons in at night," said the slender gentlemen. The ARVN officer, a double agent.

"When will the attack begin?" quizzed Sarg.

"Not sure of the date, the Cong don't want another Tet. They want to make sure there are enough weapons and insurgents in place before the military moves in."

"Work on finding logistics, so we can squash this before they overrun the country."

"My contacts trust me only to a degree," he continued. "They believe I'm ARVN, but working for them."

"Who is your contact? I need their name."

The lieutenant gave Sarg the name, and the future meeting place. He demanded more information about the meeting: How many would show up, any protection detail, how long would the meeting last? He feared being set up, which was the reason for asking for explicit details.

His antenna was on high alert, after one of his colleagues had been kidnapped, tortured, and hanged in the streets. He trusted no one, including some Americans. With the U.S. demanding the withdrawal of American troops, his only true mission was to get everyone out alive.

"I expect you to contact me tomorrow," warned Sarg.

"Don't worry, I will deliver the VC on a platter."

The two men departed; the traitor would soon discover Sarg's genius. He retreated to headquarters; work needed to be done.

"What do you think?" asked Captain Harrow. A tall, portly man, his father had fought in WWII, and his grandfather in WWI.

"I'm going to follow him tonight, set up the sting."

"Who you want with you?"

"Give me Johnson, Lang, Binh, and Dung."

"Roger that. Any ideas on who the contacts are?"

"Some, but we will arrest them all tonight."

"Sarg, are you sure he is playing both sides?" Harrow continued. "I have received confirmation he is ARVN's number one agent."

Why would the captain question the Sarg's judgment? If he were white, would he receive the same grilling? After his buddy's decapitation, he made it his mission to kill all those involved. Dealing with subtle forms of racism in the military was unfortunate, but to question him at this time put his life in danger.

"He's a double agent, *sir*."

"His intel leads to nowhere. My informant tells me he has outed operations in the past including Sergeant Richards." He paused for a moment before raising his voice. "I'm taking the son-of-a-bitch down, *sir*."

The captain sat for a moment, scrunched his chin, unsure of the resolve. He said, "Make sure you have the proof."

The captain dismissed Sarg, who saluted without receiving a return salute.

"Joker, are you in position?"

"Donald Duck," said Sarg, speaking in Vietnamese before asking if both Bonnie and Clyde were in position. A couple of reasons for Sarg's rapid promotions, his natural leadership, and his ability to speak different languages. From a young age his mother taught him French, Spanish, and Creole. He learned Vietnamese after his first tour in Nam.

The group continued to monitor the situation. What they didn't know, Sarg had a mole in the group, someone he trusted, and someone passing along intel, both dependable and brave.

"Everyone set. We go in sixty seconds."

"Roger."

"Joker and Donald, stay sharp. Anything comes out besides us, light it up."

Breaking in the door, seven members of the ARVN. The back room contained seven members of the VC and regular army. Everyone inside would be arrested without one shot being fired. Sarg got his man.

He would later learn, all the prisoners were turned over to the Phoenix project, a CIA operation, but first, he interrogated the saboteurs. All the interrogations took place at headquarters, with each interrogation taking place in a different room.

The mole, escorted away from the others. Her name, Ly Dimah, her first name meaning Lion, which fit her personality. She infiltrated the group, knowing if they found out her true identity, they would kill her.

"What did they discuss?" quizzed Sarg.

"Danh, wants to attack the central government. He is getting pressure from up north to finish this," she replied.

"Any ideas on when?"

"Three weeks, but nothing finalized. You guys interrupted before we finished."

"I didn't want anyone to escape—you are too valuable to us. If they found out you are working for us, you would be hanged," snapped Sarg.

By 1974, the fall of South Vietnam imminent, Sarg left the country to finish his tour in the States. He kept his Vietnam experience close to the vest, occasionally showing pictures or going to reunions with old buddies. The exposure to war followed him for the rest of his life. Ly, young, beautiful, and determined, would be granted U.S citizenship after leaving Vietnam. They would later marry after getting back to the States.

Chapter 5

Before the detectives met the CI, Jordan wanted to do a little research on Angelica's case. He didn't find much and hoped Brittni might fill him in later.

Sarg asked, "Where is LSU?" as he entered the room.

"I think he went to the records room," one of the other detectives answered.

"There you are. What are you doing in an hour?"

"Not much—a little research. What's up?"

"My CI wants to meet; we are picking her up off Lafayette."

"No problem. Did she say anything?"

"She will fill us in but wants to meet in person before she tells us anything."

Scratching his forehead, concerned with what his CI might provide, Sarg trusted this particular informant, and he benefited from her intel on numerous occasions. Her confidential information led to numerous arrests, and in one case helped prevent a bank heist before it happened. He made sure he took care of her, paying her exceedingly well.

The two officers headed to the meeting place. A little small talk came about during the ride. As they arrived Sarg instructed Jordan to pull over to a bench near the coffee shop.

"How are you, Jan'nell?" Sarg extended a friendly hello to the CI with a handshake.

"I am doing great, Bull Dog," she replied, using the street name for Sarg.

"Want anything to drink? My treat, and then we can take a walk if you'd like."

"Please, ice coffee."

"How about you, LSU?"

"I'm good, sir," replied Jordan.

They entered the coffee shop all together, in the better part of town. She lived in a more modest middle-class neighborhood in New Orleans. Jan'nell's connections made her a valuable information source. After losing her mother and grandmother to violence, after Hurricane Katrina, she decided it was time to make New Orleans a better place and became a confidential informant for the police. On two occasions she turned in her own relatives.

"What do you know about the murders from the other day?" quizzed Sarg.

"Destiny is moving loads of smoke. She is getting it from Mexico," she said. "She wanted a larger foothold at LSU, and Jaron became the meal ticket. He said no." She sank her head.

"How does this equate to murder?"

"Jaron told his girlfriend, and she threatened to go to the police," she answered.

"A risk for snuffing him out." Sarg, rubbing his face with his hand, verbalizing a thin accusation.

Sarg took a drink of his coffee, "There is something more than pullin' a Nancy Reagan?"

"What is a Nancy Reagan?" asked Jan'nell.

"Just say no to drugs, from the '80s."

"Oh, real old school, like pre-flight," laughing at her own joke.

"Yeah, whatever, girly. We need more than this. Who is her supplier?"

"The Garza family."

Jordan chimed in, "We've had a couple cases from their murderous ways, one dud with no legs or arms when we found him."

"Raul Garza. Is working on distributions into universities and colleges. He wants networks in every college or university." The detectives left with more questions than answers.

After getting back to the office, Jordan wrote some notes while pondering the information CI had presented. If Garza wanted to overtake school distribution, a large undertaking, with his resources it was doable. The question: Why put a contract out on a kid who said "no"? A big risk for a player like Garza.

Chapter 6

The detectives retreated to the office. As Jordan sat at his desk, a call came from an unrecognizable number. "Hello, this is Detective Matthews."

"Hi, Jordan, this is Brittni. Dylan said you may be looking into the disappearance of Angelica." Her voice quivered. After all these years the loss of her friend, very emotional.

"Yes, the FBI contacted me because she attended LSU. They are looking for someone to do some research."

"How can I help?" quizzed Brittni.

"I can't remember the specifics about what happened the night she disappeared."

"She told me about meeting a friend for drinks. Never gave me a name."

"Anything alarm you?"

"I think she planned on spending the night with her date, but wanted to keep it from me." You could hear anguish in Brittni's voice. She continued, "I should've pressed her harder on giving me a name."

"Where did they find her car?"

"In the parking lot of a grocery store in Prairieville. Didn't make sense, where they found the car."

"Did you tell the police this?"

"Yes, every word. They were idiots. They didn't care. They figured she got herself hooked up in some drug deal gone bad because she smoked." Brittni raised her voice to show her frustration with the police.

"Do you remember the detectives' names?"

"Yes, Boone and Johnson, clueless assholes. They had the gall to call her a slut to my face."

"I'll try to find and question them."

A little pause preceded the next question. "What about your thoughts on her possible date?"

"Remember Professor Calkins? A sleazeball always hitting on the girls, the ones with lower grades. She struggled in his class—maybe I'm grasping at straws."

"I do remember him, and every semester he would try to hook up with two or three of his students, according to rumors. They excused his behavior as a horny professor."

"I believed he should be questioned again about the disappearance. She said she planned on going to his house, talking about grades and graduation." She finished the sentence with a long sigh.

"I figured they questioned him?" Jordan asked.

"They did. He gave them an alibi for the night, I guess. What I don't understand is how the university continues to employ him."

"Needed evidence, I guess. Plus, what girl is going to come forward knowing they traded sex for grades?"

"I agree, but something should be done."

"Anything else you can remember?"

"A secret admirer. She got flowers like three days before, and placed them on the counter, but again wouldn't say from whom."

Brittni paused. "She kept her sex life a secret; I didn't care what she did."

"I'll contact the officers and see if I can come up with something more."

"Her parents live in Biloxi—the number is 228-900-4321. Give them a call. They may be a little angry after the lax investigation— please understand," cautioned Brittni.

"I'll do that. In the meantime if I have more questions, I'll give you a call, okay?" he said, trying to reassure Brittni he would stay on top of it.

"Thanks, Jordan. Please find her—I miss her so much."

So far no one offered anything of substance for the FBI, other than lots of questions to a puzzle. An odd case: A girl disappears, a professor with a history as a predator, a possible ex-boyfriend or acquaintance, and little evidence. Well, at least he could provide background info for Agent Blackthorn. He wasn't sure where it would lead. The FBI needed a gopher, while not tying up their resources. Jordan became the gopher.

Time to call the Baton Rouge police department. "Hello, this is Detective Matthews with New Orleans homicide. I'm looking for a couple officers, Officer Boone or Officer Jackson. Are they available?"

"Officer Boone is available. We have three Officer Jacksons. Do you have a first name?" asked the secretary on the other end of the line.

"Officer Boone will do. Can I speak with him?"

"I will put you through to his number."

The two officers spoke for over twenty minutes, speaking in general terms about the case. They agreed to meet the next day and go over more specifics. Homicide detectives don't get days off, but tomorrow would be a scheduled day off, and a drive to Baton Rouge.

The drive took around an hour. As he pulled in, a place he entered numerous times when his father and grandfather worked with the department, Jordan walked through the front door and asked for Officer Boone.

After a couple minutes Officer Boone came down the hallway. Tall, overweight, and cocky he wanted nothing to do with this case. "I'm Officer Douglas Boone." He stretched out his hand, shaking Jordan's hand in the process.

"Hello, Officer Boone, I'm Detective Matthews. Nice to meet you."

"Why don't you follow me to my desk?" The two sat at Boone's desk.

With the case file in hand Jordan asked, "Is this a copy of the case file? Can I take this copy?"

"Yes, and yes, but I'm not sure it will be helpful. The girl is a runaway or got caught in something that contributed to her disappearance."

"How so?" grilled Jordan.

"Well, she did a lot of drugs. Second, a little loose if you know what I mean." The smirk on Boone's face irritated Jordan.

"Her roommate says she smoked pot, nothing more."

"My partner and I thought she snorted cocaine."

"Your basis for this is?"

"There isn't one. Intuition, gut feeling, real police work."

"I like to look at facts," said Jordan.

"That would be the reason so many murders or disappearances don't get solved in The Big Sleazy," as Boone started to laugh.

"I think I need to excuse myself, because the only thing keeping me from knocking your block off is explaining to my captain why I let you live."

Jordan got up to leave. Officer Boone followed him down the hall for a little stretch.

"What's your deal? Why do you care about some slut?"

The detective's demeanor flipped to rage. He quickly turned around and went after Boone, who tried to back up. At six-three, 240, quick, and agile, Jordan lunged with his hand around Boone's neck and threw three punches before being subdued by other officers. Four officers would be needed to pull him off the bloodied officer. After thirty seconds he composed himself.

"Thank these men because they saved your ass. If I see you in public, I'll kick your freakin' ass into your next life."

"Hey, hey, hey, listen to me, listen to me. I've got you, let it go. It's not worth it, not for this asshole," said the man talking to Jordan, Braxton Davis, a fourteen-year veteran of the force.

"I'm calm, I'm calm, let me go, I'm calm," as Jordan peered at Boone with searing eyes.

"Damn, big dog, you are still rocked up." Jordan looked at Davis in bewilderment.

"You know who I am?'

"You played tight end at LSU, won a ring, you were the man," said Davis.

"I'm Jordan."

"Yeah, yeah, sure. Hey, why don't we take a walk?" as the two sauntered down the hallway, with Davis gripping Jordan at his elbow, guiding him.

"What ever happened with the NFL thing?" asked Davis, trying to make small talk. A seasoned investigator, and interrogator, talking became natural for the detective.

"My Achilles blew out. The damage was too extreme to be able to play in the league."

"Listen, we all want to kick the crap out of Boone."

Before Davis finished, Jordan stepped in. "I'll cut that son-of-a-bitch up in pieces and throw him in the bayou."

"You aren't the only one who wants to beat the hell out of him. Listen, from now on if you need something call me. I'll find the answers for you, and you won't need to talk with Boone."

"That works. Sorry about the mess I made."

"No problem—we will take care of it. You wanted to take his head off." Davis continued, "What's this about anyways?"

"A missing girl from LSU. The FBI contacted me and wanted me to gather some background information on her. They think there is a serial killer somewhere in the South, so I'm following leads." By this time Jordan had calmed down.

"Listen, give me her name and I'll do the digging," said Davis, his curiosity piqued from a previous situation. His family had gone through the experience of a kidnapping in the late '90s, his cousin never found.

Chapter 7

The next day, both Jordan and Sarg began sifting through information, making calls about the Garza family and looking into Destiny's background. Facebook, other social media, anything they could find that would help with the case. Jordan found something interesting on Facebook. Destiny and a couple friends had made a video of dope, money, and guns. The video showed her laughing, and rapping about her riches—not a motive for murder, but interesting.

"Sarg, got a video of Destiny and some of her friends. Lots of drugs, money, and guns."

"Maybe a cause for a warrant for narcotics, but not murder," he continued. "But a tool to put some pressure on her."

"I'm thinking maybe we should look into some of her close confidants, maybe put some pressure on them as well."

"Absolutely. What do you think about bringing 'Jonsee' in, to help with some research, etc.?"

"Sounds good." The two forged ahead looking for clues and ways to crack Destiny or her clan. The murder of her cousin headed to her doorstep, but the detectives needed facts, not innuendo.

Every day Sarg liked to take a walk, rain or shine, a habit he ingrained into his daily life. It became a spiritual, relaxing exercise. On this date, however, he wanted to take Jordan with him, a mentor walk.

"Jordan, let's go for a walk."

"Okay, sure," said Jordan, who knew Sarg liked to walk alone. With the request, even if it was out of the ordinary, you don't say no to Sarg. On this day he wanted to go for a ride, then walk along the Mississippi, down to Crescent Park.

"Get in the car, please."

"Where are we heading?"

"Crescent Park. I'm looking for a little change-up."

It took fifteen minutes to get to the spot. Walking along the Mississippi River provided a tranquil effect.

"Letting you know, I have the utmost confidence in your abilities. You are a hell of a detective," Sarg divulged with a reassuring voice.

"I know. I feel sometimes I need more experience."

"You don't. There are things you will pick up on, and other attributes you have. You will know when someone is lying to you; like with Destiny, you smelled it from the start. Your work ethic, and propensity to look for answers, are unmatched."

"Thanks. Wish we could spend a couple more years together, to learn more," said Jordan.

"You will do fine; remember I will only be a phone call away." They walked for a little while without saying a word.

Jordan revered Sarg, a legend in the NOPD, war hero, covert operator, and at all times a gentleman, no matter the situation, or regard for how someone else treated him.

"There are a few rules—maybe I'll put it in a frame for you. My laws to live by."

"They are as follows:

- Be a gentleman
- Console family members, no matter what
- Everyone is a potential killer
- Everyone is a potential lair

- Sometimes the answer is staring at you, but you dismiss it

"The last one is very important for this reason." Sarg paused for a moment before continuing. "We are human, with human emotions, or biases for or against someone. This can cloud our personal judgment— don't allow it," finished Sarg.

"These five laws will be all you need, because they cover everything, and if you f up I can still kick the crap out of you."

"Yes, you can, sir," as they chuckled.

With his old-man strength, you didn't challenge Sarg. The two men decided to sit on a bench along the river. A normal late summer day, temps in the low 80s, very little wind, a pleasant day. They sat for minutes, enjoying the sun and peacefulness, before Jordan's cell phone rang.

"This is Detective Matthews." The caller wanted to speak with the detective regarding the recent murder of Jaron. He provided vague intel but wanted to meet with Jordan. They both agreed to meet in a couple hours.

"We need more evidence on Destiny—keep pressing," said Sarg.

"I agree. This meeting might provide more answers."

"We should probably get back to the office."

Chapter 8

Elena Katrinov, born in the Ukraine, moved at age nine with her parents to the States in 1992. Full of life, she loved living in America. After graduating with a degree in marketing from Georgia Tech, she settled in Birmingham, Alabama, finding a job with an ad agency, which provided booklets and pamphlets for smaller colleges and universities. A talented designer, her company appreciated her talents.

Two weeks earlier she became introduced to someone at a local hangout. They decided to take a cruise to the Cayman Islands, Cancun, and Key West before the ship returned to Tampa. The connection with someone older did not hold her back from a chance at enjoying the cruise. She thought this would be a good chance to get to know her new friend. On the third night of the trip, they became intimate with each other. Her new lover, charismatic, intelligent, and extremely sexy. She would learn more about her lover, a professor, a scholar, an author of numerous books, who worked with the FBI from time to time.

Early evening with dinner and drinks starting the night off. Light conversation, and a few drinks, led the two of them to lose all ambition, "Would you like to dance, Elena?" asked her lover.

"I'm a little uncomfortable in front of others."

"This day and age no one cares, and if they do, so what," said her lover, trying to alleviate what the onlookers might think. They danced a few dances together, grabbing each other by the hips. Elena loved the touch, the attention. After a couple of dances, they sat back down and ordered drinks.

Her lover leaned in and whispered in her ear, "You are so sexy and hot."

"You make me feel at ease," gazing into her lover's eyes. Before she could resist, they kissed, locking lips for what seemed like an hour. She couldn't pull away from the soft and luscious taste.

"You like?"

"Yes, you taste delightful," Elena smiled.

"I would like to dance more, if you would like?"

"Me too—not yet." They continued to chat and enjoy each other's company for the next couple of hours, occasionally touching each other in a seductive way.

An hour later, "Would you like to head back to my room or yours?" asked Elena's lover.

"Can we go back to mine?"

They headed to her room, with the sexual tension running through her body, a fairy tale, her bearings being manipulated, her desires uninhibited, her body quivering with pleasure.

She opened the door to her room, with her lover walking in behind her. Feeling hands running underneath her dress, exposing the sexy lingerie. They kissed before taking off each other's clothes.

"You are beautiful. I want to make tonight unforgettable." The kissing went from gentle to biting the lower lip gently. The two of them took each other's clothes off with Elena's lover licking her nipple gently before working their way down and tasting her.

They made steamy, passionate love for over an hour. Elena would be brought to the brink of orgasm before her lover slowed down. A special and perfect night, one she would never forget.

Jordan's phone rang at 5:30 a.m. He didn't recognize the number—who would be calling this early?

"Detective Matthews, this is Agent Blackthorn. We have another disappearance. Can we meet you in your office?"

"What time?"

"Thirty minutes," pressed Agent Blackthorn.

"Okay, I'll be there."

Jordan walked into the office, one eye open and the other still sleepy, working on his second cup of coffee. A little more alert, he grabbed the case file of Angelica Lawrence. During the weekend, he looked it over, finding nothing out of the ordinary, but he also thought the police did a shabby job looking for her.

With a purpose, Koi walked down the hallway. A smart-ass officer named Fredericks chimed in with something very sexist. "You got some assets I wouldn't mind inventorying."

"Jerk-wad, the only shot you have at me is if I'm dead," snapped Koi, with a scowling glance, one of disdain for having to respond.

"Fredericks, you say another word and you will be brought up on sexual harassment charges—do you understand?" the strong language coming from Sarg.

"Hi, Sarg. No need to protect me. I can kick his ass, and embarrass him in front of his momma."

"Yes, you can, but he needs to understand that I don't tolerate rude behavior."

"I'm looking for Detective Matthews," asked Koi.

"I'll take you to him."

"How are you, Sarg?" Koi continued. "Heard you were retiring. I'm sure you are ready, but talent like yours is hard to replace."

"It's time. How are the kids and your parents?" asked Sarg.

"They are fine. Are you having a retirement party? Mom and Dad would love to be there."

"I'll let you know. Here is Detective Jordan Matthews. This here is Agent Koi Blackthorn."

Sarg paused for a split second. "She is a personal friend of the family."

"Good morning, Agent Blackthorn."

"Glad to meet you. Can I call you Jordan?"

"You may," replied Jordan.

Both Koi and Jordan sat down with Jordan, spreading the case file out over the table in the conference room. He proceeded to inform her of his findings, which didn't amount to much.

She read different notations along with information the Baton Rouge police had written down. The case file, less than helpful.

"I haven't had a chance, yet, to call Angelica's parents. I planned on calling them," explained Jordan.

"That would be helpful. You said you knew one of her friends?"

"I did. We spoke on the phone the other day. She didn't provide much. Sorry for the lack of evidence."

"Believe me, there is something here, and when we find it, we will understand the reasoning behind the kidnappings," answered Koi.

"You said you have another missing person case, possibly tied to this one?"

"Yes, we think a twenty-seven-year-old woman is missing from Birmingham. No one has seen her for five days."

"Any more details?"

"Agents are asking questions and looking through her computer, phone, etc.," said Koi. "We think based on some findings the kidnapper and the victim may have met in Louisiana."

"Okay. Anything else that would tie her to the area?"

"Nothing of substance." Koi started asking about Jordan's background, telling him about her association with Sarg and how their families went back many years. She disclosed how she worked out of the New Orleans FBI office. They talked for ten minutes before saying their goodbyes and promised to stay in touch with each other. Koi went to find Sarg and offer her congratulations on his future retirement.

With a cup of coffee in hand, Sarg walked towards Jordan. With a concerned look on his face, he sat down without speaking a word for the moment.

After ten minutes he expressed, "If the Garza family is connected, we need to tread lightly. They are ruthless." He then added, "I can't fathom Destiny is anything more than a lead dope dealer."

"I think there is something more, some deep-seated hatred or another motive for this killing." Sarg leaned back in his chair, pondering their next move.

Chapter 9

Back at her office, Koi went over notes from the investigation. With her thoughts dominated by her daughter's volleyball game later, she hoped for no interruptions while reading the material.

"Did the NOPD come up with anything of substance in the Lawrence case?" questioned Agent Cattrell as he walked into her office.

Dionte Cattrell, the director of the New Orleans office, had worked for the bureau for fifteen years, the last seven in New Orleans. Dionte and Koi showed each other the utmost respect, which did not exist in the early days of women agents.

Married with three kids, he thought of Koi as a younger sister, protecting her even though she didn't need protection, and not because she carried a gun.

"I haven't had a chance to go over the case files completely, but according to Detective Matthews the Baton Rouge PD didn't look too extensively into the case."

"How can you not work a missing person case?" questioned Cattrell.

"They thought she took off on her own or got mixed up in prostitution," Koi snapped back.

"Easy, I'm on your side."

"Some men have no business in law enforcement."

"What do you think of Matthews?" Dionte asked, grinning at Koi with a playful smirk.

"What do you mean?" demanding an answer while back scrunching her left check. "Are you stupid or something?" with a tone of disbelief as she raised her voice.

"Good-looking dude, football hero, carries a gun, fits some of your criteria for a man."

"Did you send me over there with those intentions?" frowning at Dionte as if to say, *I'll FIND MY OWN MAN, THANK YOU VERY MUCH.*

"Listen, being a football hero doesn't impress me, and second, I don't need you finding a *man* for me."

"I've been talking to Mom and we agree, you need to find someone. You are getting too ornery—she says you need a man."

"I love my mother, but you and her need to stay out of my love life."

"Reading cheap novels isn't a love life," said Dionte, not letting it go.

"Drop it, okay?" demanded Koi.

"Okay, see me after you check out the files. I'm also sending you up to Birmingham to find out what you can."

"I know you are looking out for me, but trust me, I'm okay," said Koi, knowing Dionte looked out for his sister.

"I think life would be cool if you found someone. The girls want you to find someone."

"What makes you think this?"

"Well, Kinta says she would like a dad." Koi started to tear up.

Her husband left and wanted nothing to do with her or the kids. The pain from the abandonment never left. Her focus, her girls, and her job.

With the help of her parents, the kids were in good hands, where she could focus on the job if needed.

The pain is still in her heart, from the past.

Dionte came over and hugged Koi. "I know your ex hurt you, but love is the best when it's right." Dionte added, "Kendra and I share things, playfulness, conversations, things couples share, amazing."

"If I find the love you two show toward each other, yes it would be something I long for. But listen, if you try to set me up with a cop again or anyone else, I'm going to kick your balls into your mouth." Koi smiled as she walked away. Dionte didn't doubt her ability to inflict pain, as he reached down and adjusted his stuff.

Around 5 p.m. Koi headed out to her daughter's volleyball game. She was immensely proud of her girls, Kinta and Osika. The kids, smart, determined, and helpful around the house. The girls often talked about not having a dad. Their grandfather took on the role of father figure. On some nights the eleven-year-old, Osika, would lay crying in Koi's arms at night, wondering why her father had left.

The school, the same one Koi attended. She pulled up to the school and walked into the gym. The distinct sounds of fans, moms and dads, screaming for their daughters. Her disposition, on the other hand, remained quiet during games. She never yelled at her daughters, the refs, or coaches, preferring to remain anonymous.

Kinta, a natural athlete like her mother, muscular for a fourteen-year-old, and taller than most her age.

"Hi, Mom, Dad. Where is Osika?" as Koi kissed both her mom and dad on the cheek.

"She is outside in the playground with some of her friends," answered her mom. "There are a couple of moms outside."

"How was your day, dear?" questioned her dad.

"Okay. Tough case, few clues."

"You will catch him," consoled her father.

"Can we talk about this later, please?"

The father, Choctaw and African American descent, not an odd combination in this neck of the woods. Her mother, Choctaw, brought discipline, including spiritually. Dad expressed on more than one occasion, "I'm along for the ride."

The games, exciting, as Kinta's team won 3-2. She played a large part in the team's victory.

Proud of her daughter, they hugged after the game. "I'll take the girls home."

"Okay, dinner will be ready," answered Koi's mom.

"I'm starving."

After dinner Koi helped the girls with their homework. She enjoyed this part of life, spending time with her girls no matter the activity. Once tucked in she went out to sit with her mom and dad, like they did on numerous late nights.

"Thanks for helping out today," said Koi, entering the room, thanking her parents. She always wanted to show appreciation for their help. Without their help life would be unimaginable.

"No problem, dear, she played well," Koi's mom continued, "Is the homework done?"

"Yes, I looked at their grades. Both of them are getting all As."

The girls were expected to excel at school. The idea of being self-sufficient and strong women; in other words, never rely on any man. Her heritage became an important part of her everyday life. She wanted her girls to understand their ancestry, the Choctaw beliefs, and their way of life.

Chapter 10

The next day, a confidential call came in regarding Jaron's murder. The informant said Destiny had ordered the hit on Jaron, and wanted to meet with the detectives in charge. Jordan informed Sarg about the call. This might be a break the detectives needed. One of the benefits from Hurricane Katrina, people coming forward with information on murders. With the murder rate holding steady, NOPD needed informants to solve the cases. The people of New Orleans became disillusioned from the constant crime rate, including murder.

"The meeting is set for 12—work for you?" asked Jordan.

"Yes," replied Sarg.

"Anyone we can put pressure on in Destiny's organization, to help bring her down?"

"This guy named Derron, he is the second in command."

"Let's try to get warrants for phones?"

"I'll take it to Judge Burrows," said Jordan.

After Jordan looked over the warrants for both of the phones, he asked if anyone could run the applications over to Judge Burrows. He believed the warrants would produce evidence, which in turn would lead to arrests.

The meeting with the informant took place at a sub shop near Tulane University. As Jordan and Sarg pulled in, with no idea about the informant.

"Sarg, isn't that Derron?" questioned Jordan. He recognized him from a recent photo.

"Yeah, I think so."

"He might be our contact."

"Look sharp, kid, this might be a setup, I've seen it before," Sarg took extra precaution after his days in Vietnam.

"How about if I go inside and you stay here as a lookout?"

"Good idea—stay sharp," demanded Sarg.

Jordan exited the car and headed inside the sub shop. His senses on high alert. Lacking the experience, he relied on Sarg for situations like this. He looked over the place as he entered. Exits, patrons, anything out of the norm. He walked over to the counter and ordered a six-inch sub with a drink. Sitting outside, Derron walked toward Jordan.

"Detective Matthews?" questioned Derron.

"Yes, sir, and you are?" asked Jordan.

"I'm Derron. Can we go someplace else? I don't want anyone rolling up on us."

"Want to go in my car; someplace more secluded?"

"I'll follow you. No way I can be seen in your car."

He followed the detectives to a more secluded spot. As they pulled into the area, Sarg told Jordan to stay alert.

"Okay, what information do you have for us?"

"Well, Destiny ordered the hit. She wanted him dead for two reasons, one he wouldn't push, and two she needed him dead, because he threatened to go to the cops." He lowered his head.

"But killing your cousin?" questioned Sarg.

"She became scared after he learned of her drug empire," sulked Derron.

"How do you know this?"

"I'm her right-hand man. I make sure couriers receive products, we are paid, and we make arrangements for pickups," said Derron.

"You are implicating yourself in this conspiracy?" Sarg raised his eyebrow, questioning Derron's forthright confession.

"Dog, if she can murder her own family, she can take me out," responded Derron.

"How can you collaborate this intel? Did you witness the order to kill her cousin?"

"I witnessed the order. She stared at me with cold eyes—I needed to say something."

"Will you wear a wire or set her up with a drop?" asked Jordan.

"I'm not sure. She's dangerous."

Derron told the detectives he would reach out to them when he felt more comfortable. The detectives returned to their car and watched him leave.

More pieces to the puzzle, but still not enough to get a conviction. Destiny might be dangerous—executing your own family makes you unpredictable—but the puzzle was not finished.

"Wish he was willing to wear a wire," Jordan pressed his hands together, trying to mitigate the nervous energy.

"Me too, but it took a lot of guts to meet us," added Sarg before saying, "We need to make sure he stays alive."

The detectives headed back to the office to check on the warrants. They wanted to do research on Derron, fearing he might be setting them up for an ambush. Why would he give up Destiny?

Sitting down at his desk, Jordan noticed a message from Koi. He would call her later.

"We got the okay for cell phone records, and taps on Destiny's phone," Jordan told Sarg.

"Excellent, and Derron's number?"

"I'll highlight his number."

"Okay. I think we should interview mom one more time, ask her about Destiny."

"Smart. I'll give her a call, set something up." The two detectives spent the rest of the day going over different aspects of the case. Searching past arrest records, or contacts between the police and their suspect.

Wanting to close what he hoped would be his last case, Sarg worked from all angles. Over the years, he had closed 83 percent of his murder cases, a remarkable achievement in a large city like New Orleans. His reputation became legendary all over the world.

On one occasion, detectives from Russia came to visit him in the late '90s, picking his brain, inquiring about his techniques. From his years in the military, he showed patience, which served him well on many occasions. He didn't excuse the racial biases against him, being African American, but didn't dwell on them either. The focus for the seasoned detective: convict killers and console the victim's family.

The day ended with the FBI case on Jordan's mind. Angelica and her family needed closure. The idea of a serial killer murdering her bothered Jordan. Thinking out loud, "Koi is an attractive woman. Wonder if she is single."

Chapter 11

Leaving before the sun rose, Koi headed to her destination, Birmingham, Alabama. The city became infamous during the '50s and '60s for its racial divide. Nicknamed Bombingham, after several bombings at Black churches in the 60's.

Dr. Martin Luther King preached at different churches in the city. The city offered the KKK a safe haven for its members, with little chance of being persecuted for the bombings. Like many cities in the South things changed for the better for the Black community. Still not perfect, however.

The FBI believed twelve different disappearances showed similar modus operandi, from across the South, between the ages of twenty-three and thirty, slender or athletic. All the women working in professional endeavors, and single. Communication would start by text, the phone; however, never traceable because the perpetrator used a disposable phone, or blocked the number.

The women, seduced, and never heard from again. Each victim showed different backgrounds, but all were college educated. One victim, named Kennedy, offered a couple of clues. She told one of her girlfriends about her rendezvous with someone she conversed with online, that she planned on spending the weekend in Baton Rouge.

First stop, Elena's apartment. She planned to meet the lead detective of the most recent missing person's case. The FBI believed Elena to be the latest victim in the case deemed "The Southern Belle Kidnapper Case."

"I'm Special Agent Blackthorn," Koi said, making her acquaintance while approaching the officer.

"How are you? I'm Detective Fallen, lead investigator on the Katrinov disappearance," said Fallen.

"You can call me Koi, Detective," she responded.

"I'm Jason"

"Can we go inside?"

"Yes, we can. Her parents came through a few days ago, as well as our department, and we didn't find anything out of the ordinary."

"What about cell phones, computers, anything she communicated with?"

"Cell phone is gone, but we subpoenaed her records. They should be at my office."

"What about emails?" Koi figured the detectives viewed them.

"The emails did not show us anything which would lead to a suspect, mostly work and friends," answered the detective.

"What about a laptop?" asked Koi, entering the apartment.

"She bought a new one, not much on it. The old one wiped clean and gave it to her sister." Jason gazed around the apartment, looking for anything out of place from the other day.

"The new laptop shows nothing in regard to emails, websites visited, anything which would lead to her whereabouts."

"Will the parents' mind if I take both laptops and allow the FBI forensics team to go over them?"

"Shouldn't be a problem. They are at the station." The detective started to get a little annoyed. *The FBI must think BPD is incompetent,* Jason summarized.

They both walked into the bedroom. The room was impeccable. Clothes hung or in drawers, shoes put away, bed made, nothing out of place.

"Did anyone look for DNA on the sheets or bedding?"

"No, we didn't."

"Would you mind helping me bag them, please?"

Jason, reluctant at first, but eventually helped Koi remove the bedding and sheets. "What do you hope to find with these?" asked Jason.

"This girl, based on what I can tell, wouldn't run off with any man," said Koi. "Whomever kidnapped her, she trusted. She may have spent the night with him?"

"You said she didn't trust any man," questioned Jason.

Before Jason added more, Koi interrupted. "I said someone she just met. Maybe they had a relationship for a month or two, who knows." She wanted to cover every base.

Standing in the middle of the living room looking around, she noticed a bookshelf, for some reason pulling her toward the books. She grabbed a couple of books off the shelf, mostly marketing books, or books describing techniques on how to be successful. She grabbed one more book. A piece of paper fell out, and she reached down to pick it up, an address with the name Lacroix Hotel, the hotel outside Baton Rouge. Koi theorized this might be a clue. At the least some checking would be in order.

"I guess there is nothing more here," said Koi.

As they walked down the stairs a young lady approached them. BPD interviewed all the occupants of the apartment complex.

Wanting to conduct her own interviews, Koi asked, "Young lady, I'm Special Agent Blackthorn. Do you know Elena Katrinov?"

"Seen her around a few times," replied Vanessa.

"Do you recall anything strange, or anyone with her?" asked the detective, probing for answers.

"No, she kept to herself," offered Vanessa.

"Well, thank you. Here is my card. Contact me or Birmingham PD if you come up with anything more, or notice someone odd."

"I will. Sure hope you find her—we are all scared."

"Keep track of each other. Don't go out alone, okay?" Koi said, trying to reassure Vanessa with a calming voice.

Before reaching the car, Vanessa yelled out, "Wait a minute, I do remember someone with her about three weeks ago."

Koi's ears perked up as she walked toward Vanessa. "Go on."

"About three weeks ago I saw her holding hands with this guy, dressed funny, with a long overcoat, hat, sunglasses, odd at the time."

"Would you be able to give us a better description, or provide a sketch artist a description?"

"No, it was late at night, like 11 p.m., and I only viewed them through my window." Vanessa looked miffed as she tried to recall the night in question. "The next morning I didn't see her car."

The case started to feel like rolling a boulder up a hill, each answer leading to more questions.

Back at the station, Jason retrieved the case file from his desk and handed the copies over to Koi. They went out to lunch together, where she asked more questions about the case and if there were any other unsolved missing person cases.

Koi left the city with more questions, few clues, and a defeated attitude, but only for the moment. Being a fighter, she would never quit, until she arrested the person committing these crimes against women.

Chapter 12

Wanting more answers, Koi called her boss to inform him she would be heading to Nashville and speak with Elena's parents. Even though her boss thought making a call would be sufficient, he relented and allowed her to travel to Nashville. The city, a straight shot north, about a three-hour drive.

Reaching out to her father, "Dad, I need to head up to Nashville. Gathering some more information."

"We will take care of the girls," he added. "Anything we can help you with?"

"No, Dad, I appreciate it. Taking care of the girls is a big benefit to me."

"Did you find any clues in Birmingham?"

"We did find a couple clues, but we need to be patient," replied Koi.

"Don't worry about the girls," assured her father.

"Tell them I will call after 9, okay?"

"I will. Be safe. Love you."

"Love you too."

The meeting with Elena's parents, set up for 6 p.m. She would meet the parents at their house. For the next three hours, a lonely drive, nothing but her thoughts. This case consumed many hours, phone calls, and going over countless missing person cases looking for correlation. Stress brought about moments of doubt, but Koi pressed on.

Being a single mom of two girls encompassed lots of time and energy. She thought out loud, "Do I have time for a boyfriend, and how would he react to me living with her parents and two younger girls?"

She couldn't settle for anyone. Guys seemed more interested in rolling in the hay than committing to a relationship. The love her mother and father shared, she longed for. Her first marriage, more like an arrangement than love.

She entered the city. Nashville, a vibrant city, and the capital of country music, offered opportunities for folks in all walks of life. There were areas of lower income, but for the most part the city had seen a renaissance. The nightlife brought many residents to the downtown area.

The Katrinovs lived on Beechwood, not far from Vanderbilt University. Their business, a dry-cleaning store, provided a middle-class life for the family. Elena wanted to venture out on her own, and instead of attending Vanderbilt, went to Georgia Tech.

Koi approached the house, a quiet neighborhood of both younger and older homeowners. She looked around. *A typical American neighborhood*, she thought.

A woman in her twenties, beautiful, slender, with brunette hair answered the door. "I'm Special Agent Blackthorn. Are Sergei and Marina here?"

"Yes, they are. Please come in," said Elena's younger sister, Angelina.

"I'm Angelina, Elena's sister."

"Nice to meet you, Angelina," said Koi. They walked into the living room.

A modest home with pictures adorning the wall of the Katrinovs and their daughters—a close-knit family, based on the pictures.

"This is my mom and dad, Sergei and Marina."

"I am glad to meet you, and very sorry under the circumstances for our meeting." Koi felt at ease, as though the Katrinovs only wanted an explanation for their daughter's disappearance.

"We are glad to meet you," answered Marina. Koi saw pain in their faces. This is one of the reasons she wanted to meet the Katrinovs. The pain, it's real, like Elena.

"I know the Birmingham police department interviewed you, but I wanted to interview you as well. The possibility of something insignificant is actually significant."

She cautioned Sergei and Marina, however. "I am not blaming anyone. Just want to ask a couple questions if I may?"

They spoke for about an hour, with Marina showing their daughter's room. After speaking with the Katrinovs, and investigating Elena's room, Koi came up empty-handed. She thanked both Sergei and Marina and left without any real answers.

Angelina followed Koi to her car. "I didn't want to speak in front of our parents. Can you meet me at Sip and Read, a coffee shop off Blackmore? A lot of students go there to read and drink," asked Angelina, prodding the detective to accept.

"When?'

"Give me ten minutes. I'll tell my mom and dad I am meeting a friend," replied Angelina.

"I'll be there," responded Koi.

Young adult girls typically didn't want to talk in front of their parents about sensitive subjects, usually sexual. Sisters, however, shared with each other. Maybe Angelina would furnish details about Elena's life.

Thirty minutes later, Angelina showed up.

"I'm sorry I'm late, but my parents wanted to question me on some things," trying to catch her breath and talk at the same time.

"Slow down—we have time. Would you like to go inside to get something to eat? My treat. I'm a little hungry?" said Koi, famished after traveling most of the day.

"We can do that."

"Let's go inside," leading Angelina into the coffee shop with a smile. The shop provided all kinds of drinks, plus different sandwiches, soups, and a variety of snacks. A hangout for college students and other younger folks.

They sat down after getting their orders. "What do you do, Angelina?" asked Koi.

"I work for St. Thomas Health Systems. I'm an insurance adjuster."

"I'm sure your job keeps you busy. Do you have a boyfriend?" questioned Koi. She asked leading questions, which offered her the opportunity to ask other leading questions more important to the case.

"I do. His name is Brandon. He is a doctor, works with cancer patients," answered the younger sister, smiling back.

"What was your sister like?"

"She is awesome, the best. She wanted to do her own thing." She paused for a moment before continuing. "She wanted to be her own person. Our family is close knit, but she wanted to blaze her own path."

"What can you tell me about her personal life?" inquired Koi.

"She dated, and no, she wasn't a virgin," added Angelina.

"That's okay. My dad thinks I'm a virgin, but I've had two kids." The women laughed. They understood how dads react to their daughters and their sex lives.

"When she moved away, she kept me in the loop with most of her life, but I think she hid a couple things."

"What do you mean?"

"I went to visit her two weeks ago, saw a text from a woman, sexual in nature, thought she might be bi." Angelina leaned back, showing uneasiness sharing information on her sister's sex life, but she trusted Koi.

"She likes older guys. She dated a couple older guys, and I mean twelve to fifteen years older," adding to the intrigue.

"Any idea about who she may have been dating?" said Koi, seeking more answers.

"Dating a guy but I don't have a name. I think being with a woman, nothing more than experimenting."

"How do you know about the guy?"

"She told me three weeks before she vanished about spending time with a professor." Angelina began to tear up, reliving some of the last moments with her sister.

"Did she say what school, a location for a date?" Koi's instincts told her to ask more questions.

"No, she did say she was meeting him in Pensacola, Florida," said Angelina as she reached for the agent. At this moment they became sisters.

Koi obliged by hugging the young woman; a tough time wondering about your sister. "I got you; I got you," grabbing Angelina tight. "I'll find her—I promise."

"Please find her for me." Angelina lost all control.

The two talked for a while longer about Elena, their personal lives, and how much the family missed her. The heartbreak real, the family pain real. This case needed to be solved. When she left, she cried for almost an hour after getting into her hotel room. Koi's resolve, stronger than ever. She vowed to find this son-of-a-bitch and put the needle in his arm. No one deserved to be kidnapped or killed by some predator.

She called the girls, and talked, before telling them over and over again, "I love you." The night was restless. She didn't sleep much, the case starting to affect her personal well-being.

Maybe the Bayou myth about the Devil was taking hold of Koi.

Chapter 13

The team began to view the cell records of Destiny and Derron. Jordan, with a cup of coffee in hand, headed over to Officer Benson's desk. "How are you this morning, David?"

Officer Benson came from the academy after graduating from Tulane. His quiet demeanor personified his ability to remain calm in tense situations.

"I'm good. Take a look at Destiny's cell records." David slid the records over to Jordan.

"There are numerous calls to and from Mexico. Derron's number shows calls to and from, sometimes ten to fifteen times a day," David said.

"Things are getting interesting," Jordan said, the puzzle pieces coming together. One problem, lack of evidence needed for an arrest.

"I can contact my friend at NSA," David said. "He will find out who the Mexico numbers belong to. If we can connect her to the Garza family, we may be able to put pressure on her."

"This girl is calculated, careful, although killing your cousin is spontaneous."

"She might be getting in over her head," answered David.

"She is unpredictable. We need to get her off the streets as soon as possible," added Jordan.

With a day off, Sarg and his wife planned a day together. She wanted to spend time on a steamboat, having lunch.

Ly had retired a year before from the HUD. She had worked for the people of New Orleans, finding them affordable housing. A job she loved after going through her experiences in Vietnam. Younger than Sarg, but smart. A sense of style fit into the 5'8" frame, a perfect match for Sarg.

She had lost her entire immediate family during the war. The VC raided her father's village, west of Da Nang, killing her family. For some reason the VC allowed her to live. After becoming an orphan, she decided to work for the South Vietnamese government as a spy at age fourteen. She never returned to Nam after leaving.

She encircled her arms with Sarg's as they sat overlooking the Mississippi River. He always said he would never change his life for anything, except the chance to reunite Ly with her long-lost family, thinking of others before himself.

"You know I love you," said Ly, as she winked before kissing him on the check.

"I love you, dear. Be careful—I don't have any blue pills on me," chuckled Sarg.

"I'm sure you don't need any, if I use my magic ways."

"You do bring it out in me."

"You going to miss the job?"

"Some, but like I told LSU, it's time. Time to let someone else be lead investigator. I'll miss the people, but not the death," sighed Sarg.

"We've seen our share of death, from the war to New Orleans. I won't miss the destruction of lives either." Ly squeezed her husband's arm tighter.

"I'm sorry for bringing some of the stress home to you."

Ly interrupted, "I didn't mean you were reclusive or abusive, my dear."

"I know. But some cases, heartbreaking, especially the unsolved ones." Sarg's eyes and shoulders shrunk as though he had failed somehow.

"You are an accomplished detective, with a great career. Don't let a couple cases damper your career or retirement," assuring her husband with words of encouragement.

After graduating college in 1980, he started working for NOPD. A natural leader, with keen instincts, and the ability to interrogate suspects. Oftentimes he would be an arbitrator between the public and the police. With the distrust of the police, he brought the two together.

Hurricane Katrina exacerbated the distrust between the police and the community. Some citizens used the hurricane as an excuse to never return. Sarg asked Ly after the hurricane if she wanted to move.

Her response was vintage Ly. "HELL NO," claiming she had lost one country and this time evil wasn't going to win.

Coming from a dirt-poor situation to a life as a respected detective brought joy to Sarg. His mother, important in his life, taught him self-reliance and the importance of education. He had both book and street smarts; most PhDs couldn't match wits with him.

The kids, on their own, had a sense of pride. Kendra, the oldest, and Trent, both married, Kendra with two kids and Trent one.

At lunch, with the boat ride coming to an end, Sarg grabbed Ly by her hands and asked, "Do you think you would ever want to go back to Vietnam?"

"I've pondered the idea. Guess we think alike," answered Ly.

"You are receptive to the idea?" Sarg asked again.

"Yes, I am. The country has changed over the last four decades. I need to extinguish my demons," as the tears flowed.

"After I retire let's go." Sarg pulled Ly in closer, giving her a kiss. The rest of the afternoon and early evening were perfect. The sun bright, with a slight breeze. A perfect day for lunch, a boat ride, and of course the company.

The duo exemplified the idea: *You can either make your bed, or not; the decision is yours.* The meaning: If your life is a mess, change your life with positive decisions.

Chapter 14

Back at the office, Jordan and his colleagues continued working the Lewis case. Out of the blue, Derron called.

"Detective Matthews?"

"Yes, this is Matthews. How can I help you?"

"Destiny got wind you are looking into her." Jordan sensed the fear in his voice.

Jordan thought for a moment, *There's no way.* "How did you learn this?"

"She yelled your name. She is planning to take you out"

Threats against officers were usually more braggadocious than actual threats. This, however, needed to be taken more seriously, if the Garza family was involved.

The family was well-known for its murderous ways, often cutting out the tongues of their victims and mailing them to the families. A sick and depraved way to teach law enforcement and a tactic that scared many families over the years.

"That doesn't answer the question. Why does she think we are after her?" as Jordan pressed Derron for an answer.

"I'm not sure. I'm sayin' she got the info. I'm scared that if she finds out it's me, I'm a dead man—feel me?" Derron's insistence made Jordan believe he was not acting.

"All right, calm down. Where are you?"

"I'm in a hotel in Gulfport and told her I wanted to visit family in Houston for a few days."

"Does she think you're a mole?"

"Dog, you not hearin' me. You need to come gets me, give me some protection," demanded Derron.

"Okay, okay, stay put. I'll work on things. In the meantime stay alert for anything out of the ordinary. Also, stay in touch with us every four hours, if I don't call you," said Jordan, hanging up.

He gathered the detectives working on the case around his desk. He informed the team that their informant may have been compromised and officers may be in danger. A warning to stay vigilant would be issued, since they were dealing with the Garza family—and Destiny. He sat down to contemplate his next move, then informed his partner. "Sarg, this is Jordan," in a raspy voice.

"What's up, kid?"

"Derron called. Says Destiny put out contracts on our lives. He didn't give me names, but says she knows about our investigation."

"Make sure everyone is aware. Let's kick this into high gear. If this is true, we need to arrest her before they make a move. This is serious, Jordan." Sarg never used Jordan's first name.

"I briefed the entire department—where are you?" questioned Jordan.

"Wife and I are on a boat ride, heading home soon," responded Sarg.

Over the years Sarg had received threats from the KKK, drug dealers, and some politicians. He took every threat seriously until the threat could be judged on its merits.

"Let's stay in touch. I mean everyone needs to do a check-in. Where is Derron now?"

"In Gulfport. Should we pick him up?"

"Let's bring him in, give him some protection," demanded Sarg.

After hanging up, Jordan put things in motion. He called Derron and told him the U.S. Marshals would take him to a safe house, while explaining his calls would now be recorded. He warned him to stay put, no meetings with Destiny or anyone associated with her.

A dangerous time for all involved if the assumptions were true: Destiny finding out about the investigation and ordering hits. Jordan thought about Jaron's mom and the family. Would Destiny take a shot at them or hold them captive?

The rest of the day went off without a hitch. The Marshals picked up Derron and escorted him to their safe house. Jordan wanted a chance to depose Derron more; something wasn't adding up.

"We are home, and found a present, a voodoo doll by the front door," said Sarg on the phone to his partner, explaining the warning.

"You need forensics?"

"We are making arrangements for Ly to head to the kids. She will stay with them for a few days. I ordered a protection detail for them and Ly," said Sarg.

"Anything you need me to do on my end?" asked Jordan

"No, give me about two hours. I'll be in the office."

With the voodoo warning, and the revelation from Derron, NOPD began working under the presumption that the bad guys were a serious threat.   ⚜

Chapter 15

The next morning, Koi headed straight home from Nashville—no need to go into the office. She wanted a shower and something to eat, to kiss the girls, and to unwind after a long two days. The case, exhausting, but she needed to push through, with so many young women disappearing.

Sharing her home with her parents made things easier. She owned a five-bedroom home on the outskirts of New Orleans.

The FBI offered her a chance to work out of the New Orleans office. She jumped at the chance to return home, after spending her previous assignment in Dallas.

With no one home, a chance to unwind with a glass of wine. She put the case files on the kitchen table and poured a glass of wine, before taking a long, hot shower. She meditated in the middle of her bedroom floor with the phone off, listening to the sounds of a waterfall, a moment of quiet before everyone else came home.

Koi's mom walked in looking for her daughter, finding her in the kitchen. They approached each other, giving a kiss on the opposite check. "How was your trip, dear?"

"Not too bad—got some useful info. Where is Dad?" questioned Koi.

"He ran a couple of errands and said he would pick up Kinta after her practice, if you want to stay here?" said her mom, reminding her about her daughter's volleyball practice.

"That would be fine. Would you like a glass of wine? I'm going to pour another," as Koi started to pour a second glass.

"Sure. Are we drinking for a special occasion, or is this a relaxing glass?" questioned her mother, grinning. Mother and daughter having wine, a chance to unwind, heaven at the moment.

"This one, a relaxing drink," Koi continued after pouring her mom a glass.

"After this case, I think, I am going to take some time off before Christmas. The girls will be void of games and practice. I'm thinking of heading to the Cayman Islands. You and dad are welcome to come along." Koi sat down at the counter.

"I think you and the girls need this trip alone. Get away for a few days."

"This will give us a chance to unwind before the new year," said Koi.

Both girls, active from an early age, with sports being a big part of their lives. The unfortunate part, they didn't play the same sports, which meant the seasons overlapped.

Her father exuded a strong personality, an excellent athlete in his day, playing football and basketball and running track. He attended Grambling University, playing for legendary coach Eddie Robinson. After college, he became a teacher, and later superintendent of New Orleans schools.

Koi's mom, Catori, met her dad at an education conference. They worked well together and would often be seen at city functions.

Before picking up the girls, Felton spent his day volunteering his time as an officer for the HBCU Foundation. He worked on fundraising and scholarships.

Pulling in the driveway, Osika, darted from the car, recognizing her mom's car in the driveway. "Mom, I missed you," the excitement evident.

"I missed you too, dear. How did your day go?" As Koi embraced her youngest daughter.

"Good. I got an A on my history test. My softball team has practice on Saturday—can you take me?"

"I'm so proud of you, and yes, I can take you Saturday. What time is the practice?" asked Koi.

"I'm not sure. Grandma, what time is my practice?" questioned Osika. Catori answered at 9 a.m.

"Mom, can you help me with my homework?"

"Yes, I can. Let's do it now." They sat down, with Osika opening her bookbag. As she dumped everything out, a letter fell out of the bag.

Koi quickly snatched the letter as her daughter tried to keep her from reading it.

"Mom, no, please give me the letter," demanded Osika.

Koi opened the letter, which asked if her daughter liked a certain boy. Along with an invitation to a birthday party for the boy. Koi understood these days were coming sooner rather than later. Her girls, attractive, with boys chasing them from here to eternity. She asked Osika about the letter and the boy. Was he nice? Did he play sports? How does he treat the other kids? They talked, with Koi agreeing to allow her daughter to attend the party.

Not long after the homework session she received a message regarding a missing person, a woman from Lexington, Kentucky. Her name, Izzy Caulmet. She disappeared two years ago, believed to be a part of the current serial kidnappings/murders. A business card from a professor at LSU, turned up in Izzy's jacket. The name read Professor Heath Calkins, LSU.

Chapter 16

Professor Calkins, a fifteen-year tenured professor at LSU, and second in command in the Criminology department. A graduate of the University of Texas, hired right out of college by a community college near LSU. While teaching, he received his master's degree from LSU, before being hired by the school.

The students loved his teaching style and charisma, while also keeping his classroom light, which allowed thoughtful discussions, as he delivered out praise to students when they brought insightful comments. A dark secret, he liked dating students. The administration ignored the rumors.

One reason the administration never questioned the professor was his ability to bring money into the university. He traveled across the world promoting LSU, and fundraising.

When he attended LSU, Jordan took three of his classes. Today, however, he would be questioning the professor about Angelica. The two men would meet in Calkins's office, after his 1 p.m. class.

The professor and Jordan, over the years, had lost touch. With his career, Jordan became focused on his professional life.

"Professor Calkins, how are you? You look great," extending his hand to shake the professor's hand.

"I don't do handshakes. We've known each other a long time. Staying in shape from what I can tell." The two men sat in their respective chairs. The professor continued, "How is NOPD treating you? Congrats on your promotion to Homicide, detective."

"Thank you. Promoted over a year ago. I work with a first-rate group of detectives and support personnel. A mix of newbies and veterans," answered Jordan.

"How are your mom and dad?"

"They're fine. Dad is retired, as you know. Irritates mom to no end—she says he needs a job," said Jordan.

"Professor, I wanted to question you on a former student here. I'm doing some legwork for the FBI on a missing persons case," changing the conversation to Angelica.

"Sure, no problem," said Professor Calkins.

"Do you remember a student named Angelica Lawrence? I think she was a Psychology major, but took one of your classes?"

"She completed a couple of my classes. I believe her aspirations were to work for the FBI," answered Professor Calkins, trying to remember the actual classes she took. Attractive, smart, and well liked, she often took part in class discussions.

The disappearance remained on the minds of those past and present associated with the university. LSU staff did not want the case to be a stain on the university.

"The police came and asked about her, viewed my notes and grades," said the professor, offering information about the police investigation.

The police investigation uncovered that she did like to party. She liked to drink, but never drunk. She liked to smoke pot, but never drove her car after doing either. Outgoing, an extrovert, loves to laugh, loves her animals, and always in a good mood. She carried a 3.4 as a Psychology major, with a minor in Criminal Justice. Her goal: to be the first female director of the FBI. Her studies were important to her, and her partying lifestyle never interfered with her goals.

"Do you recall any rumors or theories as to what happened?" said Jordan.

"One theory, kidnapped by a sex slave ring. The police learned about her meeting up with someone, but no names."

The two men continued to talk about various subjects related to the case, and possible students who may help in the investigation.

Before Jordan left, Professor Calkins suggested he might want to speak with another professor.

"Do you remember Dr. Denkins?" asked Professor Calkins.

"I do. I took two of her classes," offered Jordan.

"Well, she may have some insight since Angelica took one of her classes at the time of her disappearance."

"Thank you, Professor Calkins. I want to thank you for everything, including what you did for me as a student here," said Jordan.

Jordan went to find Dr. Denkins.

Dr. Denkins, a well-established professor with an impeccable reputation. Another of LSU's well renowned faculty. She wrote numerous papers on behalf of the university. Her studies dug deeply into the behavioral sciences.

The office door was slightly open as Jordan approached. It looked like he would catch a break. He peeked into the office, noticing hundreds of books on the shelves, some on the same shelves since the day she moved into her office.

LSU garb, some family photos, and photos of vacations the professor had taken over the years. A definite thrill seeker.

"Dr. Denkins, may I speak with you for a moment?" asked Jordan with a pleasant smile.

"Oh my God, Jordan Mathews, you get your ass in here," said the excited professor.

"So, you do remember me?" said Jordan.

"Of course I do. Still have the pic of you catching the TD pass in the championship game," as Dr. Denkins pointed to the photo hung above some of her photos on a side wall.

She asked, "I need you to autograph the picture before you leave. Can you do that for me, pretty please?" At forty-two, a knockout, in excellent shape. Students both male and female fantasized about the doctor.

"Of course I can, but are you sure? I wasn't the best player on the team. I am humbled." Jordan sat down after signing the photo.

Sitting down they talked about families, life experiences, and their careers. Jordan recognized a couple of Denkins's books she wrote. The art of capturing murders had evolved over the years. DNA, forensics, and video cameras benefitted law enforcement. Her books became must-reads for law enforcement agencies.

"Dr. Denkins, may I ask you a couple questions about a missing student from here, Angelica Lawrence?" asked Jordan.

"I do remember her, an excellent student," offered the doctor.

"Is there anything else you can tell me about her? I'm helping the FBI with some background information," said Jordan.

"No. She had a bubbly personality, engaged with class discussions," sitting in her chair trying to refresh her memory.

"What do you think happened to her?"

"No real concrete theories, but one thought, the killer is an LSU student. They hooked up one night, and for some reason he killed her."

"You think she is dead?" asked a puzzled Jordan, the case only a missing person's case at this point.

"After years of experience, this tells me she is dead," offered Dr. Denkins. The revelation stunned Jordan for the moment before he continued with more questions.

Ten minutes later they both said goodbyes to each other.

Chapter 17

Koi, sitting at her desk going over photos of the disappeared girls. She put together a timetable, eliminating anyone she thought didn't fit the profile. With a solid twelve missing persons cases, she needed to do her own investigating.

The first case, a young lady named Cami Douglas from Richmond, Virginia. She had disappeared in 2002, at age twenty-four. The investigation showed a long-distance romance, but no one in her family, or friends, ever met him. She worked for the State of Virginia forensics team.

No phone numbers, emails, texts—how could this be? These highly educated women knew better than to go with strangers, one or two, maybe, but twelve? The answer was in these pages, but escaping the FBI, at the moment.

The morning went into early afternoon, before Koi's stomach started to grumble. Drinking coffee keeps you alert but doesn't cure hunger. In that moment her cell phone rang. On the other end, Jordan, the NOPD detective, with information.

"Good afternoon, Detective, how are you?"

"Hello, Koi. I'm doing well and you?" answered Jordan. They talked for a few moments about the information, or lack of. The interview with BRPD offered nothing.

With Koi's hunger not dissipating, she asked, "Jordan, have you eaten lunch yet?"

"No, I've been going full-bore all morning on the murder case. Where would you like to meet?" hoping for something more than fast food.

"Let's meet at Murky Waters."

"Perfect, see you in twenty," said Jordan, excited as a teenager thinking this was a date.

He went to inform Sarg about going to lunch, but not with whom he would be meeting. "I'm going to head out for some lunch," said Jordan.

"Mind if I tag along, kid?"

"I'm meeting someone for lunch. Can I give you a rain check?" Jordan, anticipating the next question, conveyed, "No one you know," before he asked for a name.

"You would be surprised, kid, how many people I know," said Sarg, smirking as he answered.

"Her name is Loren," said Jordan, all the while thinking, *Why am I lying?*

"You want to play it that way? Old Sarg is smarter than you think," responding with laughter. "Kid, I have sources all over. You can't hide anything from me. Enjoy your date."

Late last night, Koi called to question Sarg about Jordan. He filled her in about the young detective and thought the two would get along.

Twenty-five minutes later he arrived at the restaurant. Wondering if he should call her, text, or go in. The nerves, uncontrollable at the moment, with negative thoughts creeping in. Is this a date, or is she looking to go over information, and would someone else be with her?

He decided to text her.

She responded, "I'm inside. Come on in."

Jordan's shoulders shrunk, and his mood descended into despair, thinking, *She is seeking info.*

He walked inside like a dejected puppy. Looking around, he spotted Koi in the corner of the restaurant, sitting alone. He sat down across from her. He ordered water and a club chicken sandwich. She wanted fish with rice.

"How is the case coming along?" asked Koi, making small talk.

"Okay. Lots going on, and some contradictions," answered Jordan, before adding, "What about yours?"

"Lots of confusing contradictions as well. These girls are dating someone, but no names, no texts, no phone calls," answered Koi, summarizing the research.

"I talked to two professors up at LSU. They both remembered Angelica, described her as intelligent, always participated in class discussions," passing along the information to Koi while shrugging his shoulders.

Catching killers would never be easy. The ones with calculated attributes proved more dangerous and elusive. He wondered how he might deal with the case, a dozen or so disappearances from different states. This case needed to be solved, and in some weird intuition, Jordan theorized he and Koi would be working together, and solving the case.

"Can you keep a secret? I mean when I tell you something, you tell no one, not even Sarg?"

"Yes, anything you tell me I will keep between us," as Jordan smiled at Koi.

"I think my perp is here in Louisiana, a professor, or a professional of some sort."

Koi folded her hands together and brought them up under her chin, holding up her head while looking Jordan in the eye. A tactic she had learned during her training days. Always look at the eyes; they can give you answers.

"A professor. Are the disappearances centralized during certain months?" asked Jordan.

"No, we believe the perpetrator is a professional," Koi continued. "You need too many resources to be able to do what they are doing."

"Is this a theory or is there evidence? The person may not be from this area, maybe spends certain times of the year here."

"What evidence we possess leads me to believe the perpetrator lives between New Orleans and Baton Rouge. The kidnappings, or killings, are going to continue until we stop it," followed Koi in a stern voice.

They talked over lunch, about their upbringing. Jordan, astonished by Koi's talent on the volleyball court. The discussion turned to family, what their parents did for a living, and Koi's kids. A delightful afternoon, which led to more personal talk between the two of them.

Jordan paid for lunch, and the two of them went their separate ways, for today.

Chapter 18

One week later, a day off for Jordan. He ran his usual four-mile run with some weight training included. The idea of staying in shape appealed to him. Throughout his run, his mind wandered to the information Koi had shared with him. A riddle, encircled within a puzzle, and the joker was winning. His thoughts also focused on the Lewis case.

One thing Jordan admired about his father: he didn't bring his work home with him. Some officers drink, some are violent, and some do both if the day-to-day grind gets to them. Jordan's father never displayed any of those traits.

When he told his father he wanted to be a police officer, his father could not be prouder of him. Times like this he wished his dad would've shared more about his job.

Gratified with his career, being the youngest homicide detective in the department's history, and a chance to learn from a resource like Sarg. He enjoyed soaking up everything the seasoned detective taught him.

As Jordan continued his barbell workout, he thought about Koi and their two recent dinner dates. Older, professional, intelligent, and sexy.

Single at the moment, with close to a year since his last date. Maybe he should give her a call and see if she would like to go out for dinner, or a day on a boat. He finished his workout and headed to the showers with nothing more on his agenda, except some errands.

Taking the next couple of hours to run his errands, he pulled into his driveway and recognized someone on his front porch, Koi. A tingle came over his body, and a huge smile emanated from ear to ear.

Then some self-doubt came in, *Is she here to talk about the case?* No way, she is dressed in a short skirt, hair let out, sandals.

Doesn't look like something an FBI agent would wear on a daily basis. Jordan exited his car while trying to not show the excitement of seeing her.

"Good morning. I almost left, planned on leaving you a note," explained Koi.

"Good morning. I like a strenuous workout on my days off, and I ran some errands," responded Jordan.

"I knew you had the day off—I asked Sarg." Jordan confused; should he walk up and give her a hug? He wanted to be respectful, but she looked *hot*.

"I have the day off and wanted to stop by." Reaching for Jordan's hand, she clamped down and pulled him closer, wrapping her arms around his upper neck and giving him an unquestionable sexual embrace. Jordan could smell her perfume. Confused about the hug and perfume, his mind wandered. *Is this real?*

"I am glad you are here," as Jordan continued to hold her, not wanting to let go. "I wanted to call and ask if you wanted to do something more than dinner."

"Well, yes, but for now how about we get something to eat?"

The two of them broke off the embrace, as Jordan unlocked his door and let them inside.

"I am sorry I showed up unannounced, but wanted to surprise you instead of calling," offered Koi in a soft voice. "I thought about giving up, if you hadn't come home soon," she added.

"I needed to do a couple of errands, banking, oil change, etc."

Jordan asked, "Would you like to sit down for a bit, or do you have something in mind?"

"What do you think about heading down to the French Quarter? There are a couple of restaurants we can choose from."

"Sounds great—let me change clothes. Would you like something to drink?" quizzed Jordan.

"No, thank you," she answered with a smile, which showed her dimples and attractive features.

Jordan walked upstairs to his bedroom, strutting like he had just won the Heisman Trophy. He picked out some clothes, put some cologne on, and went downstairs. His thoughts: *Don't say anything stupid or silly.*

After he came downstairs the two of them talked for a moment about Koi's girls and a couple of other of life's happenings.

Koi said, "Are you ready?"

"Yes, I am," replied Jordan.

She walked over to him, placed her hands around his neck, and gave him a passionate kiss. He was stunned by the unprovoked kiss. *Now what?* he thought. They unlocked their lips after a couple of moments.

"Your lips are soft," said Jordan, showing off a huge smile while holding her tight.

He stood in silence for another moment, before getting the nerve to talk. "It has been a while since I kissed someone."

"A long time for me as well," replied Koi.

The two of them headed toward the car, holding hands like teenagers, Jordan's heart beating rapidly.

"Your heart is beating fast." Koi said. "thump-thump-thump."

"A little. I wanted to see you. I love the kiss, unexpected."

"I can take it back."

"Don't think so," conveyed Jordan.

"By the way, you don't need to get the car door—I can manage. I am my own woman."

Thirty minutes later they arrived at their destination. They found a restaurant on the Quarter, called Muriel's Jackson Square.

"I have two girls. What do you think of kids?" asked Koi as the two of them sat across from each other.

"I always wanted kids."

"Well, my two girls are independent, athletic, and smart," added Koi.

"What sports do they play?

"Volleyball, basketball, lacrosse, and softball."

"Sounds like they are busy girls. What do they think about you dating?"

Koi answered. "They said it's time to find someone. They think I show a little attitude from time to time," the early afternoon sun highlighting Koi's radiant looks.

"You, attitude?" humorously asked Jordan.

"Of course, I can't be independent, but those moments are few," offered Koi, as she winked at Jordan.

The conversation continued over lunch, two of them getting to know more about each other. He explained how the injury had cost him any opportunity for a pro career but he had moved on.

She talked more about her Native American mother and African American/Native American father, things she left out during their lunch date. Her love of volleyball, but her life in law enforcement, her crowning achievement with respect to her personal career. The girls, her pride and joy, and she would protect them with her life.

As they finished their lunch, Jordan asked about her evening plans, and weekend plans. She told Jordan about her daughter Kitna's upcoming volleyball game, and youngest daughter's softball practice.

Light conversation continued on the ride back to his place. The time was 3 p.m. when they got back. He asked if she would like to come in.

Back at his house, he showed her around, the LSU room, the jerseys, championship ring, and different points of his career.

Suddenly she grabbed his hand and whisked him over to the couch. He looked puzzled as she pressed her hands against his shoulders, forcing him down on the couch. She lifted her skirt, straddling him while grabbing his hands and pressing them behind his back, holding him in place, controlling him. She moved toward him, kissing him. After a few moments of kissing, she worked her way down his neck while lifting his shirt over his head. He kept silent, enjoying the moment. Licking his nipple with her tongue, he allowed her to take the lead.

Koi could feel his rock-hard chest and abdomen. Working her way even farther down, until she reached his pants undoing the button, and taking them off to his delight.

Taking him in her mouth, while digging her nails into his thighs. The exquisite pleasure taking him to the top, he forced himself to slow down.

After a while, he grabbed Koi under her shoulders, lifting her up. He stood up and wrapped his arms around her as she followed his lead and wrapped her legs around him.

She said the first words. "Where are we going?"

"The bedroom," he replied.

After reaching the bedroom he took her clothes off, then picked her up, tossing her on the bed, his strength overwhelming her. Jordan grabbed her ankles and spread her legs apart. He worked his tongue on both thighs before he started to work it inside her. He started to lick her; within a minute she began to come. He kept her from escaping his clutches by firmly grabbing her ass.

"Oh my God I'm going to come again!" yelled Koi. "Don't stop!"

She pulled Jordan on top of her. He slid himself inside while holding her down, pumping himself deep inside. A little while later he rolled her over on top, a position where she felt in charge again.

"Damn, you feel so good," said Jordan. He reached around, grabbing her ass, and forced her up and down on him, causing her to come again.

"I want you to come inside me, deep inside," she begged.

"I'm almost there," he answered. She pressed her hands on his stomach and they climaxed together.

Jordan pulsating as he continued to pump her. "You feel so good, don't stop!" she screamed.

He hollered with gratification as he let loose his juices, causing her to scream with pleasure. After a few moments, she rolled off him.

"Wow, I've never done that. Please don't think less of me," she said.

"I will never think less of you. Spontaneous moments make things hot."

"I must have come four or five times," she added. "I don't want you to think I jump from bed to bed, just after getting to know someone."

"I don't." They lay together, touching and occasionally kissing. It didn't take long before round two started. She lay on her stomach as Jordan closed her legs and mounted her from behind. He pressed his hands on her shoulders and lower back, while sometimes going slow, sometimes fast.

Twenty minutes later he rolled off as they both felt the exhaustion and pleasure for the moment.

Chapter 19

Around 8 p.m. Jordan received a call from Sarg. His informant was found dead, mutilated. Her body was dumped near one of the precincts. She suffered immense torture, her nipples cut off, a hammer taken to her hands, smashing them to pieces, and a sign attached to her that read, "F off police this is what happens to traitors." Sarg's voice crackled as he spoke with Jordan.

The next morning at the precinct, Jordan said, "I know you are hurting, Sarg," trying to bring a sense of calm. Jordan continued, "Listen, we will arrest whoever did this, I promise you."

"I apologize—this one hurts. I swear to you, as much as I am about not being a vigilante, if I could get away with it, I would rip these animals from limb to limb." Sarg reached out, putting his hand on Jordan's shoulder.

"Trust me, we will find them, and they will be locked up forever."

"I plan on going to the funeral. I want you to be there, at a distance, surveying the situation. The killers may show up," Sarg added, "Also, keep a close watch and see who shows up. Get plates," demanded Sarg.

Trying to lighten the mood with a bit of news about him and Koi. "By the way, Koi and I went on a date. We had a nice time together, I like her," said Jordan.

"She is a great gal; I think you have a lot in common, with determination being one of those attributes."

"She is very level-headed, and yes passionate, is how I would describe her," said Jordan.

"Don't hurt her. You may find yourself attached to a cinder block and thrown into the Bayou, by her doing, not mine," chuckled Sarg.

Jordan sifted through information on the Garza family, dropped off by DEA. The sheet showed lots of illegal activities and ties to over fifty murders. The photos in the file, the bodies of mutilated victims, some with no heads.

A text came in, from Koi. An instant smile came across Jordan's face. She wondered how his day was going.

He responded, "Not too good. Working on the Lewis case. One of our CI's found murdered, a brutal scene."

"Sorry to hear. Garza family?" she quizzed.

"Yes, making the case more difficult," answered Jordan.

They continued to text back and forth about the case for a few more minutes, before she informed him, she needed to go.

Her last text, "What about drinks later tonight? Say Luxie's around 10?"

"Sounds good, I will be there," replied Jordan.

He went back to his paperwork, again looking for anyone who might help their case. The Garza family wielded political clout in Mexico. They infiltrated parts of the government, with bribes and death threats causing the Mexican government to acquiesce to the family's demands.

A CCN reporter a few years earlier began investigating the family. They found the reporters body tied to the fence at the border near Laredo; his family couldn't recognize him. A week later a bomb went off near the gate corporate offices. CCN discontinued the investigation soon after.

Making plans with respect to the funeral, how surveillance would be conducted, who would follow whom. These were the times Sarg showed patience when investigating a case. He wanted Jordan to learn the same attribute.

The clock read 6 p.m., quitting time, and Jordan anticipated the evening with Koi. He couldn't get her out of his mind. He wanted more of her.

He went home to shower and relax for a bit before heading out. He thought about both the Lewis case and Koi, kind of mixed emotions, work never far away from personal life.

He pulled into the Luxie's parking lot and viewed Koi's vehicle, a couple cars behind him. They both exited their cars at the same time, with Jordan walking over to her, giving her a long embrace. He whispered in her ear, "I am so glad to see you again," as he kissed her.

"Me too, but I am going to tell you, we can't go back to your place after drinks."

"I am on call tonight, and do not want to be interrupted," replied Jordan, while showing his displeasure about being on call.

"The nature of the job, I understand," responded Koi.

After sitting down and ordering, she asked, "Are you off on Sunday?"

"I am, as long as I don't catch a case," explained Jordan.

"I would like to invite you over to my house for a barbecue, if you are interested in coming. Meet my parents and the girls," she continued. "Dad is buying seafood and steaks."

"I would love to come over. What time?"

"Let's try 3, if it works for you?"

"Certainly does. What's your address?" questioned Jordan.

After giving Jordan her address, the two of them continued holding hands across the table while chatting about their college careers. The experiences, working in a team atmosphere. Koi, an alternate on the Olympic team, an experience she will never forget.

They left the restaurant a little after 11.

Chapter 20

With a murder on St. Phillip Street, Jordan arrived at the scene, with the familiar faces, officers cordoning off areas. A crowd gathering with loved ones hugging and crying. When would this nonsense stop? Jordan observed Officer Hendericks, and approached her as he got out of the car.

"Hi, Lattice, what do we have?" asked Jordan.

The paramedics took one victim to the hospital, shot in the stomach, but the paramedics picked up a faint heartbeat. The other victim lay on the ground, covered by a white sheet, blood everywhere including seeping through the sheet.

"One deceased, and one on the way to hospital, in bad shape. The deceased individual, with four gunshot wounds," said Officer Hendericks, looking in Jordan's direction.

"Any idea what happened?"

"No details yet. Officer Brooks and Officer Johnson are talking to the locals, asking questions." Officer Hendericks paused for a moment before continuing, "You know the rule, no snitches in this neighborhood, no one talks," the desperation in her tone, one of despair.

Lattice Hendericks had grown up in New Orleans. Proud of her city, unfortunately a dangerous place, one that offered African Americans little hope or opportunity. According to local legend, God is punishing New Orleans, with hurricanes and murder.

"Have you seen Sarg?" quizzed Jordan.

"Nope, but I'm sure he will be around pretty quick," replied Officer Hendericks.

"Thanks, Lattice," Jordan noticed her tearing up, life beginning to leave her body.

"Lattice, you okay? Anything I can do?"

"I'm okay. Tired of these scenes, death, destruction, utter stupidity. These people need help, opportunity, some damn dignity," barked the young officer.

"Make sure you talk to someone, myself, Sarg, anyone. Don't keep things inside. This job can depress you, okay?" as Jordan tried to comfort her.

"I will. Thanks, Jordan. You're okay for an LSU guy," as they both broke a smile. She had attended Tulane, a rival to LSU in some sports.

The detective walked over to the body, with the forensic investigator looking at the corpse. NOPD owned one of the best forensic investigation teams in the country. Police departments from all over the country came to learn from their techniques. Colleges sent professors to observe the methods they employed.

"What can you tell me, Ablah?" asked Jordan.

Ablah, from the country Jordan, a taller, thin, and attractive Muslim woman. Her parents emigrated from Jordan when she was 3. They settled in Atlanta; her father, a physician, and mom stayed home raising the family.

The NOPD, with the blessing of the mayor at the time, hired a younger, more diverse department of men and women from all ethnic backgrounds. She joined NOPD right after college.

For the young ME, a dream job. Her subjects deceased, she gave them a voice, a chance to tell their story. The two women Jordan came across would be the life of the department in the future.

Lattice didn't take any crap from anyone and would make an outstanding detective someday. Ablah, an accomplished medical examiner.

"Bad, bad all around." Ablah paused for a moment before continuing. "Our victim shows four wounds, the most damaging being right through the heart."

Sarg pulled up, tired, thinking about another senseless murder. The grind weakened the strongest of minds.

For the veteran detective, Vietnam would be the worst, the bodies of fellow soldiers, body parts mangled, or disfigured beyond recognition. *How can we do this to each other?*

He understood how war works, and what enemies do to each other, but fellow Americans killing each other, sometimes for the most minuscule of things, like looking at you in a certain way.

"What you got, kid?" asked Sarg.

"Two vics, one on the way to the hospital, the other here. I'm looking for identification," answered Jordan. He bent over the body rumbling through pockets, looking for anything that might identify the victim.

"Found something," said Jordan.

"His name, Jackson Pendergrass, age twenty-four, lives on Western Avenue." Jordan handed the driver's license to Sarg while he rummaged through his pockets.

"Pendergrass, I think I know this kid's momma; she is an English teacher at McDonogh High School," offered Sarg, hoping her son wasn't lying on the cement. He remembered she had three children, and his son dated her daughter for a brief time.

"Any idea what happened?" quizzed Sarg.

"No, our officers are making the rounds, asking questions," answered Jordan.

"What a waste," said Sarg. He started walking down the sidewalk looking for clues.

Jackson's father had been killed years before, when the kids were youngsters, remembered Sarg. He recalled Kendra remarried, nice guy, family man, stepped in and became a father to the kids, and now this.

Sarg walked over to one of the officers, "Anything Justin?"

"Well, this is Donovan," said Officer Larson. "He says he was sitting on the porch, watching our two vics walking down the street. They were approached by a black guy, skinny, not quite six feet. He goes inside for a couple minutes, hears shots, and comes out. Sees our two vics on the ground, and the other guy running toward Rendon."

"That's it?" questioned Sarg.

"Ya, man, dogs were talkin', didn't think nothin' of their chat. Next thing is they layin' there. I called 911," offered Donovan, trying to explain what he saw. He didn't want to be involved.

"Ever seen the victims or the shooter around before?"

"My mans, I've seen them around, think they hangs out together. Other dude never seen him before," answered Donovan.

"Make sure you get all his info, phone numbers," demanded Sarg.

"I knows you, the big dog, I'm tellin' you, I's got nothing more to offer," as Dovovan looked away, not wanting to make eye contact with Sarg.

One resident who didn't want to be identified by name offered a better description of the shooter. He noticed the shooter a couple times walking up and down the street, though he hung out with another guy a couple streets over.

Still shook-up by the deaths, Lattice informed the detectives that the other victim passed away en route to the hospital. The guy's name, James Jefferson Barnes. They called him "JJ."

Jordan and Sarg talked for another half hour. They wondered if these two shootings may be connected to their other case.

It's the way the Garza family worked to eliminate all loose ends.

Jordan spoke with Sarg, worried about Lattice. He thought she may be struggling emotionally, after having a brief chat with her.

When officers or detectives showed traces of metal anguish, Sarg often invited them over to the house to unload. Listening like a psychiatrist, offering points of view, and making sure if they needed to seek professional help, he would be right there behind them.

Officers seeking psychological help used to be frowned upon. Sarg took a different approach. Better to unload as opposed to letting things explode on loved ones, the public, or on yourself, in the form of suicide. He not only had experienced suicide in Vietnam, but over the years, two officers committing suicide.

Often asked why he didn't go after the chief of police position, Sarg explained, "Not everyone can be the chief. You need sergeants as well. It can be the difference between a smooth-running department, or not."

He summoned Lattice over to him, and they took a slow walk away from everyone. With the angst and desperation in her voice, he showed deep concern. The two of them talked, before he invited her over to the house after her shift ended. She accepted.

He called his wife to tell her that Lattice would be coming over, and would she put out some food and drinks? Ly understood this was one of her duties as a cop's wife, to be supportive not only to him, but those around him. They might save his life one day.

A long night: Jordan arrived home around 7 a.m. He needed to sleep before heading back to the office. While meditating in the shower he wondered, could their cases be connected? He dozed off for four hours, before his alarm went off.

Chapter 21

A cup of coffee and reports started Koi's morning. A young agent named Brett Yukolvich knocked on the door. He wanted to see Koi about some information he had followed up on.

She waved the agent to come in. "Good morning. I bring news on the Katrinov case."

"Give me some good news, please!" replied Koi.

"We found a number from a cell phone our kidnapper used to contact Elena. The number comes from a company that sells phones out of Jamaica."

"How did we come about this information?" quizzed Koi.

"The number is unlisted, with Elena's records showing no trace; however, one of our hackers tracked the number. The number came from a store in Jamaica, which sells untraceable phones. Drug dealers use this outfit a lot, to hide the numbers they use."

"This is excellent. Can I talk to the hacker?"

"Yes, you can. Would you like me to find her?"

"Yes, please, this might be a possible break," said Koi. Brett left the room to retrieve the hacker, Liz Ferguson. The FBI knew the phones were untraceable but hoped the new information would help provide a lead.

Her thoughts wondered, what might the girls being going through—their treatment, possible torture, or other unspeakable acts? An uneasiness came over Koi. This wasn't a typical kidnapper case.

The women were all gorgeous, and smart, which led her to believe the person doing the kidnapping was a genuine con artist. The perp conveyed a sense of trustworthiness, essentially a trap for these women.

About fifteen minutes later, Brett came back with Liz. "Agent Blackthorn, this is Liz. We used her last year cracking the embezzlement case on the Hamas terrorists. They funneled money through an Arabic restaurant, using the funds for operations against America."

"I remember reading your name on the reports, Liz. I'm Koi," as Koi reached out to shake the hacker's hand. Young, brash, and off the wall, Liz's talents, unmatched within the FBI walls.

"Please sit down, and fill me in on what you have learned." Koi extended her hand to show Liz where to sit.

Both Brett and Liz took their seats.

Liz, a twenty-four-year-old hacker whom the FBI found after she hacked into a DOD website. The FBI tracked her down and offered her two choices: one, prison for a few years; two, work for the FBI.

A typical generation Xer, either she wore clothes three sizes too big or very revealing. Comfortable with her body, but she disliked how men looked at her. Beautiful green eyes, nice smile, and purple hair, with a personality to match. The FBI allowed her to smoke marijuana, which curtailed her occasional angered outbursts.

She set aside her anti-government perception after the government hired her. A few friends decided to end their friendship once they learned of her new job.

Solving puzzles became her trait as did breaking into other people's computers. She did this to gather information the FBI used to apprehend and convict criminals.

Her talent became indefensible to the agency, even though her personality could be described as odd. Her superiors thought her talents outweighed her strange behavior; better working for the government, as opposed to working against them.

"You look sweet. Dating anyone?" Liz, bisexual, made no bones about her sexuality.

"Not sure it is any of your business," replied Koi, agitated with the question.

"Don't worry, I'm harmless. Trying to get a lay of the land, what type of person I'm dealing with, since I don't trust uppity ass agents who think they are perfect," said Liz, as she stared at Brett with an offbeat smile.

"Why do you work for us?" questioned Koi while crossing her arms and displaying an expression. *This girl needs her ass kicked.*

"Can't do jail, darlin'. Besides, you geniuses need my help in catching killers."

"Now we've disposed of your biases, what do you have for me?"

The young brash hacker laid things out on the conference type table. She explained about coming across a number she tracked, the number came from a store in Jamaica.

The Hamas perpetrators used the same system when trying to communicate with their operatives in the U.S., which is why she came across this number.

Both Koi and Liz stood together going over the data. Before Liz left, she brushed up against Koi, running her hand over her ass.

Koi grabbed Liz's hand, before admonishing her. "Two things, Liz. I am not into women, and I have a boyfriend. You need to stop with the sexual flirtations," Koi said while raising her eyebrows and voice simultaneously.

"You don't like girls, no problem. I'm a playful sort of girl. No harm, no foul, right?"

"Let's leave it there, and nothing more will be said," added Koi. Liz nodded and understood.

"Thanks for the information, and if you come up with anything more, I would appreciate you letting me know ASAP."

With past experience as a barometer, Koi never thought of getting a warrant through legal channels with the Jamaican government. Jamaica, a poor country that offered sanctuary for all types of criminal activity, with money being funneled to the prime minister and his cabinet. The criminal activity flourished as long as he got paid.

The FBI, with Koi being the lead investigator, pushed for arrests of certain Jamaican government officials three years earlier, when she discovered girls from all over the world were being kidnapped and taken to Jamaica. The officials sold the girls as sex slaves to rich buyers from all over the world

The evidence impelled the FBI to seek a warrant with the Jamaican government. The government relented, offering up the minister of National Security, a fall guy. The Jamaican authorities said they would handle the prosecution.

After a heated exchange with her superiors, the FBI explained they would not go after the prime minister. Koi thought about quitting but decided men would not push her away from her career.

U.S. government officials made a deal for the security adviser and received information regarding three minor drug dealers. In Koi's mind, the FBI traded drug couriers for the young girl's lives, and this didn't sit well with her.

Koi needed a break and decided to text Jordan. They texted back and forth for around ten minutes, with an occasional provocative text. He sent a pic of himself shirtless.

Koi responded, "Seen it, no biggie, lol." She found something she never experienced. Someone who would listen and stick by her side when she needed him.

Walking down the hall to visit Agent Jorgenson, originally from Norway, he came to the U.S. and enlisted in the military. He left the military after ten years, to pursue a career in the FBI, after becoming a U.S. citizen. His colleagues liked his demeanor, and stick-to-itiveness. Calm and deliberate, and searched for meaning, or reasons why certain criminals did what they did.

"Do you have any follow-up information on Elena?" asked Koi, looking for answers and more pieces to the puzzle.

"Not yet, Ms. Blackthorn," answered Gabor.

"I need some answers, Gabor," demanded Koi before continuing. "We need to stop this before the next girl disappears. I understand you are methodical, but please understand the urgency."

"Ms. Blackthorn, I want this guy caught like you. I want to make sure we don't overlook anything."

"I know, Gabor. I'm lost, like this guy is toying with us, and it's going to continue."

"We will find him; I promise you." Koi left the room. She needed Jordan more than ever.

Chapter 22

Sunday arrived, for Jordan, an extensive workout and run. During this time his thoughts were provoked by the other afternoon with Koi. Her smell was still emanating from his house. Excited about meeting her parents, daughters, and hoping everyone would hit it off. He finished off his sets on the weights, and now off to run four miles.

Koi woke up early before the girls and went downstairs for a cup of tea. Her dad in the kitchen. Felton sat quietly at the table, reading the paper.

"Morning, Dad," as Koi walked over to her father, giving him a kiss on the cheek. Being a close-knit family meant a lot to her. The girls benefited so much from her mom and dad, and their influence.

"Morning, my little panther, how did you sleep?" Her dad liked to call his daughter "little panther" when others weren't around.

"Slept good, Dad, thanks."

"What do I need to do before your man gets here?" said Felton as he continued to look at his morning paper.

"Dad." Koi paused while staring at him. "Is this the way you are going to be?"

"Mom says I need to be a perfect gentleman, so I don't screw this up for you, because you may not get another chance, if this one runs for the hills," said Felton, still downplaying the interaction between him and his daughter while turning the page of his paper.

He continued to rib his daughter. "I can't say you are on the rebound, so I need to make sure you catch this one," laughed Felton.

"Oh, my Lord, Dad, you think I'm desperate? I have plenty of suitors. This is going to be a casual afternoon lunch, okay?" responded Koi to her dad's needling.

"I'm not saying you can't attract a guy, wondering if you can keep them, my little panther," said Felton, as the oldest daughter came down the stairs.

"Grandpa, why are you nagging Mom. She is beautiful," said Kitna, protecting her mother.

"So, says Nashoba," which means wolf in Choctaw. "Can you give her some dating advice, since she has been out of the dating game for some time?" conveyed Felton, looking at his granddaughter while shrugging his shoulders.

"Be careful of the wolf and the panther, they may pounce," answered Kitna, giving her mom a high-five.

"Well, you two are ganging up on old grandpa. I'm trying to help you catch and keep a man. Like fishing, if you keep throwing them back sooner or later you run out of fish," said Felton, as he leaned back in his chair and reached his hands for the sky with a goofy smile, which he gave his daughter from time to time.

The banter between the two on occasion continued until Felton gave in by way of facial expressions such as the *I don't understand you* look or the *I give up* look.

"Men are the ones with issues. They need to follow a woman's lead, and the world will be perfect," said Kitna, as both her and her mom started a "volleyball dance" while razzing Felton.

"So, this is how it's going to be? When the two of you come to your senses, old grandpa will be here for knowledge."

He sat for a moment thinking of his next sarcastic comment, which he soon followed up by saying, "Women may run the world, but men fix it after it breaks down."

"Only because men break it," snapped Kitna while shaking her head in a smart-aleck manner.

"Okay, okay, I can see where this is going. I need to take myself out on the back patio."

"You can stay, but we understand if you feel a little defeated. Kitna, are you hungry, and how about you dad?" asked Koi, as her dad headed to the back patio to enjoy the morning sun, and his paper.

"Whatever you make is fine with me."

Koi and Kitna worked on breakfast, chatting about school, the week's upcoming games, and whether she needed a new dress for the homecoming dance coming up the following weekend. Koi said they could go dress shopping tomorrow night if things worked out after practice.

With breakfast made, Koi made a plate for her dad and herself before walking out back. She wanted to chat more.

"Here is your breakfast, Dad," as Koi placed the plate in front of him.

"Thanks, dear, greatly appreciated," said her father as he put down his paper.

"This guy who is coming over, a football player, police officer? What do you know about him?" quizzed Felton.

"He's a good guy, Dad. Respectful, determined, athletic, and wants more for the city."

"You got all this from a date or two. I'm guessing you know more about him than you are letting on?" asked an inquisitive Felton.

"Yes, Dad, we've been chatting, texting," Koi said. "There is a kinship, a bond between us. Feels right, Dad," trying to calm her father's fears.

He nodded his head in agreement and continued eating his breakfast. Koi didn't date much since her divorce, and the guys she had introduced to her parents hadn't left a favorable impression.

Fortunately, her career started to take off, which afforded her no time to date, as her father described, "vermin."

"Do I need to do anything before he gets here?'" asked Felton.

"No, Dad, the grilling will be a big help."

"Mom and I can go for a late morning walk?"

"Yeah sure, no reason why you can't," answered Koi.

"I'll go see if your mom is up. Thanks for breakfast, my little panther," as Felton pushed himself away from the table and took his plate into the kitchen.

After finishing his workout, Jordan headed home. He decided to call his mom and dad. They still attended every LSU game, and the day before LSU beat Florida. He called his mom and dad after taking a shower. They talked about the game, and current events in their lives.

Curious, Jordan asked his dad a question. "Dad, a quick question for you?"

"What you got, son?"

"You ever deal with any missing persons cases in the '80s or '90s? Where college students or young women disappeared, and were never found?" Jordan paused for a moment before filling in his father. "The reason I ask, remember Angelica Lawrence? The FBI is looking at her case as a serial kidnapper case," said Jordan to fill in some blanks.

"This one girl, linked to a professor at the community college, but the professor produced a solid alibi," said Jordan's dad. He added, "We never found the girl, though."

Jordan asked, "Remember his name?"

"Not him, son, but her, Bailey Denkins. Pretty thing. She liked the ladies."

Jordan's mom chimed in over the speakerphone, "George." She added, "Sometimes I wonder if you did any policework."

"What about the girl's name?"

"Last name Hindo. Denkins worked at BRCC. Need me to retrieve the case file?"

"No, I have a contact at the department, but if I need your help with anything, I'll ask. "They extended goodbyes before hanging up the phone.

Wow, thought Jordan. Dr. Denkins linked to a disappearance and being a lesbian. Of course, Professor Calkins suggested Dr. Denkins might be gay or bi. Jordan shook his head. *Can't be.*

The girl in question, a runaway more likely. Bailey Jenkins would never be involved in kidnapping or murder. Jordan saw her with guys. He also remembered hearing rumors of an affair with one of the state senators from Louisiana. The senator in question, married.

Ah, Louisiana politics, never a dull moment.

Chapter 23

The next couple of hours dragged on. Jordan, forgot about his cases for the day, instead focusing on his barbeque date with Koi's family. He got dressed and headed out to her place, a thirty-minute drive.

He walked up to the door and rang the bell.

A young lady answered. "Mom, your boyfriend is here," yelled out Osika.

"Osika, you couldn't let him in without yelling?" admonished Koi.

"Hi, sorry, they are following my dad's orders, being difficult," Koi explained to Jordan while opening the door.

"No problem." Jordan stepped inside and gave her a hug.

She smiled at him while softly running her fingers over the back of his hands, "Don't worry, later we can be alone."

"Nice house."

"Thanks, I'll show you around." Grabbing his hand, she led him upstairs, showing off her parents' and kids' rooms. Next downstairs, before ending up on the back patio.

"Jordan, this is my dad, Felton, my mom, Catori, my daughter, Kitna. You already met the mouth of the family, Osika."

"Good afternoon, sir, ma'am," said Jordan.

"No need, son. I'm Felton and this is Catori," said Felton, trying to put Jordan at ease.

"Heard you played college football; you don't look like you have any game," mocked Osika. Jordan rolled his lips together and shrugged his shoulders, as though he agreed with his young critique.

"I was an All-American," contended Jordan, as he responded to his young counterpart.

"All-American. Grandpa, you said he was a bench warmer," pressed Osika, looking at her grandfather for agreement.

"Not true, little one. Your mouth is getting you into trouble," said Felton.

"I'm making sure he is good enough for my mom." She turned to Jordan and continued, "If you don't pass my test, there is no chance," as she walked away shaking her head.

"Believe it or not she will be the toughest critic," bemoaned Koi.

"That's okay," said Jordan.

"Would you like something to drink?" questioned Koi.

"Yes, please. Whatever you are drinking is fine with me," answered Jordan.

Everyone sat outside eating and conversing about their lives. Felton told a few stories about himself and the family. Jordan amused everyone, regaling the family about growing up in Baton Rouge and playing for LSU.

The afternoon, perfect, not too hot with a light breeze. The kids cleared the table and went off to their rooms. Koi, Jordan, Felton, and Catori sat around the table talking and joking the afternoon away.

"I'm going to tell you a couple things about Koi. One, she is dangerous, and two, she is a little stubborn," as Felton rocked back in his chair before continuing. "Around age twelve," before Felton could speak another word, Koi interrupted.

"Dad, you are going to embarrass me with your story," added Koi.

"It's the true you, dear. So, we come home from a Christmas party on a Sunday." Felton started to laugh as he continued the story. "As we are getting out of the car, Koi asks if she can climb some trees in the backyard," taking a break for a moment to let things sink in. "Now mind you, she is wearing a cute little dress. So, I say no you can't, not in your dress."

Koi walked over to her dad and put her hand over his mouth, hoping he wouldn't finish the story.

Felton swatted away her hand and continued. "She storms out of the car stomping her feet like hell. Walks in the front door. My wife looks at me and says, 'She is like you, what do you want me to say.'

"I say yeah, yeah."

"We unload a couple of things before heading inside. So we walk inside, and her dress on the floor, but no Koi." He stood up and showed how he picked up the dress and started looking for his daughter.

"I yell for her, but no answer. I head out back, she is climbing a tree in her underwear." He began to laugh out loud.

Jordan started to laugh as well, while Koi becomes red-faced with embarrassment. She stomped her foot in a playful display.

"Mom, can you make him stop?" asked Koi, as she put her hand to her mouth, followed by a "zip it" motion.

"Don't think so, your father loves to brag about you," replied her mother with a grin.

"To continue, I walk out, ask her what she is doing climbing trees with no clothes on."

Pausing for a moment before he said, "Her reply, 'You said I couldn't wear the dress; I'm blaming you.' He shook his head back and forth.

"She asked me about stripping naked." He waved his hands back and forth to show he wanted Koi to keep her clothes on.

"I walked away, and about thirty minutes later she comes in the house, and goes to her room, and puts on some clothes before heading back outside."

He let the scenario sink in before adding, "I figured I lost, so let the battle go, going onto the next. There were plenty more after that."

Koi's mom chimed in, "One of those moments in life when you say your child has a mind of her own."

"A mind of her own, hmmm, I can see that," offered Jordan after hearing the story.

"You think I have a mind of my own?" questioned Koi, looking at Jordan mischievously.

"Authoritarian sounds right. You like to be in charge," offered Jordan with a sly smile.

"If you want something bad enough, you need to either be assertive or do it yourself," replied Koi.

"As long as you don't strip, and start climbing trees," added Felton.

The rest of the afternoon, spent with Koi's kids and parents, playing some volleyball in the backyard, chatting about the early years. Felton and Catori cleaned everything up and let Koi and Jordan spend time together, alone. A consensus between the two: they liked this kid.

Chapter 24

The alarm clock went off too early. Yesterday was a marvelous day, and now back to being a detective. As Jordan headed for the shower, he received a text from Koi. She sent a pic of herself in her sexy underwear with the caption, "Want to climb trees with me?"

A well-timed text; put a huge smile on his face. They would text back and forth while he finished getting ready.

He got into the office around 7 a.m., the office quiet for a Monday. On his desk, three messages. All the messages tied to the Lewis case.

Sarg walked in. He grabbed a cup of coffee and offered a "good morning" to Jordan.

Sensing his partner did not want to talk, Jordan went back to reading the reports.

Ten minutes later he said, "Think we should go over and ask some questions of Derron?"

"Yeah, let's plan on it," answered Sarg.

The next half hour the two detectives talked about the questions they wanted to ask. With the Marshals holding Derron, no need to rush the process.

Over the years, Sarg worked with the Marshals and found them to be professional, and excellent at their jobs.

As they pulled in both men looked around to make sure no one followed them. The safe house, hidden from the public. A man approached the car, after going through the gate. The detectives exited the car with a tall, portly man walking toward the car.

"I'm Deputy Bellows, U.S. Marshals."

"Hello, Deputy, I'm Markus Jacobs, and this is my partner Jordan Matthews," answered Sarg.

"Come on in."

"Anything you can tell me about the kid, his demeanor, his recent calls?" probed Sarg, looking for some information.

"We wrote it down for you, mostly with Destiny. She continues to press him, needs him taking care of business," said the deputy as the three walked inside the house.

"Did she threaten Derron at all?"

"No, nothing threatening," said Deputy Bellows.

"We can take down, or at least provide ample ammunition for prosecuting the Garza family, when the kid gives us the goods."

"We have never gotten close to the Garza family, wish you luck," said Bellows.

In a back room watching TV, the detectives approached the possible confidential source. "Hello, Derron, this is Detective Jacobs and Mathews. I believe you have spoken to them on the phone?"

The interview would go on for four hours. Derron filled the detectives in on the inner workings of the operation. He talked about meeting Raul in Mexico. A group, which included Destiny, flew to Mexico for an interview with Raul. He came away impressed with the drug lord. In turn Raul thought highly of Destiny.

Derron believed the two had sex at the estate with Raul's wife in another room. The estate, called La Casa de Dios, which means God's place. They continued their affair over the last couple of years, by meeting off the coast of New Orleans on a private yacht for weekend sexual excursions.

According to Derron, he believed Raul thought of himself as a God figure. He would pay for things for the poor in his region, and paid his employees quite well. With Raul's net worth estimated around $10 billion, he possessed more than enough resources to take care of the people.

The conversation continued, digging into Destiny, and her life. Derron explained to the detectives that she never put things in her name. Raul showed her how to hide money overseas, and ensure she would not be implicated when small-time dealers flipped after being arrested. With the killing of her cousin, she now caught the eye of both the NOPD and the feds.

"She scares me, dog. She makes people call her Atropos, a Greek goddess." Derron sat shaking his head before he said, "She inked herself with the tat of Atropos, on her back."

"We are going to set her up. You will testify; we will give you a new identity. Is there anyone else we need to worry about, anyone loyal to her we need to take down?" quizzed Jordan.

"Couple cats named T'Bone and Major C," offered Derron before giving the detectives their actual first names.

The detectives set up a tentative date for arresting Destiny. Sarg told Jordan he wanted to talk to the marshals, so he sent Jordan and Derron outside on the grounds to chat more.

By asking Jordan and Derron to spend some time together, Sarg figured he needed the experience of questioning protective witnesses.

"Dog, you think yous can do me one more favor, if I deliver Destiny?" questioned Derron.

"What do you need?"

"I got this girl and a little boy. I need them with me."

"Asshole, you are telling me this now. Where are they?" asked Jordan in a pissed off manner.

"Delta Mississippi, hidden, got them safe, put them up in a low budget motel. She only answers my calls."

"What about her family and yours?"

"I gots no family and my beau is single child with daddy," Derron continued. "They won't move on him—he's in a wheelchair, car accident."

"What is her name?"

"Bre'ne Chevnaux, she is French," Derron replied. "Please, dog, I need her—she's all I got."

"I'll do everything I can," as Jordan calmed down, understanding Derron's predicament, with his family in danger after talking with NOPD.

Sarg and Jordan went back to the office to plan out strategies. Some interesting information came from a CI. Destiny owned a large cache of arms. ATF followed recent purchases by T-Bone. He took the weapons to a storage facility for storage.

The team used the entire afternoon and evening for research and planning warrants. Both T'Bone and Major C, with minor offenses, showed no current warrants.

Questions arose about whom the detectives could squeeze.

One of the detectives noticed T'Bone with three kids from the same girlfriend. Her name, Sheri Burks.

Chapter 25

Going over the Southern Belle kidnapper case, Koi noticed some of the young girls traveling to Fort Walton Beach, Florida. *How come no one picked up on this before?* Something odd: none of the suspects' credit cards or bank statements showed them staying in a hotel, with only a couple of credit card purchases showing up on their cards. Following this lead might prove beneficial.

In the late morning, Liz knocked on her door. She entered with a short skirt, long orange tube socks, and a purple top with cut-off arms to show her bra underneath. To complete the outfit, she wore a necklace with the "Tree of Life" dangling, which is a Buddhist symbol.

"Can I ask you a question?" as Koi rolled her eyes at Liz's wardrobe.

"Sure," replied Liz.

"Why are you allowed to wear this outfit?" said Koi.

"I'm hot, can pull this off, and the choice of me working for the feds, or working against you, allows me to dress how I like," Liz said. "Do you like?" as she twirled around, showing off the entire outfit, front and back, and finished by pulling her shirt open from the side to show off her purple bra.

"I have a matching bra and hair," as she laughed, while Koi shrugged at the unbelievable display.

"Nice, and no I don't need to see any other matching parts of your wardrobe," responded Koi, trying to put out the fire.

She continued, "Do you have something for me?"

"I do, a couple of the non-traceable credit cards ordered out of France, Visa cards."

"Okay, they are from overseas—how is that helping us?"

"The cards, shipped to a PO box in Mobile. The name on the PO box is Brandon Mince."

"Excellent," said Koi, thinking this might be a break.

"That's not all—Brandon lives in Texas. Can you explain to me how and why Brandon is getting these cards shipped to Mobile and lives in Texas?" questioned Liz.

"Any chance he is meeting the girls close to Mobile? He might own more PO boxes all over the South to help him with this clandestine activity," replied Koi.

"Can you look into Brandon, please?" questioned Koi.

"Done. Nothing much to say. Lives alone, works forensics for Austin PD," as she passed along Brandon's personal information, further adding, "This guy is plain Jane—hard to believe he could be a kidnapper. Not my kind of guy. I like them a little risker, if you know what I mean."

She paused for a moment before saying, "Besides, women are better lovers. I only use guys as play things."

"Thanks for the info." Another piece of the puzzle, or a lead going off the trail. The question: Which direction?

By tracing the girls' movements, Koi spent the next couple of hours trying to find some connection. With no numbers showing up on their phones or emails. The kidnapper covered their tracks.

Millennials didn't use email as much, but no text messages. This puzzled Koi.

She drifted to yesterday, and the wonderful day with Jordan and the family. With her daughter playing volleyball later, she pondered about inviting Jordan to the game. She sent him a text and within a few minutes he gladly accepted. They texted back and forth for a few minutes about their day, before finishing up.

Koi texted "XOXO" before heading back to her case.

Special Agent Dionte Cattrell wanted an update on the Southern Belle case. With a degree from Johns Hopkins in Behavioral Biology and a minor in African studies, Dionte possessed smarts and a gentleman attitude. An All-American in lacrosse at Johns Hopkins, he later received a master's degree from Virginia. He was working his way up the ranks and being groomed to be the director of the FBI someday. The kinship he and Koi possessed came from them both playing major college sports, being minorities, and excelling not only in their respective sports but in the classroom.

Precise and cautious, an attribute he learned from his parents. They instilled a work ethic in him, and his other siblings. A three-time All-American at Johns Hopkins, a prestigious school. His teams won two NCAA championships while he played.

Dionte and Koi went over the case for more than an hour. They discussed recent clues.

Switching gears, he asked about her boyfriend. "How things going with you and Jordan?" Dionte questioned.

"Awesome—I like this guy," answered Koi.

"I did some checking. Glad to hear things are going well," offered Dionte, acting as a big brother.

"He came over to the house yesterday. Mom and Dad like him."

"What about the girls?" looking for a positive response.

"They like him; he played volleyball with Kitna and pitched batting practice to Osika. She asked last night, 'Did you kiss him?'" Koi added, "I'm scared our careers will interfere with our relationship."

"Balance, Koi, balance," repeated Dionte. "Learn to delegate, and if this guy understands, he will make room for you in his life. If not, he isn't worth it."

"I think he will be coming to Kitna's game tonight."

As Koi walked toward her car, a voice yelled for her. "Koi, wait up a minute." The agent screaming, James Brookside. He came to the bureau three years ago after working for the New York City police department. His specialty: cyber-crimes.

"Glad I caught you. Dionte wanted to make sure you saw this," said James, breathing heavily.

"Elena's cell phone pinged in Texas," said James.

"James, make sure someone follows up, and get a warrant for all the communication."

"Dionte, put things in the works. What do you think? Think she is still alive?" quizzed James, excited about the information.

"We can pray, James, but let's stay on top of this. I need to go, okay? Heading to Kitna's volleyball game."

"No problem, I'll keep you informed if we find anything else," offered James.

Entering the gym, Koi walked toward Jordan and her parents and gave Jordan a hug. The other moms paid close attention to the embrace, and soon the gossip started.

"You are beautiful," mentioned Jordan.

"You two can kiss in front of us, not like we don't know," chuckled Koi's mom, expressing their acceptance of the act. Koi peered down at her mom with the stare she often used on her daughters.

The game offered some excitement with Kitna playing exceptional, leading her team to a four-set victory. After the game a couple of the moms walked over. Nosy busybodies, about to explore the man sitting next to Koi during the game.

"Hello, Koi, Kitna played well," said one of the moms before the inquisition started.

"Who is this gorgeous character?" said Melody. Melody was a free spirit, divorced, and always looking for a good time. Her parents had passed away and left her a considerable amount of money. Before cashing in her inheritance, she divorced her husband and left him out in the cold. Koi didn't like her much, but their daughters played together.

"This is Jordan. He is a police officer with NOPD," replied Koi. Melody began to check out Jordan.

"You two look good together," said Vanessa. She sensed Melody's flirtatious behavior, and wanted to make sure nothing more became of the situation.

"Thank you, Vanessa." The ladies exchanged goodbyes, and everyone went their separate ways.

"I think Melody wants to make a play for you," questioned Koi, as she wrapped her arm around Jordan's arm, holding him tight.

"You think so?"

"She looked you up and down, checking out your stuff, with her chest hanging out," replied Koi.

"Koi, your friends may be attractive, but I only want to be with you," Jordan emphatically stated. "I feel like this is right, like I am part of the family. Besides, you carry a gun, and can use it.

Chapter 26

The homework done, and the kids asleep. Felton and Catori retired to the family room. Stepping inside to grab a couple of drinks for her and Jordan, Koi's mother came into the kitchen.

"Your dad and I are going to bed soon. If you want Jordan to stay the night, neither your father nor I will say anything."

"Mom," said a stunned Koi.

"A mom knows. If you don't want the girls to know, make sure he is gone early." Her parents always believed in being forthright. No reason to hide anything.

She walked over to her mom and gave her a long embrace before saying, "Thanks, Mom. You sure it's okay with Dad?"

"Your father's suggestion, but he thought you should hear it from me," providing assurance.

"I'll ask. Don't read anything negative into it if he doesn't stay—he may not be comfortable yet," said Koi.

Enjoying the moment, the peace and warmth, Jordan by her side. She had never felt love in her marriage. The question now, getting the nerve to ask Jordan if he wanted to stay the night.

Before she could ask him, Jordan spoke. "How do you think your parents would feel if I asked you to stay the night at my place on Saturday, as long as you are open to the idea? If you think we are ready for the next step? I would like an evening with only us."

"What a coincidence. My mom asked if you wanted to stay the night tonight." He grabbed Koi and pulled her in close before whispering in her ear, "I would love to stay the night. Your dad is okay with this?"

"His idea, according to Mom," replied Koi.

"What about the girls?"

"I need you to leave before they wake up, around 5?"

"I can leave by 5. I need to be in the office early tomorrow. We are working on indicting Destiny, and her co-conspirators."

"Taking her down will make the streets safer," answered Koi.

"How is your case going?" asked Jordan, showing interest in the Southern Belle case.

"We got a couple leads today." Koi paused and added, "I think it is a smoking gun, like someone is putting out leads for us to follow, and leading us away from the culprit," shaking her head.

"How did you come to this conclusion?" asked Jordan.

"The subject in question is incapable of committing the kidnappings. He has no means of keeping the girls, and since there are no bodies, how are they being transported?" Koi shrugged her shoulders, showing disbelief in the leads.

"Are you still thinking of a professional in the area?" asked Jordan, looking into Koi's mind.

"Yes. This person is calculated, strong, sexually attractive, and seductive. How else can young women fall for this?" questioned Koi, gripping Jordan tighter, showing a little vulnerability.

"You will catch him, and when you do, you will have your answers. The problem is dealing with subjects, and their thoughts."

Jordan followed up by saying, "I had a professor in college, she talked about the minds of serial killers and sexual predators. She explained criminals are not all crazy, but calculated. There are times when revenge is the answer."

"What was the professor's name?" asked Koi.

"Bailey Denkins, awesome professor, smart. She made you think about other motives, like control, as a motive. Her theory, the world offered a lot of gray areas."

"I would like to meet her."

"She does some seminars in behavioral sciences, I believe for the FBI. I remember she would often head up to Washington to give these seminars," said Jordan.

"I don't recall ever hearing her speak," said Koi, trying to remember if she'd ever met Denkins.

The rest of the evening was spent talking about movies, sports, or what books they may have read recently. By the time they noticed the clock, 1 a.m. Koi grabbed Jordan's hand and led him to her bedroom.

They stood at the edge of her bed. Koi took his shirt off, and he reciprocated the move. Sliding his hand down between her legs, he undid her zipper with her pants still on, placing his hand inside her pants, rubbing her. She moaned, dug her fingernails into his back, leaving marks. They climbed into bed. He placed his arms under her legs, lifting them high and thrusting himself deeper in her. They flipped over, her on top while he stayed inside her. She rode him hard, slowing down, speeding up, and slowing down, before coming all over him. The two of them sank deep into her bed, exhausted.

"I want more of you," whispered Koi, rubbing her hand gently over his chest.

"Would you be scared if I told you I've started to fall for you?" asked Jordan.

"No, never. I want you in my life forever. I want you as my friend, my lover, my protector."

Chapter 27

The office was busy with detectives running down leads on four different cases from the weekend. Everyone gathered around, with one detective providing intel: Destiny might leave the country. According to surveillance, they overheard the plan for her to leave by the end of the week.

Sarg implored everyone to stay sharp, fearing a desperate Destiny might act irrationally. When people are in complete despair, they are willing to steal, hurt, or kill to stay alive.

The photos of all those under suspicion, plastered on the board in front of the room. Six subjects with the hierarchy attached to each, showing Destiny at the top with an arrow pointing toward the word "Garza." The captain pointed out the importance of everyone doing their job, and not overstepping their bounds. He wanted everything to be done by the book. Operation Take-Down was scheduled for Friday.

The captain turned the meeting over to Sarg, who gave out assignments for all shifts. Jordan would be required to work with the surveillance teams.

The next questions for the detectives, protecting Bre'ne, Derron's girlfriend.

"Are the federals taking Bre'ne to a safe house?" questioned Jordan.

"Yes, I think they are getting her this afternoon. They will let me know when they pick her up."

"That's good, fantastic. Any idea where they might take her and the child?"

"No, they keep it to themselves, unless we need to interview someone."

"You think Destiny is getting nervous?"

"I do. I think she understands the heat is coming down on her. Killing her cousin brought more heat than she expected."

"Can I tell you something? Koi and I are getting serious," offered Jordan, looking for a more pleasant conversation.

"I am happy for you and her. Her dad is the best, and I love her mom—no-nonsense type of people."

"She is great, and so is her family. The girls are awesome. I think they like me."

"Treat her right, and she will be your best friend for life. The best times of my life have been with Ly. We complete each other."

Police work is a tough business, and being alone when things don't go right may lead to psychological problems. Having someone to lean on allows officers a chance to work through issues.

A call came in from the FBI. Destiny would take an early flight to Cancun, Mexico. With the FBI listening in on her conversations they requested the NOPD hold off on arresting Destiny, unless they could arrest all of those involved at the same time.

Garza's past made him a target of the FBI. He murdered anyone willing to take on the organization. After he ordered the murder of the chief of Law Enforcement for the Mexican government, the government instituted a hands-off policy. By acting with violence, it scared not only government officials, but rivals.

After the murder, the chief's body was displayed on the streets of Mexico City, in a park, with no arms, a gruesome scene. The Mexican government never went after him again.

Surveillance teams followed T'Bone's girlfriend, noticing she began to put belongings in boxes and take them to a storage unit. Guess she and her beau planned on moving?

By 6 p.m., Sarg finished questioning Derron. He provided a plethora of information regarding Destiny's operation since their last interview. He detailed how much money she'd made, and the orders to kill. To date she had ordered six people to be murdered.

According to Derron, she felt untouchable.

Chapter 28

The next day Destiny flew out to Cancun. A private flight that took a couple of hours. Once she landed, a car would be waiting for her, taking her to Raul's yacht.

This would be the best place to meet, away from prying eyes and surveillance. Looking forward to the rendezvous, she loved spending time with Raul.

Married with two kids, Raul wanted more of Destiny. Before getting on the flight, she bought a couple of new lingerie outfits, to surprise her lover.

The plane landed, with Emesto Jimenez waiting, the director of intelligence for Raul's organization, after he had been hired away from his previous employer. He trained with the CIA in America, while working for the Chilean government. The CIA trained him in spying techniques, and how to extract information from informants or enemies. He was dapper, sophisticated, and a complete intellectual.

His salary, in excess of $5 million a year, afforded him the opportunity to travel and spend. He provided intelligence on government officials and competitors. He became the calm person before the storm.

"Ms. Destiny, how was your flight?" asked Emesto. He handed the rose to her, from Raul.

"Good, thank you."

"We have the car over here. Philippe, would you retrieve the ladies' bags, please?" Emesto, a gentleman, never lost his temper. His mother had taught him to be a *Caballero*, which is "gentleman" in Spanish. This attribute served him well as a clandestine operator.

He opened the door for her, and soon, off to the harbor.

"So, tell me, what do the feds know?" questioned Emesto.

"Well, I think they are squeezing Derron. He said he is at his grandma's in Houston. The problem is my informants say he isn't there. I keep trying to contact him, but he is ignoring me. I also think they are trying to pin my cousin's murder on me."

Emesto took a moment to let the information sink in. "I think we need to sit down with Raul. Maybe we can bring Derron back into the fold."

She nodded in agreement.

Once at the harbor, Destiny would board one of Raul's speedboats, complete with a .30-caliber machine gun mounted on the back and bulletproof glass. The cost of the vessel, after modifications, $4 million. Both Emesto and Destiny, loaded on the boat, called *Zona de Peligro*, meaning *Danger Zone*.

Raul became a drug lord at twenty-eight, after learning the trade from a man named Englis Hector Lopez. Now thirty-five, his handsome looks endeared him to multiple women across the Tamaulipas region. At one time he thought about being an MMA fighter; instead, Lopez recruited him. Raul later ventured out on his own, building an empire other drug lords and Mexican authorities revered.

Destiny ran over to Raul and hugged him before whispering in his ear. "I have something sexy for you in my bags. I missed you."

"Sounds great, my dear," as Raul lightly pressed his hands against her cheeks before kissing her.

"Why don't we head to my cabin? We can talk business later." Raul reached for Destiny's hand, and they headed off to Raul's cabin.

As the door closed behind her, Raul reached and locked it. He picked her up, and she wrapped her legs around him. He took her over to the ottoman and forced her on her knees. Grabbing her hair, he pulled her head back, and stuck one of his fingers in her mouth to suck on.

She reached, and unbuttoned his pants, and dropped them to his ankles. He forced her to take him in her mouth. She obliged, and worked him with her mouth, licking the shaft with her tongue when he pulled out. It wasn't long before she ended up on the ottoman with her skirt up. He slid her thong to the side and slid inside, her feeling her wetness.

She screamed, "Yes."

Pressing his hands on her stomach, his repeated thrusts made her scream. "How do you want it?"

He flipped her over, and mounted her from behind while pulling her hair and spanking her ass on occasion.

"Where do you want me to finish?"

"Inside, leave it inside," demanded Destiny. The sexual encounter continued for a little while longer with playful banter between the two of them before Raul came inside her. With his juices inside, Raul wanted to pull out, but Destiny curled her legs and made him stay inside her a little while longer before she reluctantly let him go.

"You are the best lover, ever," said Destiny, embracing Raul by wrapping her arms around his neck and holding on tight.

"You are better than my wife. She is ordinary in bed, missionary only, no excitement," replied Raul.

"We need to do this more often"

"We will be able to do this more. Why don't you nap for a while? I'm sure you are tired."

Raul went to the conference room to speak with Emesto and see what he had learned on his recent trip to the States.

Back in New Orleans the detectives learned the name of the shooter, Derrick Jones, in Jaron's murder. He lived in Shreveport and worked as a private investigator. The investigator gig, a front for his real job, contract murder.

Sarg wanted him picked up and held at the Shreveport police department. Four hours later, Shreveport PD called to say they had Derrick in custody. With no formal charges, Derrick asked to see his attorney. The Shreveport authorities said detectives from New Orleans would soon offer an explanation for the arrest.

Chapter 29

Raul, Emesto, and Destiny ate breakfast in the state room. Sailing to Raul's home base, Ciudad Madero. They discussed who would remain loyal to the organization, who needed to be eliminated, along with contingency plans if Destiny needed to leave the country. With four jets and an airstrip near his home, getting Destiny out of the country would be no problem.

They used code names for the airports, along with other secret ways of communicating. Emesto excelled in this covert activity, the ability to hide and communicate. Destiny's code name, Xzal, which is the short version for the Aztec Goddess Xochiquetzal. Xochiquetzal, a feminine deity of beauty, sexual love, and power.

After the morning breakfast, and meeting, both Raul and Destiny decided to sit out on the front deck of the ship. A chance to be alone discussing the meeting, making sure that both of them were on board with the decisions, no mistakes or impulsive decisions.

Raul didn't agree with killing Jaron, and his girlfriend, but understood why Destiny had ordered the hit. She wanted to make sure her message would be understood. *Do not cross her.*

Sitting quietly, she decided to take her top off, and soak up the rays. Not shy about flaunting her body, a black goddess. She swung her bra over her head before she tossed the garment to Raul.

He got the message and grabbed her hands, pulling her closer to him. While kissing, his hands firmly gripped her breasts, before he started to suck her nipples. She straddled him, grabbing his head, imploring him to continue. The boat captain and security, getting an eye full.

Destiny loved this. She loved to be watched when having sex, a complete turn-on, and more times than not, her orgasms more intense.

After standing up and sliding off her bathing suit bottom, she worked on top of him. Pressing her hands, forcing him to lay flat, they continued the sexual encounter until she climbed off, after he had finished.

T'Bone called Destiny to inform her about Derron working with the feds. "What the hell! After all we did for him, and his family, he is going to rat me out?!" screamed Destiny.

"Well, I guess Derron flipped, working with the feds," said Destiny reaching for Raul's hand.

"Don't worry, my love, I will handle it. I will find some of my guys who can do the job and disappear. No amateurs," proposed Raul. "I'll make this go away. Any ideas on where they might be keeping him?"

"No, it might be close to New Orleans, though, to be able to transport him to court."

"I'll put Emesto on it. He has contacts inside the State Department who will tell us where they are hiding him." Raul took his fingers, running them over the back of Destiny's hand, as a way to calm her down and relieve the stress.

Liz found something on one of the victim's Facebook posts. A photo of eight people, at a conference. The account belonged to Shelby Davidson.

After being kidnapped from Little Rock, Arkansas in 2006, she worked as a Forensic Scientist for the state. The photo showed participants with name tags on their chests, while others showed no name. In the photo, Shelby, with a gentleman whose name tag read Professor Calkins.

She believed this meant something. With keen intuition, she quickly ran out of her office looking for Koi.

As Liz ran down the hall, "Koi, Koi, here is something you need to see. I think it is important to the case. This photo here, I found on Shelby Davison's Facebook account. All of these people, at some sort of conference. We need to identify everyone, see if they remember her," demanded Liz.

Koi gazed at the photo, and rolled her eyes. Why would this be so important? It's people at a conference; does Liz think the killer is in this photo?

"How does this tie into kidnapping?" questioned Koi.

"We are looking for tie-ins. These girls are meeting their fate, or a person before they get kidnapped," offered Liz.

"Do you know what type of conference?"

"No, but I can make out one name on this name tag, Professor Calkins. Maybe we should track him down, and ask him some questions?"

Looking closer at the photo, Koi decided it may be time to speak with the professor.

"I have a hunch that this means something, like Shelby wanted me to find this photo. What's weird, this is the only photo of her at any conference."

Putting the photo in her pocket, Koi wandered down to Jackson's office. She needed him to track down the professor's recent movements.

After speaking with Jackson, she called Jordan, asking about the professor. "Hi there—how is your day?" asked Koi.

"We are making real progress on the Lewis case, and might make some arrests by the weekend, or next week at the latest, if things fall together. How about you?"

"Not too bad. Wanted to ask you something. Some information came to my attention today. One of the kidnapped girls is photographed with Professor Calkins. Can you tell me more about him?" quizzed Koi.

"Yeah, he is a good guy, criminology professor with emphasis in psychology. Is he involved somehow, or you think he might have seen something?"

"Not sure. You think he would talk to us, fill in some blanks?"

"Absolutely he would, loves to talk about criminals and psychology."

"Did you ever take any of his classes?"

"Yeah, a couple of classes. This photo, is it just him, and the girl?" asked Jordan.

"No, there are eight or so people in the pic. Why?"

"Word around campus, Professor Calkins dated students," offered Jordan, believing it wouldn't lead to anything, but he felt obligated to tell her.

"Thanks, Jordan. I appreciate you helping me out."

The professor needed serious attention, if nothing more than to exonerate him from the kidnappings. Looking at his career, social media, and anything else that could provide a clue. She found something interesting. The professor traveled a lot, to different conferences, but also to Key West and the Cayman Islands. He recently took the same cruise as Elena.

Chapter 30

Sarg and Jordan studied the surveillance information from yesterday, and the night before, along with texts and phone calls to and from Destiny's mom, sister, and aunt. The texts, all in code.

Breaking the code, something Sarg excelled at. "I think they are making a move on someone, potentially Derron," said Sarg, while he continued to read the coded message.

"What makes you think this?" asked Jordan.

"Well, code name Bozo says he needs to be followed, and report to Xzal. Not sure who Xzal is. Someone high up in the Garza family."

"Text here to T'Bone, says 'move all the furniture.' I assume this means drugs need to be out of any stash places."

"I would concur with your assessment. Derrick Jones is being brought here today? Both of us will question him if he talks to us," said Sarg.

"Sounds good. What time?"

"Got a text, he should be here around 11 a.m.," replied Sarg.

With more clues and evidence, the detectives started to become more upbeat about the case, and progress. Standing by the coffeepot, taking a drink, Sarg reminisced about the thirty years. His home away from home over the years offered numerous memories, some good, some bad. The feeling of extreme satisfaction came over him; he had helped people recover during their worst times.

Jordan's phone rang, Koi, calling. "Hi, what are you up to?" asked Jordan, as he answered the phone.

"I'm heading to Baton Rouge, to talk to Professor Calkins. My boss thinks I should interview him alone, sorry you can't go," answered Koi, hoping Jordan would not be disappointed.

"No problem, I am pretty involved in the Lewis case. Are we still on for dinner tomorrow night?"

"Yes, we are. Mom is making tacos, and cheesecake for dessert, so bring your appetite."

"Will do, look forward to seeing you, wishing you luck. If you need anything when you are there, call me."

"Thanks love, muah," said Koi before hanging up. *Hold on a second*, thought Jordan, *she said "love." Is this her way of saying goodbye?*

The next morning Koi set out for her 9:30 a.m. appointment with Professor Calkins. The drive, under normal traffic, took an hour and a half.

A much larger campus than Georgetown. So much activity, young minds looking to be molded. She entertained the thought, *What fertile ground for a kidnapper.*

The problem, all the girls except Angelica had graduated college before they went missing.

Fall time in Louisiana is all about college football. Koi exited her car, noticing numerous students wearing LSU gear. A smile came across her face as she figured students may have worn Jordan's jersey when he played here.

Up three flights of stairs, she reached the office of Professor Calkins. A young lady sitting at the desk greeted her, and asked how she may help.

"I have a 9:30 appointment with Professor Calkins," answered Koi.

"I will tell him you are here. Your name is?"

"Special Agent Blackthorn with the FBI," said Koi.

Five minutes later, an early-forties, attractive gentleman walked toward Koi, and extended his hand. One thing she noticed, his eyes, alluring. She understood how college girls may fall under his spell.

"Hello, Agent Blackthorn. I am Professor Health Calkins. Would you like to come to my office?" asked the professor.

"Yes, please."

"Follow me," responded the professor.

"Thank you for seeing me on such short notice," offered Koi. She wanted to portray herself in a non-threatening demeanor.

"Absolutely. You said it had to do with Angelica Lawrence's disappearance—I am more than obligated to meet with you. The LSU family, including me, want to find out what happened to her."

"We are working on some leads. My first question is: Did she take any of your classes?

"She did. She took two of my classes. I documented both classes, and her grades. A bright student, although sometimes I think she partied a little too much."

"What makes you think she partied too much?" questioned Koi as she took the documents from the professor.

"Well, you overhear kids talking in class. They sometimes give a little too much information."

"Anything specific you can remember?"

"She and another student were talking one time, and I overheard Angelica say she got drunk over the weekend. She said she spent the night with one of the football players. I got the impression it was a one-night stand."

"Anything else you can remember?"

"She sat in my office one time. We discussed her declining grades. I pressed upon her the importance of finishing on a high note."

"How did she respond?"

"She said her personal life began to take up lots of her time, as well as her other classes."

"You definitely need a balance between school and private life," said Koi, talking from experience.

"A respectful student, took part in discussions."

Koi sat back in her chair writing down the notes. She sensed the professor might be hiding something. A secret he wanted to share.

Needing to clear his conscience, he described a chance happening one day as he walked by the doctor's office. The door cracked open, with Angelica embracing Denkins, and the two of them locked in a passionate kiss.

"Isn't this against your university's policy, having a relationship with students?" asked Koi.

"Yes, but I did not want to be involved," replied the professor.

"Well, thank you professor, you have been helpful."

"Do you know Jordan Matthews, a detective from NOPD? He questioned me a little while ago about Angelica. I can put you two together, if you would like?"

A smirk came over Koi's face, before she answered. "Yes, I sent him up here."

"You sent him, interesting."

"He performed some due diligence for me," answered Koi as she got up from her chair.

Leaving the professor's office, she stopped by the secretary's desk. "Is there a chance Dr. Denkins may be available for a few moments?" asked Koi.

The secretary called the doctor. "She said she would be out in a moment."

"Thank you," said Koi.

The two women chatted for forty-five minutes. Nothing of real substance came from their chat. The doctor offered the same sentiments the professor had provided. A bright young college student, with a free-spirited attitude, disappears without a trace or anything unusual being detected.

The drive home, a time to work the puzzle. Two professors both accused of sleeping with students, with one of the students disappearing. Koi pulled into her driveway at 5:45 p.m. She entered the house, smelling her mom's cooking, and gave her mom a kiss.

"Hi, Mom, I'm starving. What are you cooking?"

"Hi my little butterfly, Italian. Jordan went to pick up the girls."

"How long has he been here?"

"Got here around 5:15. He came here early to help me. I guess he cooks. He might be a keeper," offered Koi's mom.

"Yeah, I think so," said Koi.

The girls came in and ran up to their mom, giving her hugs and kisses. She questioned them about homework and their day.

Jordan followed the girls in, giving Koi a hug.

"Mom, why are you acting like we don't know?" said Kitna.

"What do you mean?" as Koi gave her daughter an idiosyncratic glare.

"Please, you can kiss him—we aren't stupid."

"I think you should take a shower before dinner," as Koi swatted Kitna on the butt, sending her off to the showers.

After dinner, Jordan and Koi took a walk together, by a river close to her house. She pulled him in close to her and said, "I'm starting to fall in love with you, Jordan Matthews."

Chapter 31

A decision to take down Destiny's co-conspirators came from the top. The judge and prosecutors believed the detectives provided more than enough evidence for a conviction. The surveillance teams viewed Destiny's crew unloading safe houses. They watched, and took pictures of transactions taking place between the wholesale operation and seller.

This organization, according to the FBI, is one of the best-run drug operations in the U.S. The FBI agreed to allow NOPD to arrest all the suspects.

The FBI confiscated bank records for all those involved, with a few accounts showing six figures in them. The investigation uncovered twenty individuals, all close confidants of Destiny. This prosecution would be costly, but worth it.

"Any word on when Destiny is coming home?" quizzed Sarg, as Jordan entered the room.

"No, not yet. The FBI lost her. She may be on a private yacht." NOPD did not want to move on Destiny's gang until she returned to the U.S. per FBI orders. They feared she would stay hidden if they arrested the others first.

Sarg experienced this with the NOPD, after the FBI took down the Beggin crime family in the late '80s. Ashe Beggin flew out of the country before he could be apprehended. He hid throughout the Middle East and would never be brought to justice. Making the same mistake again, not an option.

The FBI learned that Destiny would be flying back to the States on Tuesday. They would move on Destiny at the airport. NOPD would arrest all those associated with Destiny at the same time.

"Sarg, this came in from surveillance. T'Bone is loading up and heading out of town. What do you think we should do?" The young man asking: Officer Benjamin Clothier.

Over the years the department got younger. The younger generation was exempt from some of the biases the older officers carried, which created a more diverse police force.

"They think he is skipping town?" asked Sarg.

"His Tahoe, and a trailer, are packed," offered Clothier.

"Let's keep track of him for now. Ask if the feds can put a tracking device on the Tahoe?"

"I'll ask."

Anxiety started to set in within the department. Sensing the need to lessen the fears, Sarg ordered lunch for the team. They told stories and laughed, forgetting the assignment for the time being.

"Jordan, I want you to take Saturday off. I need you, however, to check in. You need to call in no matter the time," demanded Sarg.

"I will be with Koi. Kinta has a volleyball game Saturday, and I plan on going."

"You like this girl?"

"I do," replied Jordan. The detectives seldom discussed Jordan's personal life. With Sarg having a connection to Koi, and her family, he would not be overstepping his bounds.

"Be good to her, she will be good to you," expressed Sarg.

"We have a lot in common, like kinder souls. The only thing I worry about is our jobs, the ability to compartmentalize, and free time with each other."

"A tough gig, Jordan. You need to make time for her and the kids. Believe me when I say this, the girls are your kids as well, if this relationship progresses."

"I know, I know. I'm a little scared about finding a balance."

"You are a smart guy. Believe in your path with Koi; this will lead you in the right direction."

Destiny began to send messages to her underlings. Nothing would be left to chance. She wanted her close siblings to leave the country with her.

After talking with one of the lieutenants, Raul made arrangements to bring someone else into the business, taking over the southern Louisiana area. He decided on one of his lieutenants running the business out of Vegas. The underboss in Vegas, Jonathan Plidas, would be promoted and take over in New Orleans. The game plan, keep the shipments flowing, the distribution network intact.

Keeping his number one girl in the family became a priority. Besides, he loved spending time with her. She would need to lie low for a while and relocate to a different part of the country in a year or two. He worked with her, and the family, transferring money out of the country.

A master plan would be instituted if everyone needed to skip town. With safe houses picked and escape plans set in place.

During a lunch date, Jordan informed Koi that the FBI would be working with NOPD to take down Destiny and the others. The ability to bring Raul Garza to justice, a different animal, however.

"Sounds like you guys are going to be busy this weekend?" asked Koi, wondering if she would be able to see Jordan.

"I have the whole day off Saturday. I plan on attending Kitna's game, and I'm free for the rest of the day."

"Wow, thanks, Sarg, for taking care of things," said Koi with a smile.

"Do you want me to spend the night?"

"Of course."

While eating lunch, Koi talked about an interesting find, the Lacroix Hotel, and the possible connection to the case, becoming more confident every day that her perp lived in Louisiana. The FBI continued to follow the lead, the young kid out of Texas, but Koi did not believe he would be capable of kidnapping or murder.

Getting up the nerve he asked about her meeting with his professors at LSU. At this time, Koi believed the professors had nothing to do with the girls' disappearances.

She did ask about Dr. Denkins' sexuality.

Jordan answered, "I think she is bi. My dad investigated her once regarding a missing person's case."

"Wait, what? Who was the missing person?" questioned Koi.

"Can't remember the name. I'll ask my dad. Think it's tied in somehow?" Jordan wondered, looking for Koi's angle.

"No, not at all, but she may lead us to someone else," offered Koi. She wanted Jordan to believe in the professor's innocence, ignoring their indiscretions.

"Serial criminals, as you know, like to throw you off their trail. Look how Destiny made up a story about her cousin."

Jordan and Koi both came to a consensus: Criminals will do anything and say anything to conceal their crimes. Even fingering their own family.

In one particular case, Koi remembered involving a brother and sister collaboration. They blamed their mom for operating a prostitution ring with illegal immigrants. To this day the brother and sister still believe they were wrongfully prosecuted.

The next couple of days would go off without much of a hitch. Most of Destiny's co-conspirators worked on logistics before leaving town. Surveillance provided more information for the prosecutors. Derron informed Jordan about the accountant Destiny used. How they laundered the money. With mountains of evidence, each member of the gang would receive ten years or more.

Chapter 32

Saturday came, and Kitna's game against Mandeville. You needed to cross the Lake Pontchartrain causeway to reach the school. With Kitna required to be at the game an hour earlier, Jordan and Koi took her.

The starters circled on the court before the game, with Kitna giving the pre-game speech. After their pre-game ritual, she ran over to her mom and Jordan.

She gave a fist-pump to the both of them. "Kick ass," said Jordan, knowing Koi would not disapprove of the language.

"Always," replied Kitna.

"This is new. She approves of you being here," said Koi.

"I think so, hope I'm not a jinx."

The game would match two of the better teams in the state. Kitna played outstanding and led her team in kills and service aces. The Mandeville team included one of the better players in the state. She blocked three of Kitna's shots during the match, with a fifth set needed to decide the outcome.

Kinta listened intently to her coach. Koi never coached her daughter from the stands. She wanted the girls to understand, *Listen to your coach.*

After getting the instructions, Kitna looked up at her mom and Jordan. He suggested she start using a cut shot. He showed her with his hand motioning the way to perform the move. Kitna smiled and nodded back at Jordan.

"Jordan, what are you doing?" asked Koi, admonishing Jordan.

"She needs to use the cut shot. The blocker is a couple inches taller; she will block her shot almost every time."

"She struggles with it—you better hope it works," confessed Koi.

"She has the talent—watch."

The first time Kitna tried the cut shot, she sent it three feet out of bounds. She glanced up at her mother with an *I got this* expression.

Mandeville took an 8-3 lead, before Kitna's turn to serve. She took a deep breath and delivered another ace along the left sideline. By the time Mandeville got the ball back the score was 9-7. Points would go back and forth until the score became 13-11 Mandeville.

One of her teammates passed the ball to Kitna, for a big hit. Mandeville's blocker went up to block the shot. She raised her right arm back, as though she was going to hammer the shot, but instead hit a cut shot away from the block, to everyone's delight.

The team set up strategy; Kitna said a few words to her teammates. "Get me the ball—I'll finish this off." After hammering two more shots through her opponents, she sensed her opponent getting tired. The final serve went back and forth three different times before Kitna received a pass for a spike. As she rose, her opponent got into position to block the shot. Adjusting quickly, she sent the cut shot for the match winner.

"Well done," said Koi, as she pulled Jordan in close and kissed him on the cheek.

"Thanks. Sorry if I overstepped my bounds. We worked on the shot in the backyard."

"You taught her how to hit the shot in the backyard? Where did you learn to play volleyball?"

"At LSU, sand ball. The volleyball girls from LSU taught us some things, playing two-on-two."

"Well, I'm glad you taught her. I tried, but she struggled with the execution," as Koi grabbed Jordan's hand.

The next morning, Jordan got up early to head into the office. As he opened the bedroom door, walking toward the back of the house, he encountered Osika sitting at the bar-high counter in the kitchen.

Startled by the young girl, she said, "Hi, Jordan. You and Mom don't need to hide. We know you are staying the night," expressed Osika.

"You and your sister are okay with me staying?"

"Yeah, it's okay. Mom's old, you're old, and that's what old people do," giggled Osika. "I have a question, though?"

"Go ahead."

"Will you go to my next game?"

"I will definitely go to your next game," said Jordan.

Osika jumped off her chair and rushed over to Jordan, giving him a hug before going back to her room.

Chapter 33

Elena heard someone coming into the compound. She was trapped in a fenced area, which kept you isolated from the outside world, and hidden from onlookers flying above. Rays of light came through the trees, which offered plenty of shade from the heat of the day.

Drugged every three days by her kidnapper, the drugs kept her in a zombie-like state. Her mind, highly functional, but unable to process more complex thoughts. The house, complete with all the amenities needed for survival. The kitchen area offered the residents ample opportunity to prepare food, with food being delivered with each visit.

Two weeks had elapsed since Elena's kidnapping. Her kidnapper believed they loved each other.

"Elena, you are so beautiful. I like the dress you are wearing," said her lover.

A wardrobe of clothes hung in the closet. The property included an above-ground swimming pool, and workout room. How could such a house be built this deep into the bayou? The owner of the home dug a pipeline, which transported natural gas from another property five miles away. This kept the house running, complete with air conditioning and other amenities.

Her lover walked over and kissed her. "Thank you. How long are you going to keep me? What is this about?" asked a perplexed Elena.

Thoughts of being turned into a sex slave crossed Elena's mind.

"I am going to let you go next week."

Smiling, Elena let go of her anxiety for the moment; the nightmare would be over soon. She and her kidnapper headed to the bedroom.

Sunday morning, and for Koi, and the girls, a pancake morning. After breakfast, Koi needed to read more files pertaining to the case. No sports scheduled for the day, no practices or games, only a quiet day at home. With her parents deciding to take the girls to the zoo, Koi had some needed alone time.

"Good morning, girls," as Koi continued to make breakfast, seeking a response.

"Good. Oh, Mom, don't worry, Jordan and I talked before he left this morning." Koi dropped the bowl of pancake mix, while coughing at the response from her daughter.

"Um, what do you mean?"

"Mom, don't try to hide Jordan staying here. I was up early and talked with him after he came out of your room. We are okay with it, so no need to hide anymore," as both Osika and Kitna whispered to each other, while giggling about catching their mom and Jordan.

"You girls are comfortable with him being here more often?"

"Yes, he is like a dad."

"If you would marry him this wouldn't be an issue," as Kitna spoke up trying to offer her mom a solution. "You need to propose," finished Kitna.

"Why am *I* supposed to ask *him*?"

"Mom, this is a new age. Besides, you like to be in control," explained Kitna, as she looked at her sister, and they both shrugged their shoulders.

"I like to be in control? Girly, you are writing checks you can't cash," claimed Koi looking down at her daughter, as if to say, *Keep running your mouth, girl, and I'll show you control.*

"I may not be able to cash it, but Grandpa can so nah, nah, nah."

"I don't believe this. What about more kids? What else do you girls have figured out?"

"No on the kids, especially if you end up having a little boy. Boys are so annoying," clarified Kitna.

"I agree, no boys—eek," said Osika.

"Jordan is a boy, and from what I unearthed, you held hands with Bratford," answered Koi, looking at her daughter Kitna, with the *mother knows* look.

"Don't change the subject, Mom."

The rest of the morning was spent discussing boys, homework, and weekly schedules. Koi felt more at ease knowing the girls had expressed a positive vibe toward Jordan. With the girls growing up so fast, the thought of Jordan being a father figure put a smile on her face.

Felton and Catori came in from their walk. The girls, busy getting ready. Osika, the first to come down.

"Grandma, did you know about Jordan staying the night here last night?"

"Little girl, that is between your mom and Jordan," said Catori, trying to squelch the conversation.

"Don't worry, me and Kitna decided it's okay."

"You decided, and what house bills do you pay, giving you the authority?"

"My cuteness, duh."

"Cuteness does not pay the bills," replied Catori, holding out her hands in a *trust me* manner.

"Well, for me, consider the bills paid. Listen, we like Jordan, and don't want Mom to lose him, so we are making the decisions."

"I guess it's settled?" as Catori peered at her granddaughter.

"I guess so. I'll relay the decision to Jordan. I'm sure he will be excited to hear he has no say in this," replied Koi.

"He doesn't. He marries you or we throw him in the bayou," answered Osika, as she stormed out of the room, snapping her hips from side to side like a queen who had made the final decision.

Everyone loaded in the car for the trip to the zoo.

Koi texted back and forth with Jordan, explaining the morning's events, and the girls' decisions on their relationship. He laughed, sitting at his desk, knowing full well this might be the obvious next step in the relationship. He cut the conversation short, explaining his need to pay attention to assignments being handed out on the Lewis case.

Spreading the case file out on her large desk, Koi laid out the twelve women the FBI believed may be victims. The four cases she focused on showed the young women staying in or around Fort Walton Beach.

With the revelation, a PO box as the drop-off for untraceable phones and credit cards provided a definite tie-in. The FBI tracked two of the hotels the women stayed in. The security cameras offered nothing in the way of evidence. With no cameras in the hallways to capture the girls going in and out of their rooms, and with whom, this made finding the guy more difficult. The perp used these hotels for this purpose. The only reason the FBI knew about the hotels was that two of the victims used their debit cards at those lodgings. Confusing the situation more, two different hotels. Koi suspected the kidnapper used four different hotels. The other issue, she believed the suspect might be using an alias. The kidnapper used extreme caution; they wanted to remain hidden.

She wrote down notes to herself. One thing she wrote down, the FBI needed to account for the professor's whereabouts during the kidnappings. She believed he knew more than he was telling.

One case, Koi, delved into with great curiosity, the missing girl from Athens, Georgia. Her name, Kylie Housner. She disappeared four years ago, after attending a forensic scientist conference in Miami. The FBI interviewed two professors from the University of Virginia. The professors were the last to see her alive before she got into her car. They offered solid alibis. She pondered, *Could two men be involved in this case?* Time to interview the two professors again.

Another baffling element. Kylie had dropped her car off at the airport, but no record showed her boarding any major flights, no buses or rental cars. What about being kidnapped at the airport?

After three hours of reviewing the case, Koi got up for something to drink, and stretched her legs a little, after sitting at her desk for a couple of hours. As she poured herself a glass of tea, a thought popped into her head. *What if someone planned meetings at small airports and flying them to destinations using a small aircraft?* Small planes aren't required to file flight plans, and with smaller airports, a limited number of flights, any person could hide from the authorities by using small air travel. Time to find out if anyone owned a pilot license.

The girls came home from the zoo, tired and ready for a nap. In an hour or two Jordan would be coming over for dinner.

Felton asked, "Do I need to prepare the grill?"

"I'll take care of dinner, Dad. Thank you, though."

"Good, means I get the rest of the day off. The Saints are playing at 4:30—gives me a little time for a nap as well."

Koi retreated back to her office, to continue reading the case files.

It wasn't long before Catori brought in a snack for her daughter. "Have you eaten anything since breakfast?"

"No, focused on bringing meaning to the Southern Belle case."

"Are you getting closer, any suspect in mind?"

"Nothing concrete, like this person is in front of me but yet hidden, if that makes sense?"

"Using a different name maybe? Do you think going public will bring the person out, or make them going deeper underground, or stopping all together?" quizzed Catori.

"Not sure. On one hand, informing the public would make them stop, but we may never find them. Then again, I might feel responsible for more kidnappings if something doesn't happen quickly," as Koi buried her head into hands, showing her disgust at failure.

"You know the story of the panther, and how she is a warrior for her people? A noble creature who fought for her tribe and brought forth victory. The panther lies in you, and you are fighting for your tribe. These young girls are your tribe. You will find this bastard," as Catori grabbed Koi's shoulders and squeezed them as though she was trying to relieve some stress.

"Thanks, Mom."

Chapter 34

The arresting teams gathered around, receiving their assignments, with the idea the arrests would take place on Tuesday. Sarg wanted to make sure things went smoothly. Destiny's flight was scheduled to land at 10:30 a.m. The feds would handle this arrest, with more than fifteen agents taking part and escorting everyone on the plane to federal jail.

Jordan became more comfortable with the planning. The only fear, someone getting hurt. With tracking devices attached to all the vehicles, NOPD would be alerted in case anyone decided to leave town before Tuesday. With nothing more needing to be done, Jordan headed off to the range, for some practice.

Sarg sat Jordan down, after he got back from the range. He wanted to relax his mind, with such a larger operation taking place.

"LSU, I know you won't be able to sleep Monday night. Make sure you rest and sleep when you can," advised Sarg, speaking from experience.

"I will. I might stay the night at Koi's, have someone to talk to," replied Jordan.

Being involved in tension-filled football games did not compare to the expected undertaking.

"You possess the right pedigree for this. I've seen you in action, you will do fine. Make sure we stick to the plan, and cover for each other, and things will go off without a hitch."

"No problem, and don't worry, I'll get my rest."

After the talk, Sarg went for his afternoon walk, to clear his head. The teams, full of youngsters, lacked experience, worrisome to some, but at the same time, the energy exuded confidence. They brought talent, and a can-do attitude.

Three females would take part in the operation. Sarg requested every one of them. They had proven themselves in other situations, and he believed they would be more than capable of handling any situation. Coming through the department in the late '70s, and one of four African American police officers at the time, the diversity showed that the department had grown from his early days. Today, the department consisted of 65 percent minorities, including two women in key management positions. The number one autopsy doctor, a Muslim woman, wore her burka. Her talent immense, she found important clues, leading to murder convictions.

While out on his walk, he received a phone call from his old division leader in the military. He wanted to inform Sarg about next year's reunion, the place, Pittsburgh, Pennsylvania. The two men talked about their covert operations during the war. The division leader recalled a certain mission Sarg led in Nha Trang. A dangerous endeavor, which almost killed him.

Working with an informant, he suspected two colonels and a major worked for the NVA. When it came time to turn over his findings, the CIA stepped in to inform the military they would not be allowed to arrest the three individuals. They didn't give a reason why. Sarg followed one of the colonels, who led him to the CIA operative. The CIA operative worked with the NVA, shipping drugs out of the country, and to the U.S.

Working the case, on his own for another two months, he put together undeniable evidence. Writing a report, he handed it over to the general in charge. The report mysteriously vanished. A week later, the two colonels' bodies were found, executed, by the CIA.

The major fled to North Vietnam, while the CIA operative was transferred out of the country. Someone in the company wanted the case closed.

Sarg's source for information, a young Vietnamese woman named Ly. Yes, the Ly who became his wife.

Chapter 35

Both Sarg and Jordan walked into the interrogation room. Sitting alone, Derrick Jones, as Sarg, introduced both Jordan and him, before sitting down. Derrick, about six-three, around 210 pounds, and well-conditioned. He went into the Army right after high school, and spent six years in. In the military, he picked up surveillance skills. After leaving the military, he formed his own company, Eagle Investigation. An expert with weapons, he hired himself out as a hitman. You needed to contact a man named Julius, who provided the information to Derrick on the potential hit.

"Good morning, Derrick, do you need anything?" questioned Sarg.

"What is this about? No one explained the reason for my arrest. I have been in lockup for two days," professed Derrick, a veteran of the interrogating game.

"Well, we are seeking some answers in regard to your affiliation with Destiny Young."

"Never come across her," shot back an annoyed Derrick.

"You sure this is the way you want to play?" responded Sarg, looking straight at Derrick, with steely eyes, which made some cringe.

"Listen, I said I don't know who she is. What else do you have, because you are costing me money?"

"Do you recognize the number highlighted?" Sarg pushed a piece of paper toward Derrick, showing his phone records.

"Nah," said Derrick as he looked away from Sarg. By not making eye contact, the detectives could tell he was lying.

"Look at me. We are busting up the Garza family operation. The situation is this, you can help yourself, meaning you can keep the needle out of your arm, or you can play it like you are right now. Either way, you are going to prison for the rest of your life," said Sarg, delivering a strong message to the hitman, emphasizing he possessed the goods to convict him.

"So far you have zilch. I'm telling you I'm a private investigator," said Derrick incredulously.

"You don't recognize the number?" asked Jordan as he stepped into the conversation.

"No, wrong number. I receive lots of calls every day."

"Do you own a gun?" asked Jordan, as he and Sarg pressed on with their questions trying to find a little crack in Derrick's answers.

"Of course, I do, all three registered," said an inquisitive Derrick. He made sure to follow the rules and regulations regarding private investigators.

"Where are these guns now?" asked Sarg, using an interrogation technique he employed numerous times. He would ask one question, with the other agent following up with a separate question. They would repeat the questions, but with different agents asking the previous questions. On occasion, the question switching tripped up the person being interviewed. The technique, dubbed the "suppressing technique;" the theory, bombard a defendant with questions.

"The police confiscated all the guns. Listen, I'm done here. Either tell me what this is about or I'm walking out of here," demanded Derrick.

Unsure of the evidence against him, but confident in his lawyer, he continued to press the detectives for more answers. His lawyer, Jeffery Argyle, from Atlanta. An infamous lawyer who had defended some high-profile clients in the past. Argyle was on Raul Garza's payroll and defended family members exclusively.

"You aren't going anywhere, Derrick. This is about the death of Derron Lewis. We know you killed him. You executed Derron for Destiny, along with his girlfriend," explained Sarg, laying out the case.

Derrick started to laugh uncontrollably, shaking his head. "What is so funny?" questioned Jordan, as he leaned in, a form of intimidation.

"Man, you guys are a clown show. Whoever this Derron guy is, I didn't kill him," as he stared down Sarg with a stone-cold face, before turning his attention to Jordan.

"And you, puppy, you are not ready for this. You got no proof, and once my attorney finds out the timeline, I'll produce an alibi, you can bet on that."

"We have the goods on you, trust me, dog," indicated Jordan, showing a confidence, not unlike when he played in the SEC against Bama or Florida.

"All right, I'm done here. Get my lawyer—his card is in my wallet. Don't steal my money—you pigs are all crooks," said a cocky Derrick, thinking he would be out of jail once his lawyer learned of the charges.

"I'll make sure to send the bill to the New Orleans police department for false imprisonment. As a favor I won't ask for your badges. Wow, what a comical show you guys put on. This good cop, bad cop routine, it's like the amateur hour at some dive bar."

"I don't care who your lawyer is, you are going down, and I'll be sure to send you Christmas cards at Angola," said Jordan, as the two officers excused themselves from the interview room.

The interview went as expected, with no confession. They were hoping detectives would find more evidence at Derrick's house, forcing him to turn on Destiny.

None of the guns confiscated matched Derron's or LaTonya's wounds. This made sense; most hitmen used throw-away weapons, or destroyed them after performing a hit.

Some interesting evidence did come from his second home, one he thought no one knew about. The prosecutors kept quiet about the findings and asked for no bail.

Sarg remembered Derrick's attorney, when he defended a suspected killer in New Orleans back in the '90s. The case didn't belong to Sarg, but he followed the case, hoping to one day cross paths with Argyle.

Chapter 36

In the New Orleans FBI office, a scheduled training day with meetings later on was on the docket. Koi needed a passing score with her weapon. She headed to the range to complete the qualification. For Koi, shooting came naturally, but she continued to hone her craft. With her dad, they spent many hours at shooting ranges over the years. She continued this practice, during her career, to ensure she would not fail the qualifications.

The rest of the day, spent in class, learning about new techniques, how the FBI gathered information, surveillance, and government oversight.

The oversight part displeased Koi. She believed Congress should be afforded the right to oversee how the FBI conducted themselves. However, her personal dealings of disdain, aimed at one particular congressman, Thaddus Larue, from Connecticut.

A stiff character, whose family was extremely well off. He got into politics for no other reason, except control. He believed the FBI budget should be reduced, and their ability to prosecute cases should be overseen by an agency that reported to Congress only. Koi believed he had torpedoed her Jamaican case. According to the congressman, if young girls were being kidnapped, the blame lay with the young girls and their parents.

After lunch, Koi and some thirty other agents sat down to go over different aspects of their jobs. A mind-numbing process. Her mind wandered to Jordan, and how his day may be going. The arrests of Destiny and others, the operation in the final planning stages.

After a break, the agents all reassembled into the room, where the subject of budgets would be discussed. Federal agencies for years had screamed they needed more funding, with the FBI no different. Ten minutes into the presentation, the proposal from Congress, from none other than Thaddus Larue, suggested the FBI needed to cut its budget by 10 percent.

"Where is my gun?" shouted Koi, under most circumstances, reserved. The room erupted in laughter.

"This bastard is increasing congressional budgets for his staff, but wants to cut the FBI's budget," screamed another agent.

"Koi, please, I understand your frustration. We will stop his insidious and arrogant behavior he displays toward our agency with facts, I promise you," offered Agent Isaac.

Agent Isaac, an agent with the bureau for the last twenty years. Worked with different administrations and politicians over the years in Washington, and politics. A former Army Ranger, who became the chief of staff.

"This is a ploy, a tactic; the 10 percent is not the end game, Peter. However, it is a negotiating tactic to decrease our budget," explained Agent Longstreet. Longstreet's great-great grandfather, General James Longstreet from the Civil War. James Longstreet, a scapegoat for the Confederate loss at Gettysburg. He disagreed with General Robert E. Lee, which led to the disastrous "Pickett's Charge."

Agent Longstreet never agreed with his great-great-grandfather's position, fighting for the Confederacy, but remained proud of his name. His wife, an African American; together they had three kids. His family name tied to the Confederacy, but Nathan Longstreet showed pride in his family, moving on from the Confederate cause.

"I agree with Nathan, and believe me we will fight this. He is pushing, with other congressional officials, and two senators. They all want to decrease the budget. Their reasoning for decreasing our budget, to increase other domestic and foreign programs," said Agent Isaac.

The argument continued, with back-and-forth between agents and Peter Isaac. Until Dionte spoke.

"Listen, folks, this is as Peter said, the age of decreasing budgets. I will be attending a series of meetings with Peter and the director. What we can't do is give these people ammunition, by going off either in the field or in front of members of Congress, or their staff. We will show value in our abilities."

"Dionte, you understand the inner workings of Washington. We need to show them the value the bureau brings to the United States," said Agent Beckett.

"I agree. Koi, you just volunteered to help me with the project. I'll assign an administrative assistant to you; they will perform the legwork," professed Dionte.

"Dionte, my time is limited. You know I am invested in the Southern Belle case," replied Koi, hoping Dionte would select someone else.

"Koi, you are the most qualified. You know about budgets, the inner workings, and the benefits with specifics to each district office. I need someone with experience and knowledge. I'm sorry, but I…we need you." Dionte, always careful with his words. A master motivator, who persuaded his agents to agree with his decisions.

She rolled her eyes as if to say, *I don't have time for this.* Unenthusiastically she accepted the assignment.

"Okay, Dionte, I'm in, but you owe me. I'm thinking maybe you should pay for my next vacation."

"Who gets vacations?" asked another agent.

Taking the data, grudgingly, Koi set it aside.

Wow, she thought, this might be a dealbreaker for Jordan; more responsibility, and less time with him. Time for a little getaway, the two of them, and soon.

By the time the meeting ended, the clock showed 5:30, time to head home. She told her father she would pick up Kitna from practice, if he would pick up Osika. She left the congressional information on her desk. No time for bullshit, she reasoned.

The thought of getting her hands on Congressman Larue, the idea of inflicting pain, followed by a swim in the Bayou, complete with cement shoes, crossed her mind.

Chapter 37

Getting to the school just in time as practice finished, Koi pulled into the school grounds, looking for her daughter, and noticed her standing next to one of the mothers and her daughter. The two girls, in a deep conversation. Koi wanted to head home, but decided to chat as opposed to being rude.

"Hi, Mom," said Kitna as she smiled while her mom approached.

"Are you about ready? Jordan is coming over so I would like to beat him home if we can."

"Sure, we can leave."

"How is your hunk doing? Better watch for Melody—he wants to make a move on Jordan."

"Vanessa, this isn't the time or the place," admonished Koi, hoping Vanessa would get the hint, and not discuss this in front of young girls.

"Don't worry, the kids all talk," replied Vanessa, implying the girls knew that Melody liked Jordan.

"Well, she doesn't possess my intellect and beauty, plus I carry a gun," confided Koi, with a stern voice, all the while hoping the message would get back to Melody: *stay away.*

Koi and Kitna walked toward the car without saying another word. Koi trusted Jordan. Melody, on the other hand, displayed a propensity for being, shall we say, a little *loose* sexually. Her reputation cemented by spending time in bed with a couple of the moms' exes, which is where she gained the nickname Kermit, because she jumped from one bed to the next.

Before going over to Koi's, Jordan stopped at his house. He wanted to pack a bag for the next day. With his confidence brimming, proud of his earlier interrogation. He wondered who his partner would be. He wanted his next partner to be Detective Nelson. Nelson, with twelve years on the force, and a current homicide detective. They reassigned his former partner to a different department.

The mutual respect that Jordan and Nelson shared—they would make an excellent team. First, however, solve the Lewis case, arrest the suspects, and allow Sarg to retire, knowing they'd arrested the guilty parties. The bag is all packed; off to Koi's.

They both arrived at her house at the same time. She thought this might be a rarity with the kind of jobs they worked. Felton followed up a minute later. Kitna ran into the house to get a shower before dinner, plus she wanted to use her mom's shower. Osika worked on her homework, with her mother's help.

Dinner, homework, and chores took place over the next couple of hours. Koi noticed Osika, with a look of despair, and followed her to bed, as any mother would while trying to comfort their child. They lay in bed together for some time, chatting about the day's events, the week's happenings, and of course Jordan.

"Mom, is Jordan going to stay the night?"

"Yes, he is, but he is leaving early. He has some important work to do tomorrow. He is going to take some bad guys off the streets," said Koi, before she leaned over and kissed her daughter on the forehead.

"Cool. I feel so much safer when he is here."

"Why? I can protect you, and Grandpa can protect you as well," said Koi.

"It's hard to explain. It's like he is…" She paused, not finishing her sentence.

"He is what?" Osika teared up. Koi feared this might be something else, besides Jordan being her protector.

"Mom, if you marry Jordan, do you think he will let me call him Dad?"

"Yes, he will. Are you okay with him being your stepdad?" asked Koi.

"Yes, but I'm afraid he won't like me," said a frightened Osika. She never knew her biological dad, and as little girls sometimes do, she felt anxiety over being liked.

Koi hugged her daughter tight while stroking her long hair. "Jordan loves you, believe me. Our relationship is strong, he is here to stay, and he will treat you as his daughter."

Looking up at her mom, she smiled. The sickness dissipated. The thought of calling Jordan dad brightened her mood.

"I'm feeling much better, Mom. Do you think Jordan could come up here so I can say good night?"

"Sure, I'll tell him to come up," said Koi.

"Jordan, can you go upstairs? Osika wants to chat before she falls asleep," said Koi, as she approached Jordan, pulling him in close.

"Sure. Anything I should know before I go up?" asked Jordan.

Displaying a pained look, she shook her head. "No, no, go up. She wants to say good night to you." She squeezed him tightly; with the premise she was never going to let go. Once she released his hand, he headed up to the upstairs bedroom.

Jordan reached her bedroom door and knocked. "Come in," from the other side of the door.

"Wanted to say good night, and hope you sleep well," as Jordan approached the edge of Osika's bed. Osika flashed a huge smile and reached for Jordan's hand, forcing him to sit at the edge of her bed.

"I'm doing much better. I think my mom loves you. How do you feel about her?"

"Well, I care for your mom, you, and Kitna. I love your mom."

"You should ask her to marry you," said Osika, prodding Jordan to ask Koi for her hand in marriage.

"I'm sure it will happen, but don't be alarmed. We are still working on our relationship, building it to last forever. We love each other."

"Can I ask you a question?"

"Sure."

"Can I call you Dad?"

"Yes, you can. You can call me Dad anytime you want." Osika reached up, grabbing Jordan. He held on and kissed her on the forehead before wishing her a good night's sleep.

"Thanks, Dad," said Osika as Jordan left the room.

"You are welcome. See you tomorrow."

Jordan walked downstairs to find Koi. He found her sitting in a swing set out back. With anxiety setting in, the thought of things moving too fast, the kids wanting Jordan to be their father, brought about some nerves. "I don't think Osika was sick. She worried you wouldn't like her," said Koi, breaking the silence around the sounds of the evening.

"I think so too. She wants to call me Dad. Is this okay with you?"

"Of course. I think she believes she gets left out, like we spend more time with Kitna than her."

"You are an amazing woman, juggling kids, practices, games, work," replied Jordan, offering a description of the hectic life she led. "Osika will recognize your strength."

"My boss added another chore to my duties today. Some congressman from Connecticut wants to cut our budget 10 percent. I'm being tasked to put together data showing our worth, like I need more on my plate."

"Listen, if you want me to stay around more, I can, but understand I may leave early if I catch a case."

Rising from the swing, Koi grabbed Jordan, as she steered him to the picnic table. She forced Jordan to sit first and straddled him while wrapping her arms around his neck.

"I would like nothing more than for you to stay the night as much as you would like," said Koi, as she struggled with the words a little before resting her head on Jordan's shoulder.

"You know I have to leave early tomorrow. I am part of the detail arresting T-Bone," said Jordan.

"I want to sit a little while longer. You be careful tomorrow. I want you to come home to me every night."

"I will, I promise. This is a no-nonsense arrest," offered Jordan.

"Treat the situation as if it were something more, please," demanded Koi, reminding him situations change in a split second.

"What about your Southern Belle case? How is it going?" pressed Jordan.

"Let's not talk about it, okay?" They proceeded to sit together for a couple of hours, whispering into each other's ear.

Chapter 38

The office bristling with activity at 4 a.m. The arresting and backup teams, being briefed in the conference room. Jordan and Sarg, part of the team arresting T-Bone. The last communication from surveillance said that T-Bone was asleep with his girlfriend, and kids at his house. With the kids sleeping in the house, Sarg, fearing things may get tense, he selected the teams for this reason. After experiencing arrests, with children present, Sarg wanted to ensure their safety. The Fugitive Apprehension Team would be assisting Jordan and Sarg. The remaining subjects would be handled by the other tactical units

"Sarg, are we all set?" quizzed Jordan. The longtime detective brought the calmness needed.

Wanting to ensure nothing happened to his partner, Jordan asked, "Sarg, you sure you need to be a part of the arresting team? Why not handle things from a distance?"

"Jordan, I appreciate your concern for me—I'll be fine. I'm getting older, but I can still handle myself. Watch out for T-Bone, and the girlfriend. When cornered, certain people react violently."

"I'll will take precautions," answered Jordan.

The two men sat drinking coffee, before Jordan got up the nerve to ask Sarg a question.

"Tell me about your last assignment in Nam," asked Jordan. He wanted to see how the elder statesman would react. They rarely spoke about Nam. In fact, outside of his fellow soldiers, Sarg only confided in Jordan.

"Smart kid, you think from my last experience, might conjure up thoughts of sitting this one out," as the detective reached over and grabbed Jordan's shoulder.

"My last assignment in Nam, I lost two covert operators. We never found their bodies. Word got back to me, before I left the country, the VC cut their throats and threw them in a river. I'm haunted by losing my fellow soldiers, but my experiences do not interfere with the current task."

"I'm not saying you aren't capable; I want to make sure nothing happens to you," said a sullen Jordan.

He reassured Jordan he would be fine, and nothing would happen to him.

"I stayed the night at Koi's last night," said Jordan, changing the subject.

"I am happy for you guys; she is the best. Ly believes you two are perfect for each other," responded Sarg, as he leaned back in his chair.

"Her youngest daughter, Osika, wants to call me Dad. I'm hoping I don't disappoint her. Those girls are very special to Koi, and I want to make sure I'm right for them."

Taking in the comments, Sarg sat silent for a moment. "The Choctaw have a saying: Search for yourself, by yourself. Don't allow others to create your path for you. It's your road and yours alone. Others might walk it with you, but nobody can walk it for you." Sarg added, "You, Koi, and the girls are together for a reason; this is your path."

Time to roll out, as each group headed for their destinations. Everyone was confident, as the superintendent stopped in before everyone left, and wished them well. He understood the danger, and importance of the mission. There would be numerous arrests taking place, along with the feds arresting Destiny. The arrests would receive national news coverage.

"Be careful. God's speed," as the superintendent prayed with those wanting to take part.

Once Jordan left, Koi found it hard to fall back asleep. She tossed and turned knowing full well the events taking place in an hour. The fear, receiving the knock one day. How would the girls be affected if Jordan didn't come home? The thoughts made Koi cry, with her nerves on the fringe. She decided, time for some tea, and headed to the kitchen.

"Good morning, Dad. How did you sleep?"

"I'm fine. You didn't sleep much?"

"I'm good, Dad."

Before she spoke another word, her dad spoke up. "Koi, this is love. You are worried about him. Believe me, your mother and I beg God to bring you home every time you walk out the door with your gun strapped to your hip. I see the pain in your face. The two of you are where you are supposed to be at this moment in time."

She walked over to her dad and hugged him, as tears rolled down her face. She never worried about someone like this before. Sure, she worried about her parents and the girls. This was different, however. Jordan's job, dangerous, even for a homicide detective. She hung on tight to her dad, not wanting to let go, as Kitna came downstairs.

"Mom, you okay?" asked Kitna as her mom wiped away her tears.

"Thinking about Jordan."

"Mom, don't worry. He is a badass—he will be fine," said.

"Thanks, little one. Want some breakfast?"

With everyone in place, the word came down. The entire team sprang into action, as the tactical team rushed to the front door, ramming it in. The detectives followed them in. Sarg and one of the female officers headed toward the kids' bedroom; surveillance pinpointed the bedroom. He wanted to make sure of no mistakes with the kids. If anything, the kids' protection would be on his shoulders, as he feared they would be frightened enough.

Jordan and others busted in the door to T-Bone's and his girlfriend's room. "NOPD! No one move—stay put!" yelled one of the officers with guns drawn.

T-Bone tried to get up, tackled by one of the officers before making any dangerous moves. His girlfriend started to hit the officer. When one of the female officers pointed her gun at the girlfriend, she froze, and another officer handcuffed her. T-Bone screamed as another officer came to help, keeping the situation under control.

"What the hell is this all about? Call my lawyer—I'll have your badges!" announced T-Bone to no one in particular.

"Terrance, I'm Detective Matthews, with the NOPD, and once things settle down, I will explain why you are being arrested," said Jordan, as he tried to calm this situation.

"Casandra, will you please take Sherry to another room with her kids? I believe Sarg will be in the room. Will you ask Sarg if he can meet us in the living room?" asked Jordan.

Jordan picked T-Bone up from behind and guided him out of the bedroom. Sarg soon entered the living room.

"Terrance, you are under arrest for drug trafficking. The evidence we collected shows you are involved with Destiny Young and her organization. Your girlfriend and kids will not be arrested, but you, sir, are under arrest," said Jordan, before reading T-Bone his rights.

"Ya'll is f'ed up. I got nothing to do with her. I'm not talking," answered T-Bone, acknowledging his rights.

"We are going to search the house. Sherry and the kids, need to find someplace to go," claimed Sarg as he informed T-Bone that the detectives were in charge. Twenty minutes later things calmed down.

With three officers, guns drawn, they allowed T-bone to dress. Sherry and the kids packed a small bag. With their car being confiscated, the team needed to give Sherry and the kids a ride to her mom's house on the outskirts of New Orleans.

After placing T-Bone in the cruiser, the team headed to the precinct. All the other arrests went off without a hitch, except one.

The plane carrying Destiny landed at Lakefront Airport, a small airport used by operators for private jets. The agents waited until the plane shut off its engines and opened the passenger door. Several cars surrounded the plane, as agents rushed up the stairs looking to arrest anyone in sight. The FBI arrested four occupants on the plane, but no Destiny.

They found a doll sitting in one of the seats, with a note attached. "Hello FBI, nice try—Destiny."

Raul and Destiny had outfoxed both the NOPD and the FBI. Word got to Sarg: *Xal package not on the plane.* This could be problematic for the investigation. They hoped to arrest everyone, but with Destiny still being on the loose, how would the others react?

The detectives took T-Bone into an interview room and left for a brief moment.

Jordan sent a text to Koi, telling her the operation went down without too many issues. He did convey, "Destiny, not on the plane."

She learned earlier about Destiny conveying to Jordan the FBI would work diligently to find her. She texted Jordan "I love you" with her last text, and he followed up with the same text.

Back at the station in an interview room, "Mr. Ferguson, I would like to introduce myself. I'm Detective Jacobs. I'm going to lay it out for you. You work for Destiny. Our investigation has uncovered she is a large distributor of drugs throughout Louisiana, Georgia, Florida, Alabama, Mississippi, Tennessee, and Arkansas. We believe we can help you, but understand this, you are going to prison for a long time. The question is, will you be tied to murder, or cooperate with us?" as Sarg shuffled a couple of photos showing T-Bone handling shipments of drugs.

T-Bone, Sarg, and Jordan went back and forth on different aspects of the case. The detectives did not want to lay out the entire case in front of him, but wanted him to deduce whether to help himself or go down with a long prison sentence.

The detectives informed T-Bone of the other arrests, as they continued talking. He laughed off their assumptions; he knew no one would talk. Those who worked for Destiny understood that if they talked, death would soon follow, even if they were in prison.

With the interrogation going nowhere, and the detectives finally rationalized, T-Bone planned on staying quiet.

"You don't understand who you are messing with," mumbled T-Bone as the detectives left the room.

"We are aware of Raul. Trust me, everyone involved is going to prison. I promise you, Terrance," growled Sarg, informing T-Bone, the detectives knew who ran the organization from Mexico, Garza.

With the interrogation over, time to rest. A productive day, except that Destiny had escaped capture, and neither Derrick nor T-Bone implicated her in any illegal activity.

Thaddus Larue called NOPD. He would be representing Derrick, T-Bone, and Major C. He wanted a 9 a.m. meeting with the arresting officers and the prosecuting attorney.

Before the teams left for the day, Sarg told the team how proud he was of their performance. He wanted everyone to get a good night's sleep, and, if inclined, toast one another with a drink.

He asked Jordan to stick around a little while longer. "This isn't going to be easy, Jordan, since Destiny escaped our clutches. We will attempt to make one of them flip, but if they fear Destiny, and know she hasn't been apprehended, the attorney may tell them not to cooperate," as Sarg illuminated the situation while rubbing his forehead.

"You have a headache?" asked Jordan, before reaching for some aspirin.

"No, kid, a little tired," said Sarg, with a yawn, which demonstrated his zapped energy.

"She cannot hide forever. After we meet with the attorney tomorrow, I think we should pay a visit to the FBI. Maybe they will be able to produce her whereabouts," said Sarg.

"I agree, we will find her. Think we should put some pressure on T-Bone or Major C tomorrow, even with the attorneys present?"

"Let me ponder our next move. I want to make sure they don't make bail."

"Rest up, say hi to Ly. I'll see you in the morning," said Jordan, walking over to Sarg. He shook his hand, thanking him for teaching him everything.

"Thanks. I'm so glad you have been my partner," responded Sarg, before adding, "Say hi to Koi," as Jordan walked out the door.

"I will."

The sun out, shining brightly, Destiny and Raul relaxed poolside with a drink. He spent most of the morning answering calls and making demands. The idea of anyone taking a plea deal, not acceptable.

The attorney would convey the message, *If you work with the police or feds, la muerte*, meaning death in Spanish.

Through his contacts inside the State Department, Emesto learned of the operation to arrest Destiny. Keeping the sources from Raul provided him insulation from harm. A tactic he had learned from a young age.

Needing to speak with his boss, he entered the pool area. "Raul, the FBI is going to stop at nothing to arrest Destiny. My source tells me she is going to be No. 8 on their Most Wanted List," said Emesto, as he sat down near both Raul and Destiny.

"Here that love? You are #8," laughed Raul at the notification from Emesto.

Raul was extremely cocky, and confident the feds would never take him or her into custody. Before going out on his own, Juan Perez taught the future drug lord a valuable lesson: intimidation is a great motivator. The ex-partners agreed to allow Raul a chance to run his own operation, with one caveat; he would never attack any other cartel.

By working his way into the Canadian and European markets, Raul blazed his own trail, which netted him millions. After tapping the college market, he became the second richest man in Mexico.

"Well, Emesto, you were right," said Raul, congratulating him on his intelligence cue.

"Thank you, but I would suggest Destiny stay in Mexico for the time being. We need to fly the family out of the States as well."

"Make it happen with the family. You okay with living in Mexico, dear?"

"Yes, love. Is there a house close where I could hole up for a while?" asked Destiny, hinting about the need to house her family.

"I'll look into it, and make sure their stay here is comfortable," said Raul, leaning over to kiss her.

Chapter 39

Four other agents joined Koi to rework each kidnapping. She wanted others to look over each case file with her, and maybe they would find something the other investigations missed.

One agent revealed an uneasy feeling about one particular case, Veronica Mussel, who disappeared from Clemson University. She had begun to work on her master's degree in Criminal Psychology while working for the university.

One night Veronica informed her roommate that she planned a date with a professor from LSU. The date would take place in Atlanta, as a weekend excursion. She told her friend they'd met at a conference, and struck up a long-distance relationship.

The friend never found out the name, but the revelation steered Koi to Professor Calkins. With his presence documented at one conference, where a young lady had disappeared, and now a possible second abduction, too coincidental. Time to look into Professor Calkin's life and travel habits more.

"How come we never came across this information before?" derided Koi, wondering how the FBI missed the information up to now.

"Buried deep in her file," offered Lana.

The interviewer did not think the confession from Veronica's friend provided any clues, and buried the data, using only footnotes to describe the date.

"We need to find out if Professor Calkins attended the same conference as Veronica."

"I'll put Bryce on the task," answered Nathan.

"Do we have anything else that might tie them to the professor?"

Everyone took three to four files each, and looked for collaborating evidence. Nothing more came from any of the files. The fact Veronica met someone at a conference explained how the kidnapper might be meeting the young victims.

Bryce searched for all the conferences Calkins had attended, going back to 2006. Writing herself a note, Koi wanted to interview Veronica's roommate. She excused everyone from the room, needing a little time alone to meditate.

Sitting in silence for twenty minutes, her mind completely closed off from the world. The only thing she could hear, the occasional bell coming from her phone.

With Calkins being more of the focus of the investigation, agents began to dig deeper into his life. Koi on the other hand sensed that the task force was being played.

After breaking off the meditation, she called Jordan. They talked about the missed opportunity, arresting Destiny. She would speak with someone, inside the FBI, about a possible leak, and whether they knew of Destiny's location. Pleading with him to go home and rest, Jordan said he wanted to attend Osika's game.

The game featured some excellent plays, with Osika's team winning. Jordan rode with Felton and Catori to the game, but would ride home with Koi and the girls after they picked up Kitna from her practice.

With little conversation on the way home, the adrenaline started to wear off for Jordan.

Sensing the subdued attitude, Koi asked, "Do you mind if I stop at the pharmacy before home?" She turned her head to Jordan, winking at Jordan.

"Yeah, sure. Do you want me to stay in the car with the girls?"

"If you wouldn't mind."

She walked into the pharmacy and grabbed some special oils, ones she would use on Jordan later, giving him a complete body massage. Hoping the massage would help him relax, after the day's events, time to *calm his mind*. She came out of the store with a small bag of goodies for Jordan and her.

"So, Mom, what is in the bag?" asked Kitna, as she leaned toward her mom with her playful smile.

"It's not for you, Kitna. Jordan has a couple aches and pains, so I bought some medicine," replied Koi, figuring the conversation would end.

Kitna looked at her sister, and shook her head in a "no" fashion. "I think Mom is the medicine," said Osika. The girls laughed.

"You two are smarter than you should be at this age," said a sly Koi, continuing with the ruse.

The evening, a normal night, with no mention of the day's events.

Felton, Catori, Koi, and Jordan retreated to the living room. With no TV in the room, a place for serene conversation or quiet time. This evening, however, one of dialogue, the dangers of Raul and Destiny, and the caution they needed to take.

Koi's parents reassured their daughter they would be diligent, and keep a sharp eye on their surroundings. Koi did not believe Raul would take a shot at the family, but wanted everyone involved to remain alert.

They all agreed. Taking a shot at Jordan, Sarg, or the NOPD might bring the weight of the federal government down on the organization. A smart leader, Raul decided against poking the government bees in the U.S. He summarized that other cartel bosses might work with the feds to facilitate his arrest. A similar situation happened after Colombian Drug Lord El Nino murdered hundreds. Other cartels pinpointed his whereabouts. He later died in a shootout with the Colombian Army.

Felton and Catori excused themselves, heading to bed. They both came over, and got a kiss from Koi, as they exchanged good nights.

"Do you want to go to bed?" asked Koi as she playfully ran her hands over Jordan's chest.

"You mind if we sit here for a bit? I haven't quite wound down from today," replied Jordan.

She circled her arms with Jordan's, "Absolutely, love. I'm so glad nothing happened to you today. I know you didn't arrest Destiny, but you will."

"It will be a little more difficult with her in Mexico. How much the Mexican authorities will help us is anybody's guess," Jordan said.

Inside the Mexican government, certain officials worked with Raul, since he spread millions of dollars throughout the region. He sent $4 million to the government as a bribe in 2008.

"I've been caught up in my case. How are things going with yours?" quizzed Jordan.

Reluctant to tell Jordan what the team had found, she also knew that hiding it from him might hurt their relationship, and believed he might find out from someone else.

"Professor Calkins from LSU, our research links him to some conferences where two of the kidnapped victims attended. We are looking into his whereabouts, and some cell records." The pain in Koi's face evident with stress after sharing the intel.

She buried her face into Jordan's chest, hoping he would not disapprove of the confession. The professor, a person of interest, but not a suspect.

"Listen, honey, wherever your evidence takes you, I am behind you 100 percent. I will never compromise your investigations."

Her heart beating at a frantic pace. She usually kept her emotions in check, but being with Jordan, and disclosing the possible professor's involvement, proved hard for her to hold in emotionally.

"Not sure how much he is connected, but we need to look into every avenue. Maybe he can tell us of others who attended, and lead us to a suspect," said a relieved Koi.

"His track record for seducing college students, a definite reason for concern."

"Would you like to go to bed? I bought a couple of oils I want to use on you, give you a full body massage," said Koi, kissing Jordan, before they headed toward the bedroom.

The lust reached a fever pitch when they got into the bedroom. Jordan came up behind Koi and worked his hands all over her. He undid her pants and ran his fingers down her pants. With his other hand, he went underneath her shirt, with both her shirt and pants coming off.

Lying naked, with Jordan sitting on top of her while she lay face down on the bed. He rubbed oil all over her. Soon he slid himself inside her. She moaned, feeling his immense strength, pleasing her. She would later force him on his back while she rode him until they both finished.

Chapter 40

The next morning, after showering together, Jordan and Koi sat on her settee, a quiet moment together. After a half hour in silence, they headed to the kitchen.

Felton sat at the table with his coffee, as both Koi and Jordan walked in the kitchen area and poured a cup of coffee and sat down, after asking Felton how he slept.

Koi asked, "Dad, can you and Mom watch the girls? I need to head into the office." She needed to go into the office.

He agreed to take care of the kids. She explained the possibility of being at the office long into the night.

A message from Jessica Lathrop, Veronica's friend, accompanied Koi as she walked into her office. She called Jessica, without hesitation, asking her recollection of the events.

Her only recollection, the professor worked at LSU. She never learned his name.

The previous month Veronica kept to herself. She took two trips to Atlanta before the fatal third trip, which she never returned from.

The police never found Veronica's phone. This case resembled the others, a disposable phone being used to communicate back and forth.

The FBI learned more about the PO box and the phone's possible usages. An agent photographed a young man picking up the phones. The phones ended up all over the country, after being mailed out.

The young man, being used as a go-between, sending out phones. The recipients did not want their calls traced. He wrote down a couple of the addresses. The uses, cheating spouses looking to keep their affairs secret.

After the FBI interviewed him, they concluded that neither the young man nor the phones were part of the Southern Belle case.

After digging into his travel habits, Bryce came into the office with some new findings. Professor Calkins, over the years, had attended numerous conferences. Most of the conferences dealt with the psychology of criminals. In most of the cases, the conferences showed one hundred to two hundred attendees, including FBI agents from time to time. He wanted to show Koi his findings.

The professor offered a wealth of facts and theory. He would often speak at these conferences. Young women frequently attended the conferences, which provided the tie-in. Looking at the professor's cell phone showed no connection between the professors and the kidnapped women.

After Bryce left, Koi sat for some time. More clues, but something amiss, she concluded. She didn't want to confront the professor yet; she wanted discernible evidence tying him to the disappearances.

From a distance, the distinctive voice of Liz coming down the hall. She made comments about everyone she passed.

"Koi got something for you," as she sat down with Koi looking across from her at her desk.

"I hacked into Shelby Davison's cell phone, one no one ever knew about," she continued. "I found a pic from the night she disappeared," as Liz handed a copy of the photo to Koi.

A photo of two women in bed together, with Shelby on the bottom, the other woman hidden. Liz, believed the woman on top, might be wearing a wig or hair extensions. The pic deleted from the phone, but

Liz found the pic after recreating her cell phone with a program she built.

The photo offered no clues, other than the possibility that Shelby might be a lesbian. As she left, Koi thanked her, and said she looked nice.

The meeting between Sarg, Jordan, the attorney, and defendants went as expected. The attorney told both detectives he would be suing the department for false imprisonment.

"A judge will deny bail, I promise you," said Sarg.

"That's bullshit. My clients are innocent of the charges. Your so-called evidence is flimsy. They are law-abiding citizens with everyday jobs," expressed Mr. Argyle, with a forceful stance.

"Look, our investigation will deliver guilty pleas, showing your clients are major players in the Garza drug family," said Jordan.

The attorney laughed off the assumption before Jordan said, "They work for Destiny Young."

"What? You are out of your mind," replied Argyle, chuckling at the assumption.

"Your clients can help themselves or not, but make no mistake they are going to prison," asserted Jordan, hoping the suspects would help the officers out, but figuring it might be a feeble request.

"We will see you in court tomorrow, gentlemen," said the attorney, as he rose to leave, informing his clients to not speak to anyone without him present.

The attorney left in a huff, angered by the idea his clients would not receive bail. He called Raul, to inform him of the news.

Near Baton Rouge, a twenty-minute drive, Professor Calkins purchased a home. The home allowed the professor a place to take students. Secluded from neighbors, the nearest neighbor some five miles away.

The house inside the city limits offered no privacy, so he never took his students to the Baton Rouge home. On this day, a day off from teaching, one of his students came over, Tiffany Bachiles. Smaller in statue, blond, with a cheerleader's body. Most people notice her eyes when first meeting her, very sexy.

Infatuated with the younger-looking professor, Tiffany enjoyed spending time with him. Calkins, in his early forties, but looked much younger as he kept himself in excellent shape.

"I have some papers to read. Why don't you step outside, soak up some rays, lay by the pool?" questioned the professor.

"I would love to. Don't take too long, because I'll be sunbathing nude," as Tiffany took her top off, and flung the top at the professor. Tiffany knew this would not be a long-term situation, and believed other students spent time with the professor.

The relationship had started two weeks prior. Calkins wanted to remain discreet; he paid for everything. In turn, she would receive a favorable grade, no matter how she performed on tests.

Later the professor walked outside, and began spreading tanning oil all over the front and back of Tiffany. He started by sucking her chest, before going down on her, taking her clit into his mouth.

Wanting control, she rolled the professor on his back, and began to ride him, with his clothes on. She took his shorts off, licking her way up, before sliding his erect penis inside. She teased him, not allowing him to fully enter inside her.

She let loose of her control, and allowed him to go deep inside her, moaning with pleasure. After they finished, a quick swim in the pool followed. The professor went back inside to grade more papers, with Tiffany staying outside, soaking up the sun.

She ended up staying the night at the professor's house. They repeated their lovemaking two more times. By morning they headed separate ways, one to class, one to teach.

Chapter 41

Neither of the cases Jordan and Koi were investigating brought little progress over the next couple of days. Koi would leave in the morning for Washington, DC. She planned a meeting with a veteran agent. The agent, credited with catching eight serial killers during his distinguished career. She wanted to pick his brain about the case.

Jordan's case became more complicated with the attorney now involved. The defendants decided against cooperating with the police. The case started to receive more attention nationally, which brought more scrutiny.

Koi's plane landed around 8:25 a.m., with a car waiting for her. She was eager to meet the legendary Robert Murphy. He brought a sense of etiquette with his investigations. Calm and collected, he believed his subjects deserved some dignity, and often found that brash, in-your face interrogations seldom brought the intended results.

He had grown up in a well-to-do family from the East Coast. After graduating from Harvard, he later received additional degrees from Georgetown and VMI. His FBI career afforded him the opportunity to write over twenty books on psychological profiles, investigations, interrogation techniques, and the simple way of obtaining evidence. Both Koi and Robert shared pleasantries as they sat down.

With Koi and Robert being Hoyas they had an inner kinship. Hoyas will always be Hoyas, even though Robert got his bachelors from Harvard.

They shared a few stories, including about a couple of professors whom they took classes from. Robert told Koi how he followed Georgetown volleyball during her time there.

They delved into the Southern Belle case. Robert offered his opinion on a couple aspects of the case; she concurred with his assumptions. The two agents agreed, the kidnapper was a professional, not a loaner. The girls, quite intelligent, beautiful, and driven in many ways, would be fearful of the loaner look.

Falling for a serial killer, like Randall Woodfield, especially this many young women, did not fit the profile of someone like Woodfield. The perpetrator, sophisticated, debonair, and able to garner trust.

"Do you have any suspects, or a place of origin?" asked Robert, seeking some background on the suspects, or Agent Blackthorn's thinking.

"I believe my perpetrator lives in Louisiana. They need resources, need seclusion, and time to do what they are doing," answered Koi.

The former agent put his hands together, rubbing them. "You can trust me. I believe you know more; I will never do anything to harm your case," said Robert, reacting to Koi's vague hypothesis.

Koi's reputation within FBI circles, exemplar, after talking with a few current agents, who said, "Koi, is hyper-intelligent, and difficult to match wits with." He wanted to learn more about how she differentiated falsehoods from evidence in such a difficult case.

"Sir, I do trust you. I'm guarded with some of the facts, and it isn't that I don't trust you, but if you say something to someone else, they may repeat it, jeopardizing my case," explaining her position.

They would spend the next hour sorting through the case file, and placing data they believed important to the case in a different file folder. Robert used this strategy on all of his cases. He felt it helped steer him in a certain direction, once a fork in the road became apparent.

"Thank you, Robert, for your help. If I need to contact you, is this the number I should use?" pointing to the business card he gave her.

"You are welcome, and yes, it is," answered Robert, leaving the office, with Koi heading back to New Orleans.

She found renewed energy after talking with Robert. He shared his expertise, and knowledge, which she believed would be beneficial.

One thing mystified her. The last thing he said was, "Sometimes the answer is right in front of you."

A warning of sorts, with Koi questioning, *Am I heading in the right direction?*

Destiny's sister, mom, and aunt boarded a secret flight out of southern Texas; their destination, Raul's private airport. They would only be allowed to bring the necessities.

Destiny's other sister, Malisa, the sole owner of the home, and most of the cars, could not be touched since she ran legitimate businesses. Her hair-nail-spa business showed income around $600,000 a year. The financial division of the FBI looked into the business taxes and could not find anything out of the ordinary.

Raul and Destiny waited for the plane to land. The family stayed in a hacienda on the beach not too far from his place. They held hands tightly as the plane landed. When the doors opened, she ran over to the stairs to greet her family.

"I missed you guys so much. I'm so happy you are here," said Destiny, as she hugged each member of her family.

"We thought the feds were on our tail, a false alarm. I don't think they realized we skipped town, until it was too late," replied her sister, Neesea.

Destiny introduced the family to Raul, with one of Raul's helpers grabbing the bags and putting them into the SUV, before driving off to the hacienda.

A gated area, excluded from prying eyes and police observation. Destiny began to decorate the house, with Raul paying the bill.

"What do you think, Momma?" said Destiny, showing each one of them their rooms, and the rest of the house.

"It's beautiful dear, and I would like to thank you, Raul, for your hospitality and getting us out of the country," said Destiny's mom, with both Neesea and the aunt following up with the same sentiments.

The estate would be complete with servants and cooks. Gardiners would attend to the outside needs, with a pool service person handling the pool. Outside beyond the pool area, a private beach. Guards patrolled the grounds to ensure safety.

Getting ready to leave, Destiny pulled Raul aside. "Want a quickie before you go home to your wife?" asked Destiny, sliding her hand toward his private area.

She followed, "Hmmm, I think you do, based on what I'm feeling," while biting his earlobe.

"I really should go," said Raul, trying to fight off the urge to take Destiny up on her proposition.

She ripped open her shirt, exposing her chest, and within a second grabbed his head and forced him to start sucking on her nipples. His hand slid under her skirt. He put his finger inside her; he could feel her wetness.

"Let's go to your room," prodded Raul. The stairs, magnificent, reminiscent of an eighteenth-century castle.

After they finished, Raul started to dress when Destiny said, "Think of me when you are doing your wife tonight." He replied that he would. They confirmed the next day's meeting, to talk about business, before he left.

Back at the estate, Raul greeted his wife, Gabriela. She came from an athletic family. At a young age a couple of modeling agencies offered her a contract based on her elegant looks. They hugged and kissed each other. She could smell Destiny on him, and the smell of sex. She quickly pulled away, as he tried to keep her close.

"You son-of-a-bitch, you are screwing someone else?" demanding to know the answer she already knew.

"What are you talking about?" asked Raul, stunned by his wife's language. He thought to himself, *Oh shit, did I get caught?*

"You bastard, don't lie to me. I can smell her scent on you," snarled Gabriela, walking away. He chased his wife, and within a couple of steps spun her around with his hands holding each one of her arms.

"Listen, I will do as I please. I take care of all of your needs, and when I am through with you, I'll make that decision." This is the first time Raul ever showed anger toward his wife. She ran out of the room in tears, after Raul let her go.

Ashamed of the relationship, but he concluded that Gabriela needed to know her place. After all, he presumed, his wife belonged to him. He paid the bills. She lived in a nice house, no limits on her spending, and she traveled outside the country on private planes.

Chapter 42

Waking up early, after going to bed early, Jordan and Koi decided to go for a walk. She wanted a sense of normalcy with their lives, which might prove difficult with the both of them working in law enforcement. They held hands, not saying much.

She spoke first. "I need to head up to Baton Rouge and interview Professor Calkins." She exhorted him to never speak with anyone at LSU. He complied with the request, and said he would never undermine her investigation.

They continued to chat about the events scheduled for the next few days. As Jordan and Koi walked into the house, the girls were up eating breakfast. Osika grabbed Jordan's hand, pulling him close, followed by a hug.

"What, no hug for me? Excuse me, but I am the one who gave birth to you," said Koi, with a smile on her face.

"Love you, Mom," quickly responded Osika.

At the office a secretary handed Jordan a message, before he had a chance to sit down. Destiny's family had left the country the previous morning. The youngest sister, still in New Orleans. Fifteen minutes later Jaron's mother phoned. She heard that her family might be associated with her son's murder. She wanted to meet the detectives today! They consented to the meeting.

Meeting at a coffee shop off Huey P. Long Avenue, the detectives provided little information about her niece's involvement.

A hard worker, Julie became a nurse, and worked at the university Medical Center. She paid for Jaron's college education; he was her only child. Family was so important to her, but she became distant from her two sisters, and niece, Destiny. Over the last couple of months, Destiny visited the house more. Julie wondered why.

The three of them talked for over an hour, with Julie forcefully asking pointed questions. Jordan explained their investigation: ongoing, they continued working all avenues, and they wanted to question Destiny more, "filling in some holes."

Sarg begged Julie to not speak to anyone about her niece's possible connection. An intelligent woman, and she understood the detective's motives, dancing around the subject, but her intuition formed the opinion that her niece was an intricate part to the murder.

She became infuriated at the thought, her own flesh, murdered her only son. As she became enraged, Jordan calmed her down. She told the detectives, "I will allow you to continue the investigation."

She did offer a warning, before they all went their separate ways.

"If I get a hold of Destiny before you, you will have two murders on your hands," as Sarg hugged Julie, trying to comfort her.

Not only was her son dead, but her kin had murdered him. How could her two sisters allow this to happen? Close growing up, but they drifted apart once Destiny and Neesea became successful. Her sisters often flaunted their wealth, which caused tension at times.

Julie cared very little about the wealth; her son was her wealth. He became a bright young man, volunteered to help kids with reading at the local Boys/Girls club. She hoped to one day work in the same hospital, like their own family business, she reasoned, caring for people.

The detectives got back into the office and received a message from the FBI: they should meet as soon as possible. Sarg told Jordan to make the call and set it up. He called and the meeting would be at the FBI office tomorrow morning.

Jordan asked if it might be wise to sit with Major C, real name Bernard Jackson. He was the only provider for his younger brother and sister. Bernard's mom struggled financially; he took care of the family financially, moving his mom and siblings into a middle-class neighborhood. A recent finding, a safe deposit box with over $900,000 in cash. The feds confiscated the money as part of the investigation.

The question of the day: Would the feds be willing to allow Bernard's mom to keep the money, and help the family if he decided to work with NOPD? Sarg thought the idea needed to be pursued.

Chapter 43

One of the agents, helping with the Southern Belle case, sat in Koi's office, discussing the case. According to research, Professor Calkins and five of the kidnapped victims attended the same conference, together. A revealing piece of information. Koi requested more resources, to uncover every aspect of the professor's life.

Liz came calling. She looked giddy, like she'd discovered something important.

"Koi…Koi guess what?" as she bunny-hopped into her office. At times, Liz acted a little immature, but her full-of-life personality gave her the green light for such foolishness.

"Slow down, Liz. Do you have something for me?"

"I uncovered our sleazeball professor; he stayed the night with Shelby in Atlanta. He used a different name, Mark Holden, and they stayed at the Holiday Inn outside of Atlanta."

"How did you come across this information?" she asked Koi, looking puzzled.

"You don't want to know! I think it best if the secret stays with me for now," answered Liz.

"Okay, this is helpful; you are sure they were together?"

"Positive. This receipt shows Holden and guests. An assistant manager said she remembered the guest's name, Shelby Davis," said Liz, handing the receipt to Koi.

"You are becoming a valuable asset to the agency, and if we catch this person, I guarantee you will receive an accommodation."

"A raise would be more useful," said Liz, lifting her eyebrows, and shaking her hands as if to say "duh."

"If not the raise, how about you and I go to a nightclub with some of my friends, loosen you up a little? You can bring your boyfriend," grinned Liz, hoping Koi would accept the invitation.

"I don't think we should, but we will see," said Koi.

Dionte and Koi met to go over the new findings. Koi asked if questioning the professor, a grilling, would be in order, after learning of the recent developments about Shelby and the professor.

Taking a moment to ponder the question, Dionte agreed. The added pressure on the professor might produce a lead, or possibly implicate the professor.

He suggested waiting an extra day, with Jordan coming to the office tomorrow.

She replied, "I think my presence is not needed. Allow everyone to focus on their cases, not Jordan and me."

"Everyone knows—in fact, everybody is wondering—when you are going to ask him to marry you," laughed Dionte, with the assertion that the entire staff knew about the relationship.

"What do you mean I should ask him?" said a baffled Koi.

"You are a take-charge type of woman—time for you to act."

"Sometimes I want to kick your ass, but I would have to explain it to Washington!"

"I am your brother; you would do that to me?" asked Dionte.

"In a heartbeat, and Charron wouldn't say a thing," answered Koi, referring to Dionte's wife's acceptance of the beatdown.

"Charron is actually hoping you will ask her to help plan the wedding," responded Dionte.

"Wow, you guys are going fast—can I catch this bastard first," said Koi before asking, "By the way, I would like to take some time off after this case is over. Think Jordan and I will go somewhere."

"Moving too fast, huh?" as Dionte raised his folded hands underneath his chin.

"I've got work to do," as Koi started to step out of his office before adding, "Thanks, Dionte, you are the best."

Looking deeper into Professor Calkins, Koi wanted to ask him certain questions, and brought Special Agent Rockman into her office. With Rockman acting as the professor, she asked questions, giving her feedback on what the professor might say and how she should follow up.

When Agent Rockman left, Koi felt more confident with her interrogating technique. She called the professor to set up the meeting. *Kind of tying up loose ends*, as she explained.

With the kids asleep, Jordan and Koi found time to relax together. She expressed the need to visit the professor again, and ask more questions.

"Guess our relationship is news in the office," as Koi leaned her head on Jordan's shoulder. "We are married, according to the office scuttlebutt."

"I would like to be married," offered Jordan, while stroking Koi's hair. He added, "Question for you, though. What would you think about you and the girls going up to my parents for lunch on Sunday?" asked Jordan.

"That is a great idea, plus give my mom and dad a day to themselves," said an enthusiastic Koi, as she turned to Jordan and grabbed his face before kissing him.

"You are so good for me. My mom and dad are going to like you. They can't wait to meet you and the girls," replied Jordan.

As they got into bed, Koi asked Jordan what he thought about having a child. A discussion they both needed to talk about. Jordan always believed Koi did not want more children. He wanted kids, with the idea of adopting being tossed about.

"I can still have kids," said Koi as Jordan reached under her shirt.

Chapter 44

Since accusing him of cheating, Gabriela spoke very little with Raul. He never thought his wife would find out about his infidelities, but now, he needed to restore the marriage. His angle, *tell her how much I care for her*, while still carrying on with the affair.

"Gabriela, you are going to have to speak with me at some point," demanded Raul, taking a drink of his juice.

"What the hell do you want me to say? You are planting your seed in another woman. Why? Do you remember your vows? Is there something I have done wrong?" asked a pained Gabriela.

"No, you haven't. You need to understand, I will do anything for you, and the kids."

"Don't lie to me—hollow words. You are getting your dick off. Does she do something for you I don't?"

"Gabriela, I am going to be truthful. I'm going to keep seeing this woman. I will not flaunt this in front of you or the kids, but our relationship is business."

"How in the hell am I supposed to answer? A side piece, and I am required to accept her as business? Am I allowed a side piece?" grilled Gabriela.

"No, you are not allowed. If I catch you with another man, I will make you watch as I torture and bury him alive," said an angered Raul, as he left the table.

Dumbfounded by her husband's admission he would continue with the affair, she needed to accept the fact. Under the current conditions, she would be unable to inform her father, or anyone else. Her thoughts: *How many other business partners does he screw?*

Afraid for her family, she made the decision: protect her kids. She would find a way to punish her husband, one day, but not today.

Meeting in the estate room, to talk business, Raul and others discussed the four individuals who would take over the New Orleans operation. The distribution of drugs would be at full capacity within the week. A question came up: How to handle if anyone turned against Destiny? Raul asserted he would kill anyone to protect Destiny. Emesto believed no one would turn. The attorney communicated his beliefs to the defendants, believing they would receive light sentences.

"Emesto, how can we be so sure no one will turn?" grilled Raul.

"Raul, I cannot offer you a 100 percent guarantee. I can only tell you, your message of death will be communicated. We will not allow any betrayal," said Emesto, before adding, "Maybe offer better positions or a chance to live somewhere in the Caribbean?"

"I'm sure we can accommodate any reasonable demands. T-Bone and Major C are important clogs to the organization—wouldn't you agree, honey?"

"I agree. They need to be a part of any new setup," answered Destiny.

"Let's make sure they get out, at any cost."

Raul and Destiny spent the next few hours touring the town and areas of interest. He believed Destiny would be safe around town, but warned her, she should not go outside of the city, unless she took protection with her and informed Raul.

Ciudad Madero, a tourist town, with a large oil/gas refinery. The city had transformed itself into a tourist town while showing no effects from the drug wars being experienced in other parts of Mexico. Five years ago, Raul decided to make this his home base.

Close to the ocean, and the people accepted him. He made sure the people received healthcare, money in their pocket, and an education. In turn the town protected him, at all cost.

The detectives entered the FBI offices in New Orleans. The office, on the north side of the city, not far from Southern University. This would be the first time Jordan visited the FBI offices. Sarg had visited a couple of times over the years.

Security buzzed the detectives in the building. Once inside, Special Agent Nelson Batcker greeted the two men. They exchanged pleasantries and headed off to his office.

Nelson informed the detectives that assets had begun to monitor Destiny, and her family. The Mexican government, however, would not allow the United States to follow Raul, in any fashion. The detectives were mystified and outraged at the disrespect the Mexican government showed toward the U.S.

"Gentlemen, we do conduct clandestine operations without the Mexican government's permission. We need more time," said Nelson.

He continued, "We will continue putting assets in place. We need to proceed with extreme caution. Rest assured, we will track Raul, and who he is talking to. It's going to take a little time getting the assets in place," explained Watkins.

"What about Destiny? Anything of substance?" asked Sarg, hoping the agent would offer better news on her surveillance.

"No phones yet, but working on assets, on the ground, and we are working to facilitate moles, who report back to us only," said the agent.

"Has anything of substance come from following her so far?" asked Jordan.

With this being his first experience working with the FBI on a joint operation, Jordan discerned that the FBI was treating the NOPD as children. Nelson relayed a message from Washington. NOPD would be provided information on a *Need-to-know basis.* The State Department wanted to ensure that relations between the two governments would remain positive. A murder case in New Orleans, of little concern to the State Department.

"As you are aware, Destiny's mom, one of her sisters, and her aunt left the country. They are all together in Ciudad Madero," mentioned Agent Batcker. The agent knew the FBI had dropped the ball on the family. Continuing the conversation, the agent reiterated that the sister, Malissa, was not part of any current investigation. They were, however, tapping phones, believing she might be contacting Destiny.

The three men discussed the FBI's role, and how they would communicate with NOPD, if Destiny or her family came back to the U.S. They thanked each other for the cooperation.

Before leaving, Jordan spoke up, and asked about the chance the feds would allow Bernard Jackson to keep his money if he worked with the police. Agent Batcker said he would pass the request up the chain of command.

"What do you think, Sarg?" asked Jordan, as they left the agent's office.

"Definitely going to be much harder to bring Destiny back. With the Mexican government protecting Raul."

"I agree, the two governments made our jobs much harder, not unlike 4th-and-30 with thirty seconds left and you need a TD," rationalized Jordan, trying to use a football metaphor to lighten the mood.

"You are taking us to lunch by the way?" questioned Sarg.

"Who are *we*, and I'm buying?" asked a puzzled Jordan. Dionte convinced Koi to stay around the office.

"Kid, I told you before, old Sarg knows everything."

Dionte appeared and introduced himself.

"Good morning, Sarg, how are you, old dog?" said a spirited Dionte. Their friendship went back a few years, and with the connection to Koi, and her family, the friendship grew. They considered each other family.

"Old dog, boy if I didn't know your wife, I might take you outside and show you some old dog tricks," laughed Sarg, responding to the ribbing from Dionte.

"Koi said the same thing to me the other day," as they shook hands.

"This must be Jordan? I'm Dionte Cattrell. Koi might not admit it, but I'm like her brother in some ways," said Dionte, expressing their relationship.

"She did mention you needed an ass kicking the other day. I told her to go work out on her punching bag. I think she said your name every time she threw a punch or kick—maybe I'm wrong," replied Jordan, offering up one of the ways Koi used to burn energy.

"When she bought the bag, she named it Dionte," said Dionte before continuing, "Let's hope she never renames the bag Jordan," as the three men laughed.

"What's so funny?" asked Koi, approaching the three men.

"Oh, wondering when you might rename your punching bag Jordan," expressed Dionte, in a sarcastic manner.

"Dionte, I will never rename the bag," shot back Koi, as she grabbed Jordan's hand and smiled at him.

"Thanks, sis. I appreciate how you show your love," said Dionte. Before leaving for lunch, Dionte asked if Sarg would be interested in getting up a game of chess in the near future.

"Glad to meet you, Jordan," said Dionte, before heading back to his office.

At lunch Koi, Jordan, and Sarg talked about Destiny, and the future communication between the two agencies. The explanation, with respect to the surveillance of Destiny, did not sit well with the two detectives. Koi expressed her dissatisfaction but concluded that the State Department would be giving the marching orders. She clarified the U.S. position by saying, "They are cautious idiots."

The two governments began negotiating joint operations. The State Department felt if the U.S. infringed on Raul's organization the negotiations would go nowhere. The consensus, this is a ploy to restrict U.S. involvement, since she figured certain Mexican politicians did not want Raul apprehended.

Her theory, the U.S. government wanted to placate the Mexicans, as they did with the Jamaican government a few years ago.

Sitting at Kitna's game later in the evening, Koi asked Jordan about taking a vacation, sometime before or after Christmas. The kids would be off from practices, games, and they all needed the time off.

He responded, "I will submit a time-off request."

"How does the Cayman Islands sound?" asked Koi.

The beaches and hospitality, first-rate; the islanders loved tourists. He agreed that it would be a perfect spot for their first vacation together.

Chapter 45

Making the trip to Baton Rouge, again, Koi started out early, with an expected appointment at 9 a.m. Sifting through the evidence brought bouts of confusion. Could someone be providing false leads for the FBI to follow? The abhorrent professor, sleeping with college students, and maybe the kidnapper. Why would the LSU administration at least not look into his conniving sexual ways?

On the way up, however, Koi made a point to think about her relationship with Jordan. The way the kids and her parents accepted him, a relief. She looked forward to Sunday, and the lunch date with his parents. She wondered if Jordan would accept living in her house. The idea made more sense than moving everything to Jordan's house.

Approaching the desk, Koi informed the secretary about her scheduled appointment with Calkins. Five minutes later the professor came out, unaware of the uncomfortable position he would be put in soon. "Thanks for seeing me on such short notice," said Koi as she sat down.

"No problem. Are you getting any closer to finding your perpetrator?"

"Well, may I ask you a couple of questions, regarding your attending and speaking at certain conferences? Some of our kidnapped victims attended the same conferences. Maybe you could help me. Do you recognize any of these names." Koi slid a piece of paper over to the professor.

The professor's temples started to bulge, while starting a nervous twitch with his hand. Professor Calkins tried to be discreet with his relationships. He deduced the agent might know about his indulgence.

"Do you know Shelby Davison?" quizzed Koi, looking for facial expressions and tone with the professor's answer.

"I do. Why do you ask?" said Calkins, raising his voice.

"Professor, please no need to be defensive. What I am trying to do is fill in some blanks. My thinking, the girls met someone at one of these conferences, and since we found a connection with you and the young women, we thought you noticed something out of the ordinary," admonished Koi.

"Okay. I began to wonder if you are implicating me in these disappearances. I do remember seeing her at the conference, bright girl. We discussed different psychological profiles, and how evidence is sometimes overlooked."

"Did you and Shelby meet outside of the conference?" The professor looked away, a sign of embarrassment.

"I think we met for dinner."

"Nothing more?"

"Not that I recall. Why do you ask?" prodded Professor Calkins. He wanted to find Koi's angle, before answering.

"Listen, the two of you are adults and I'm not here to scold you on any relationships you might have off campus. I'm trying to put all the pieces of the puzzle together, and why young women are disappearing."

"We did spend time together, romantically. We broke things off a couple weeks after meeting in Charlotte. The distance between us caused the breakup."

Koi rattled off the four names, all names of women who had attended the same conferences as the professor. Taken aback by the implication, he recalled being involved with two of the four names. He wanted to end the interrogation, but withdrew the sentiment, figuring Koi might dig deeper into his life, something she began doing three days ago.

The professor offered other names who attended the same conferences. Koi wrote everything down, but recorded the conversation without the professor's knowledge. The recording, inadmissible in court, did not matter to her. She wanted a word-for-word account of the conversation.

This might be the only chance to ask the professor questions without a lawyer. With the professor providing vague answers, the idea of bringing him in crossed her mind, but she relented, keeping her cool. After a couple of seconds, she calmed herself down, knowing the professor would ask for an attorney, making a task more formidable.

This might be a time when a suspect began to offer other names as a way to throw the FBI off the trail.

Leaving the office, Koi believed the professor needed deeper scrutiny. She questioned the ability of the professor to carry out the kidnappings, believing he would be more cautious in the future. If Koi needed to interview him again, she surmised, he would want an attorney present.

Heading outside the building, Koi ran into Dr. Bailey Denkins. The doctor, walking to her classroom.

"Agent Blackthorn, how are you? What brings you to our beautiful campus?" asked Dr. Denkins.

"Asking follow-up questions about conferences Professor Calkins attended."

"I may have attended a few of the same conferences with him. We occasionally travel together," said Dr. Denkins, offering up the information.

"Interesting. Any chance you observed anything out of the ordinary when attending the conferences?"

"No, most of the attendees are psych professionals. We discussed criminal behaviors. If I think of anything, I will give you a call."

"Sounds good. Thanks, Doctor," replied Koi as she headed to her car and back to New Orleans.

On the ride home, she pondered different scenarios. *What about an accomplice?*

As Dr. Denkins noted, she attended the same conferences, and the professor offered up a few names of individuals who also attended. More clues with endless answers.

Koi felt like a dog chasing its tail. Her mind drifted to Jordan, and instantly put a smile on her face. She would look into travel plans tonight, after getting home.

On this morning, Jordan spent it in a courtroom testifying on another murder case. The case went back two years. He needed to re-familiarize himself with the aspects of the case before testifying. Pleased with his testimony, the prosecutor later informed him that the defendant had pled guilty to second-degree murder, after hearing Jordan's testimony. Another murderer behind bars.

During the afternoon the detectives arrested Jackson Pendergrass's killer. The case, not related to the Lewis case. Sarg and Jordan drove to Jackson's mom's house, to tell her of the arrest. She thanked the detectives for their prompt attention to the case.

After getting back from speaking with Jackson's mom, Jordan found a message from the FBI on his desk, from Nelson. He called the number, and reached the agent. The feds were willing to let Bernard keep his money, for family purposes, if he helped convict Destiny. Great news. Now how to approach Bernard?

Around 9 p.m., before the girls went off to bed, Koi asked if they wanted to go to Baton Rouge and meet Jordan's parents. Excitement illuminated the room, at the prospect of meeting his parents. Jordan said he would show them the LSU campus, his old dorms, and the stadium.

"I need to ask your mom something? as Osika looked at Jordan.

"Well, I'm sure she will try to answer the question."

"Oh, she better or I'm calling this whole thing off," said Osika, showing what she thought was her rightful place in the hierarchy of the family.

"Little girl, be cautious. You might bite off more than you can chew," said Koi, speaking up before sending her off to bed.

Koi and Jordan retreated to her study. He spoke about his day, and the FBI allowing Bernard to keep his money in exchange for his testimony.

"How did your interview go with Heath Calkins today?" asked Jordan, approaching the subject.

"I feel like I am getting the runaround. Everyone is offering answers, but not the right answer. I think he is still someone we need to keep an eye on, but for some reason I believe he is being set up," said Koi, shaking her head.

"Is there anything you want me to do to help you?"

"Not really. The professor gave other names to investigate; they attended the conferences." Koi paused for a moment, adding, "Dr. Denkins also told me she attended the same conferences, on occasion. Now I added one to two hundred more to my suspect list."

"I have faith in you. You will catch this maniac," offered Jordan.

"Thanks, love," as both Koi and Jordan headed off to bed.

Chapter 46

Professor Calkins wanted to spend time with Tiffany. He couldn't help his urges, and with young college students willing to succumb to his sexual prowess, it became an aphrodisiac for the professor.

On this night he started by taking her from behind. Getting a little rougher, she allowed him to continue, loving the pure ecstasy of the moment. He spanked her ass, repeatedly. Tiffany remained helpless, with Calkins overpowering her. She begged for more. Pulling her hair, he tried to push himself deeper and deeper. He turned her over on her back, and cuffed her to the bed.

At first scared, but she consented. The role-playing continued, with Calkins moving her legs in different positions, first above her head, one leg up, and ended with her legs spread, clutching her ass with a firm grip before coming inside her.

The next morning, Calkins asked Tiffany if she'd heard about any weird happenings on campus. Like a stalker or student with a kinky fetish?

"The whole campus is freaky—why?" replied Tiffany.

"An FBI agent interviewed me yesterday. They believe a serial kidnapper may be on campus. I am trying to help them."

"The word on campus, you like getting your freak on with students. In return, favorable grades. Your secret is safe with me," said Tiffany, before kissing Calkins on the cheek.

"I am worried. Be careful and let me know if anything out of the ordinary happens."

They each headed in different directions, one to class, the other to teach.

Sarg made arrangements for him and Ly to visit Vietnam. This would be the first time they stepped foot on Vietnam soil since the day they left, the country and the war behind.

His excitement, overshadowed by Ly's apprehension. She assumed distant relatives still lived in the country. She told herself on the day she left, "I will never set foot on Vietnam soil again."

Now, with the war and memories behind her, she needed to make amends, and let the past stay in the past.

The country, different from the mid-'70s, now an ally of the U.S., still a communist country, with a capitalist economy. The plan, visit Ly's old village and areas where both of them worked, during the war. Afraid of how she may handle her emotions, she would lean on Sarg and the family for support. The unknowing: Did she have family in Vietnam?

"Good morning, LSU," said Sarg, entering the room dancing.

"Shake your stuff, Sarg," said Lattice, as a few of the officers joined in, encircling Sarg while he strutted about.

"Damn, Sarg, you got some moves," as another female officer danced with Sarg.

He stopped for a moment to explain his joyful mood. "One week after I retire, Ly, the kids, grandkids, and I are heading to Vietnam. Time for Ly and me to visit, a place that is a part of our young lives and brought us together." Sarg stopped dancing, before adding, "A dark place, but out of darkness, I found the love of my life, and we created two beautiful kids. This is why I believe God sent me into darkness, with the idea that two stars would come together," said Sarg, showing his religious fervor.

"You are beautiful, Sarg, and I am so happy for you and Ly," said Lattice, embracing the Sarg with a kiss on the cheek.

Sarg and Jordan sat down to discuss the offer to Bernard. With Derron on board, but questions about his psyche, or possible second thoughts. If the detectives could turn Bernard, and keep Derron on their side, the probability of convicting Destiny increased.

They figured on interviewing Bernard the next day, as long as they didn't catch a case. Jordan shared a bit more news with Sarg. He asked if he would be interested in having his retirement party at Koi's house. He told Sarg they had talked it over, and agreed the backyard offered more than enough space. Koi and Jordan would handle all the catering, and other logistics. Sarg said he would ask Ly, and figured she would love the idea.

"Are you going to ask her to marry you soon?" asked Sarg.

"When we go on vacation to the Cayman Islands, I will ask her. I'm going to ask the girls if I can marry her, and ask her on the beach. What do you think?" replied Jordan, believing his suggestion would ease Sarg's mind.

"Sounds like you gave this some thought?"

"Don't say a word. I want to surprise her."

"I will keep your secret."

Chapter 47

Word from the FBI, they were able to listen in on Destiny's conversations. A contractor, working with the FBI, planted a listening device inside the home. Nothing of substance came from the recordings. The conversations consisted of legitimate business decisions between the sisters.

One thing of interest came to light. Raul's wife learned about the affair with Destiny and sounded quite dejected about the affair. The FBI believed this might be an opportunity. By offering Raul's wife asylum, she might be willing to spy on her husband. First step, find a way to speak with her covertly.

The next day came around with both Sarg and Jordan waiting for Bernard to be transferred to the interview room. Sarg told Jordan to take the lead.

Bernard, and husky man with a beard, came in with a nasty disposition. He informed the detectives he would not talk without an attorney present. Jordan laid two pics on the table, Bernard's brother and sister.

"Yeah, so, it's my brother and sister," said Bernard sarcastically.

Jordan, without saying a word, opened his file and took out a picture of Bernard's mom. Bernard blew up, with the only thing restraining him being the handcuffs, which secured him to the table.

"You bastards, I'll cut you up in pieces! Let me get up out of here!" screamed Bernard, getting angrier by the second.

"Bernard, I got a deal for you, one which comes from the top echelon of the federal government," said Jordan, in a calm voice.

"Bitches, you got nothing on me. I'm getting' out of here once my attorney gets a chance to straighten out the judge," shouted Bernard, while leaning across the table and looking at Jordan face to face.

"Bitch, I know who you is. You that tight end played on LSU national championship team. You didn't have enough freaking talent to play in the league—another no-talent cracker," added Bernard while lowering his tone.

"Bernard, we are burning this bitch down, you feel me? Raul replaced you with four dudes from Vegas. They are running the show. Once you leave our protected custody, you will end up like this person." Jordan flipped a picture of one of Raul's victims, showing no arms, his face unrecognizable.

He paused for a second, adding, "Your world is your family, and us."

"We confiscated the $900,000 you stashed at Liberty Bank," said Sarg, explaining. "You are penniless."

Jordan proceeded to tell Bernard the feds would be willing to allow his mother to keep the money in exchange for his testimony against Destiny. The detectives wanted Bernard to tell them everything about the organization, whether Destiny ordered the hit on her cousin or any others. Jordan laid out the proposal for Bernard to view.

He reasoned with the suspect, "Destiny skipped town with her lover, and her family, leaving all her subordinates to take the fall."

Jordan disclosed the feds were willing to reduce his sentence to five years. He would be out in a year or two at worst.

He finished the interview by stating, "Derron is in protective custody, and he will testify against Destiny and implicate the Garza family."

Bernard calmed down, and listened to the two detectives lay out the proposal, and the evidence against him. He told the detectives he needed a couple days to think about the offer. They left the proposal with Bernard, but wanted an answer by Monday.

Chapter 48

Sitting alone at her desk, a call came in. A number from New York. Koi answered the call, on the other line a young lady who attended the University of Tennessee. Her name, Jackie Warner, and she wanted to speak about Professor Calkins.

She proceeded to tell Koi how the professor hit on her at a conference in Orlando. She expressed the professor's insistence they 'hook up later,' his words; together for drinks after the conference. She told the professor her boyfriend would not approve, which ended the proposal.

Later, she observed the professor hitting on another young woman, Veronica Mussel. Jackie and Veronica struck up a friendship, after meeting at a previous conference. She believed Calkins and Veronica hooked up later in the night.

Koi thanked the young lady for calling and passing along the information. Before Jackie hung up, Koi asked, "How did you get my number?"

"I got a call out of the blue, from the FBI. The agent said they wanted to know if I ever came across Professor Calkins, or any dealings with him?" replied Jackie.

"Who called you? I didn't!"

"Some man. His name, trying to remember, oh yea, Special Agent Lattimore."

"Okay, thank you. If you can think of anything else, please call me."

With no recollection of Agent Lattimore helping with this case, she asked an assistant to look up the FBI employee list. The assistant came back ten minutes later after not finding anyone named Lattimore. Had Jackie heard the name correctly? She seemed pretty sure about his name. The next question: Who is pretending to be an FBI agent?

An agent laid documents on Koi's desk, which showed cell numbers, hotels, conferences, and places the professor had visited over the last ten years. It took time getting all the data, with the travel information the most difficult. A large undertaking, going forward, sifting through the data. Three agents would work on evidence gathering the entire weekend.

Sunday could not come quick enough, but it was finally here. Felton and Catori planned on going down to Bourbon Street, and people watching. Koi, up early, allowed Jordan to sleep in a little longer. She was excited about meeting his parents, along with a day of no games and practices.

The kids came down around 8 a.m. looking for breakfast. Koi warned them about eating too much, with the cookout planned for noon. Jordan arose, and walked into the kitchen, where her mom and Jordan were kissing.

"Awe, how cute," said Kitna, a smart-aleck remark, as she rolled her eyes at her mom and Jordan.

"Are we going to start this early in the morning?" responded Koi, with her arms on her hips while addressing her daughter's comments.

Jordan sat patiently, while getting exposed to how long young girls take getting ready. Koi did not take too long with her natural beauty. She used little makeup and could be ready in twenty minutes.

The oldest daughter, Kitna, however, made up for her mom's lack of time getting ready. By 10 a.m. everyone loaded up and the car, rolling toward Baton Rouge.

Jordan's parents had lived in the same house for thirty-five years. The house, on Vice President Drive in the Old Jefferson neighborhood. Everyone got out of the car, as Jordan led everyone to the backyard, where he expected his father to be cooking on the grill.

"Hey, Dad, how are you?" said Jordan, giving his father a hug before introducing Koi and the girls.

"It's great to meet all of you," expressed Charlie, Jordan's father. Koi gave Charlie a hug, while declaring she was glad to meet Jordan's dad after hearing so much about him.

Jordan's mom came outside. "Hi, Mom, I would like you to meet Koi, Kitna, and Osika," as Jordan pointed to each of them when saying their names.

"Nice to meet all of you," said Lorena, before asking, "Is everybody hungry?"

Everyone sat at the table. Before too long, Charlie began telling Koi and the girls about Jordan's youth. The girls laughed at the stories, with Jordan hiding his head with his hands.

Koi talked about her heritage, and upbringing. The conversation switched to the girls, and their athletic accomplishments.

Jordan's parents were quite impressed with Koi, and the well-behaved girls. She later described her FBI recruitment. Being in law-enforcement interested Charlie more than Lorena.

At the same time, Kitna, Osika, and Lorena conversed about Jordan. Lorena talked about what a good kid he was, although he did things boys mischievously do.

Without asking permission Kitna bellowed out, "Mom, Osika and I think Jordan is good enough for you to marry." Everyone chuckled at the proclamation.

"I'm so happy you settled the discussion," said Koi before adding, "I agree, I think we should keep him."

"Me too," said Lorena.

After lunch, Jordan drove the girls to the LSU campus. He proudly showed them the campus, places he took classes, and Tiger Stadium. Later, they visited the historic district in Baton Rouge. A great day had by all, before heading home to New Orleans.

Chapter 49

A message came from Bernard. He wanted to meet with the detectives as soon as possible. Both detectives welcomed the news. If Bernard wanted to meet, he might be willing to flip. After talking with Sarg, they set the meeting up for the next day.

The day's news got better when Raul's wife reached out to authorities, through an intermediary. She might be willing to give up Raul, working in secret.

Sarg thought the FBI should pursue any possible opportunity to arrest Raul. "This may be a huge chance for us."

The FBI later communicated they were on board. They, however, said they would be cautious. The Mexican government would not be pleased about the covert operation. Only four FBI agents learned of Gabriela's request. They planned on keeping the information from the State Department.

"Definitely a feather in our caps—who is the contact?" asked Jordan.

"Someone within the FBI, and she is willing to help bring down her husband. I will stay on top of it," offered Sarg.

"Sounds good."

Needing to clarify the information from Jackie, Koi called her to verify the name. Jackie confided with Koi; the name was correct. Pressing Jackie about the number that called her, she replied, "Unlisted." Another dead end.

The case started to drag on Koi's psyche, with frustration setting in. Time for another opinion, from Dionte. She laid out the case, and data, on the table. She wanted to bring Professor Calkins in. He was against the idea, deciding instead to use more resources, following the professor's every move. She reluctantly agreed to continue the surveillance, but expressed her faith that the professor was her primary suspect.

Koi retreated to her desk, with Liz sitting in front. During the last two days she hacked into all the current suspect's accounts, and each of the victim's accounts. She found a message, two women talking on the phone. One, Elena, the other, undetectable. The recording, done without the other person knowing. They talked sexually to each other. Elena did not hide her feelings; the other person was more discreet.

Offering her opinion, Liz said the kidnappings might be a team effort. Koi entertained the idea; this might be something, a couple executing the kidnappings.

"Is this the only recording?" questioned Koi

"For now, this is the only copy. The discretion by the other woman makes me believe the two women met up not long after this phone call."

"How long before she disappeared after this call?" asked an inquisitive Koi.

"Her family lost track of her the next day. This person is involved somehow," expressed Liz.

Koi instructed Liz to continue digging, find out who this person is, and whether they kidnapped Elena. While hacking, Liz said she would explore some of her lesbian networks in the area, ask if a couple might be asking for unusual sexual requests, like handcuffs, or blindfolds.

From Liz's experience, women would approach her for a sexual encounter, only to find the woman wanted a threesome, with her husband or boyfriend. Liz told Koi that at a club, one time, a couple wanted to have sex with Liz in a coffin, and film it. She declined the invitation.

Expecting the kidnapper would be coming around during the day or evening, Elena wanted a precise timetable for her release. She planned on being more forceful.

A car pulled up to the house. The house and surrounding area offered a large front and back yard, cut off from the outside world, with barbed wire fencing.

Elena and her kidnapper spent the afternoon together. She asked, fearing the answer, "What are you going to do with me?"

"Well, in a couple of weeks I will let you go," he said in a sullen voice.

"Why am I here? Why are you holding me captive? I wanted to be with you," said Elena with a fearful expression.

Her kidnapper told her, "Fear nothing—you will be going home soon." After dinner and a bottle of wine, a romantic night. Elena believed she would be released soon.

Koi and Jordan went for a walk after the evening's normal activities. They talked about meeting Jordan's parents, and the girl's upcoming games. She asked about the case against Destiny.

"Bernard might be willing to turn on Destiny." The case started to take shape, a chance to bring down one of the most powerful drug lords.

During the walk, she reiterated her beliefs about Professor Calkins possibly being involved in the kidnappings.

"You think a couple is kidnapping the women? Makes sense; easier to control someone with two," asked Jordan, probing Koi's thoughts.

"It does make a little more sense. My issue, Calkins is a control freak, and secretive with his sexual exploits," answered Koi.

"He is secretive, and sounds controlling."

"The FBI is going to start following him more. I wanted to bring him in, but Dionte said no, wants more evidence."

"Sounds palatable. I mean you don't want him getting off and leaving the country, if you find more evidence."

"Tell me something, what do you think of Bailey Denkins?" questioned Koi, poking around. She knew Dr. Denkins had a previous relationship with a student, at least according to Professor Calkins. Plus, the fact that Jordan had described an investigation with a female student.

"She is an excellent professor. Worked her ass off for her doctorate degree. All the students like her, both male and female—she is cool. Wanted you to think for yourself, not accept the answer," replied Jordan, wondering about Koi's direction.

"Well, I met her the other day after interviewing Calkins. She told me she attended the same conferences. Now we learn Elena may have been with a woman before she vanished," said Koi, believing this may be too coincidental for a chance encounter.

"Do you think she and Denkins spent time together? A little thin. She might like women, or be bi, but kidnapping? She is respected in the law enforcement community," reacting to Koi's assumption.

"I know it's thin, but my perp lives here in Louisiana."

They left the discussion, switching gears to the upcoming vacation. They looked forward to the time off.

Professor Calkins spent the night with a different student at his hideaway house. Her name, Kylie. They took the sexual excursion outside, under the moonlight. She loved the ferocity of the professor's sexual power. The professor forced her against the hood of his 1964 Chevy Impala. Lifting her skirt, he pulled down his pants, and worked himself inside her. Holding her down on the hood, the sex intense.

A night of hot sex including light spanking, hair pulling, and different positions, continued inside. She enjoyed her first time with the professor.

Chapter 50

Raul made arrangements to visit one of his Venezuelan contacts, who produced drugs for his operation. The flight plans and other logistical arrangements, set up by Emesto. He planned on being gone for three days, after which he and Destiny would go to Jamaica on the yacht. With a protection detail on the yacht at all times, he never feared an attack.

Gabriela informed her husband that she had come around to his indiscretions. As long as Raul did not flaunt his promiscuity in front of her or the kids, she would accept his affair as business.

He thanked her. "I love you with all my heart."

Secretly, Gabriela began plotting against her husband. A mutual contact, a former adversary with the U.S. national women's soccer team, was her contact. They stayed in touch over the years and met in the States or Mexico on a couple of occasions.

A three-time NCAA champ at North Carolina, Paige Lawson played on the National team, which won two gold medals and a World Cup during her time as a player. Her father, a former CIA operative who made inroads with the FBI through her daughter, which led Gabriela to the FBI.

Gabriela had a scheduled flight for the same day as Raul. The flight would land in Atlanta, the meeting with her friend Paige, and the FBI.

On the phone she told Raul, "I'm taking the kids with me."

As an ex-soccer player on the Mexican national team, Gabriela never experienced trouble traveling back and forth into the States. Anxiety began to set in. If Raul found out about her meeting with the FBI, he would murder her.

The detectives walked into the interview room, Bernard sitting alone, handcuffed to the table. The detectives sat down and offered Bernard something to drink or eat. He declined.

"So, I am still thinking about your offer. My problem: how do you plan to protect my family?" said Bernard, struggling with the thought of turning against Destiny and the Garza family.

"Are you thinking of some sort of witness protection?" questioned Jordan.

"Yes, plus my welfare in prison needs to be addressed. Raul will pay someone to kill me."

"We can talk to the feds. We need to protect your immediate family? Brother, sister, and mom? Does anyone in the family need a job?" inquired Sarg.

"Yes, plus relocating me with them, and a job when I get out," as Bernard clarified his position and requests.

"We will ask the feds; they make the call. What can you tell us, we need something to take to the feds, so they know you have the goods to offer," said Jordan.

"She ordered the hit on her cousin. I was there when she gave the order to Derrick over the phone," responded Bernard.

Now the detectives could place two people in the room when Destiny gave the order.

"Anyone else in the room when she gave the order?" asked Jordan.

"Derron, T-Bone, and myself."

"We will check it out, but this is only a start. We will need more. You will need to testify against Destiny," insisted Jordan.

"You keep me alive, keep myself and the family safe, I'll help you bring her down. She is at the point she may be uncontrollable," said Bernard, as the interview finished.

Sarg and Jordan retreated to their office area. They chatted about Bernard's confession. The feds allowed Derron and Bernard, along with their families, to enter the witness protection program. If they delivered Destiny, with a chance at apprehending Raul, a small price to pay for bringing down a drug lord

They wanted to make certain Derrick would go down for pulling the trigger, and Destiny convicted for authorizing the hit. Sarg wanted Jordan to interview Derron, confirm Bernard's account.

Before Jordan made contact with the U.S. Marshals, he texted Koi. He wanted her opinion on Bernard's request. She thought the DOJ would go for the deal.

Jordan returned to the office after questioning Derron. He confirmed Bernard's recollection of the events. He also provided more information on the safe houses, and the probability the houses may be in use, to store drugs.

The next call, to Special Agent Batcker. The two men chatted about Bernard's willingness to help the feds and NOPD in exchange for federal protection for him and his family. Nelson said he would speak to his superiors, but with both Bernard and Derron being on board, he believed the government would protect both families. The only issue, capturing Destiny.

The next day a private plane landed at Hartsfield-Jackson Atlanta International Airport. On board, Gabriela and her kids. She looked forward to seeing her friend, with sightseeing planned.

"You look so good," said Paige before adding, "I'm so glad you came to visit. We are going to have fun."

"Thanks for having us," as Gabriela turned to her kids, introducing them to Paige. Both kids, one boy and one girl, were polite and educated. The daughter followed in her mom's footsteps, becoming quite the soccer player. The boy, more into nature and the ocean.

Everyone piled into Paige's SUV. Off they went to her house where she lived with her wife, Alexa. Paige, retired the year before from the national team. They planned on having kids after Paige's retirement. The women lived in a modest home, outside of Atlanta in Lawrenceville, in the downtown area. Paige started a soccer training facility, and her wife worked for the state of Georgia as an environmentalist.

The women chatted on the way to Paige's house, catching up. Gabriela proudly spoke about her daughter becoming a little soccer prodigy.

Paige reached over grabbing Gabriela's arm. "You will be safe with us."

After exiting the vehicle, Paige took Gabriela to the side and said they needed to find a time to meet with her dad and the FBI at the same time. The plan, the next day at Paige's facility.

By 5 p.m., Alexa pulled into the driveway. She requested the next couple of days off, with the three women planning on visiting the capitol, the Georgia Aquarium, and other attractions around the city. Alexa, from Georgia, had graduated from the University of Georgia. She met Paige through Alexa's brother, who attended North Carolina at the same time Paige did. Alexa's friends teased her often: "Your brother found your wife for you."

After introductions, Alexa hugged Gabriela as though they were old friends. With a bottle of wine open, the women sat at the bar talking about life. The kids in another room watching TV.

Before going to bed Alexa called her dad to confirm the meeting with Nelson in the morning. He would fly up from New Orleans and meet with Gabriela.

Chapter 51

In a secret hearing, Bernard stood before Judge Jackson with Sarg representing law enforcement, and vowing for his information. The judge wanted Bernard to understand, in exchange for his guilty plea, he was willing to testify against Destiny. The three men discussed the information, along with the validity of his knowledge regarding the inner workings of the organization. With the deal struck, Bernard would need to tell the truth on the stand, or be prosecuted, with the prosecution allowed to prosecute him with no restrictions.

Inside the briefcase sitting next to Bernard, private ledgers, which he'd confiscated after Destiny left the country. She forgot to take them, thinking her mom would be responsible for their safe keeping. On the evening Destiny left, he opened the safe, without anyone's knowledge, taking them into his possession. The ledgers offered detailed accounts, shipments, payments, contacts, all tied to Destiny. A bible of sorts, which made the prosecution case much easier. With over 100 names, the ability to put pressure on underlings, by offering reduced sentences for their testimony, assured the judge, with the federal prosecutors agreeing. All the prosecuting parties agree, Bernard's family would be able to keep the money.

On Koi's ride into work, Dr. Denkins was on her mind. Koi believed she may be hiding something, but what? Professor Calkins continued to be her prime suspect, with more data coming in daily, implicating him.

Koi summoned Liz, asking if she might be able to hack into the doctor's email, phone, or other personal accounts.

With no warrant in hand, she told Liz to keep the search private, "You cannot under any circumstances tell anyone. I am feeling a little desperate. We need to catch whoever is doing this before another girl disappears."

"I will keep my actions quiet. I will not take the fall, so we understand each other."

"I and only I will take the fall, I promise."

Liz high-fived Koi and said, "I'm starting to like you more and more. You are a badass chick, with a gun. Sexy as hell. Damn, too bad you only like men."

Caught off guard by the compliment, Koi responded, "Thanks. I think you are attractive, a little young for me. If I did like women, you and I would be hanging out." The thought of being with a woman never crossed Koi's mind. She wanted, however, to compliment Liz with the idea she would keep the hacking a secret.

"By the way, how come I'm not allowed to carry a gun?" asked Liz.

"You are a computer operator; you are not field personal. With your felony charge sealed, we would be forced to open the case file for all to view."

Going to work on Dr. Denkins' background, Koi began her search as far back as her high school career. Her social media accounts offered a few names to contact. She needed to keep this covert, and didn't want to alert the doctor.

An FBI agent handed a detailed sheet, showing the doctor's extensive travel during the last ten years. Denkins, coincidentally, traveled to some of the same cities as the missing women, and at the same time. Koi didn't believe in coincidences. This only meant that a more an in-depth search of Denkins' life would be ordered.

Two hours later, Liz walked in. She informed Koi nothing out of the ordinary in her cell and emails, except text messages between Denkins and a state senator from Louisiana. The messages showed the two of them carrying on an affair for three years. The relationship, according to Liz, broke off nine months ago. The sexual encounters took place at a house, secretly owned by Denkins. The house, not in her name; belonged to a company she owned. Liz found the company by searching the state's business lists.

The question: Why hide a house inside a company? Did Denkins use the house to meet the senator or others?

Growing up in a middle-class family, after high school Denkins attended UAB. She began teaching at community colleges while working on both her masters and doctoral in behavioral psychology from North Carolina. By securing numerous grants for the purpose of studying criminal behavior, this skyrocketed her career. Law-enforcement agencies sought her expertise, with cold cases.

The chance to collaborate with Calkins further endeared her to agencies throughout the United States, including the FBI.

Koi thought, *What a big goose egg*, perplexed by the lack of substantive evidence.

"She is having an affair with the senator. This does not mean she is kidnapping any women," as Liz showed Koi all the interactions between Dr. Denkins and others. "She does travel throughout the country, with a few trips to Europe to deliver speeches."

"I don't know, maybe I'm barking up the wrong tree. What do you think?" asked Koi.

"I'll do some more digging to see what I can come up with. If anything, we can eliminate her from the suspect list if it leads us nowhere," replied Liz, trying to mitigate the conflict between their gut and the data.

Two days later Koi received a packet that showed Dr. Denkins was using credit cards under a different name. She wanted Liz to dig deeper into the doctor's life. Lots of circumstantial and odd clues started coming in. Not only did Denkins use the unauthorized credit cards, but there was some evidence of untraceable phones showing up on the card's statements. Koi decided to keep the information to herself for the time being.

Destiny and Raul landed in Venezuela along with Emesto. They landed on a private airstrip south of Calabozo. The drug lord who owned the airstrip, Manuel Hoztas. Exempt from Venezuelan authorities, after making a deal with the government for $20 million a year, and other perks. Manuel, a large, overweight man, with heart trouble over the last couple of years. In the near future, he would turn the business over to his two sons and wanted Raul to meet them. The day, spent touring the facilities, distribution centers, and the overall drug trafficking operation.

The two sons, Rafael and Miguel, discussed the impending take-over and ensuing transfer of power. There would be no real changes, but Raul wanted to get some insurances about pricing and distribution. They all sat down for lunch to discuss the future and assure everyone things would be status quo.

Later in the day, a tour of Manuel's zoo, complete with giraffes, lions, cheetahs, wildebeests, and other exotic animals. An impressive enterprise, but a waste of money, thought Raul.

Raul and Destiny flew back to Mexico the next day, and their planned vacation.

Chapter 52

Gabriela followed Paige into her office; her cover, a vendor. Agent Batcker walked in not long after both Paige and Gabriela. Dressed as a salesman, he introduced himself, and Paige walked out the side door of her office undetected.

With two bank accounts in her possession, Gabriela passed them onto the agent before revealing her knowledge of her husband's operation. She expressed her willingness to explore and provide details about all the aspects of his operation. Agent Batcker discussed planting listening devices throughout the mansion. He also hoped she would be willing to provide computer information, allowing FBI agents to hack into the system. Taking a huge risk, Gabriela accepted the assignment.

"Nelson, I'm scared of my husband. I don't think he would do anything to our kids, but me on the other hand, who knows," blurted out an intimidated Gabriela.

"You are being extremely brave, and rest assured the agency will do everything humanly possible to ensure the health of you and the kids," expressed Watkins.

"Can you take down Raul?"

"Gabriela we can do our part. The question is, will the Mexican government consent to a joint operation if we need their help?"

She crossed her legs, leaned in, and said, "I do have a little pull within the government. I need your assurances you will do everything in your power to evacuate my kids and me, if I deem he is aware of my involvement with you."

"Outside of starting a war, I will do everything necessary to keep you and your kids safe," replied Watkins.

"War will be no issue for Raul. You may need to kill him. You also need to keep track of his intelligence officer."

"Do you know his name?"

"Emesto Perez."

"When can we meet again, and maybe someplace a little more secluded?" asked Batcker.

"Two weeks in LA."

"I'll make the arrangements. In the meantime I'll put together everything we need you to do."

Leaving the office together, Gabriela felt stronger about her conviction. If the FBI came through as Nelson proposed, she and her children would be able to start a new life, away from her husband.

On the field, Paige barked out orders for her players. An hour later, they left for lunch. Nelson flew back to New Orleans with the wisdom that the FBI might soon know Garza's every move. His informant was playing a dangerous game, one putting her life in danger.

His plane landed; he called his superiors before he sat in back of the car that escorted him back to the office. Ecstatic over the news, but concerned for Gabriela, the deputy director agreed to provide all needed resources for the operation.

Later, during the night, after the kids went to bed, Koi decided to indulge Jordan with her theory about Dr. Denkins. Incredulous about her theory, Jordan remained quiet, not offering an opinion. She continued to lay out her case, with reasoning and intuition. Jordan started to express his disbelief, by explaining law enforcement's admiration for Denkins, including the FBI's admiration. After an hour of going back and forth, Koi asked Jordan to leave the room for the night.

Lying on the couch, Jordan tossed and tumbled until falling asleep a little after 3. Koi sat in bed, going over her notes, her mind racing, with no chance to calm herself and sleep. She listened to Jordan's rebuff of her theory. He had said he would always back her; now the first real test, he failed.

At 5 a.m. she walked into the living room. Jordan, startled by Koi, opened his blanket, where she slid next to him with her back to him. He wrapped his arm around her. They fell asleep for two hours before the start of the next day.

Waking up first, Koi turned to Jordan and said, "I'm sorry for asking you to leave last night. I will work on being more patient with you."

Jordan kissed Koi on the forehead. "My attitude, I'm sure, caused your anger. I will listen to more of your theory after we come home tonight, if you want to show me?"

"I will show you all of my evidence. It is circumstantial, but still more than a coincidence."

He folded the blanket, then put it away before joining Koi in the shower.

Chapter 53

Before driving off, Koi walked over to him with the girls in her car. "I believe Denkins needs more investigation by our team. I'll bring all my evidence for you to see for yourself," said Koi, leaning into Jordan's car.

"I think you are wrong; she wouldn't do this. I will work as her attorney so you can eliminate her as a suspect," said Jordan.

"I don't want this to become between us. Be objective when you look at the evidence," replied Koi.

"I will." Koi grabbed Jordan by the face and kissed him before telling him she loved him.

Mortified by Koi's insistence about Dr. Denkins, he told himself to be patient—*after all, she is a seasoned FBI investigator.*

He needed to remain calm, but after walking into the office he snapped at Monic. "Where is my file?"

"Who in the hell do you think you are, pretty boy?" demanded Monic. "You may be a detective with some hottie FBI girlfriend, but I'm not someone you can abuse at your pleasure—you understand me, boy?" screamed Monic, letting loose anger no one had witnessed before from her.

"Monic, could you please give me a moment with Jordan?" asked Sarg, while giving her a silent command with his head.

"You take care of this, Sarg, or we may have issues," with Monic storming out of the room.

"Jordan, let's take a walk," with Sarg grabbing Jordan by the shoulder. Moments like this made Sarg the leader everyone listened to, a skill Jordan lacked. The two of them walked outside, not saying a word.

Apologizing for his terse attitude, Jordan explained the reason for his current mood. Sarg implored Jordan to listen to Koi. She possessed experience Jordan lacked. Over the years her talent and ability to find underlying evidence had produced results.

Sarg delivered a firm, "She is the best thing to ever happen to you. Don't let your ego destroy your relationship. My ego almost cost me Ly."

"How so, Sarg?"

"I didn't believe her when she told me about a CIA agent playing both sides. I finally listened to her. If I continued to ignore her, I would be dead." The men sat silent for a few moments.

"Now you need to go into the office and apologize to Monic, make things right before she slices you like Sunday dinner. Second, leave your ego at home before Koi sends you packing."

"Thanks, Sarg." The two men walked back inside where Jordan headed to Monic's desk to apologize for his behavior.

She accepted his apology. "You're the best, Monic, thanks," said Jordan, walking back to his desk.

"Darlin', don't forget what you said—I am the best," professed Monic in her southern accent.

Koi texted Jordan around 2 p.m., wondering if his mood had changed. Five minutes later, they talked by phone. She expanded on her beliefs by providing some facts. The investigation hit an obstacle, and she hoped Jordan might be willing to interview the doctor.

Running the idea by Dionte, he agreed with the calculation. Sending Jordan in made sense since Denkins would not suspect he was doing anything more than gathering information. The thought Denkins might become suspicious about a second interview with Koi was outweighed by the need to solidify her theory.

Sending Jordan to do the interview made sense from only one perspective, a ruse, with the FBI looking for different suspects, and not at Denkins.

Kio called Jordan, after speaking with Dionte. "You and I have the green light to interview Denkins."

"You take the lead; let her control the conversation. I will have a set of questions for you to ask."

Around 10 p.m., Koi and Jordan retired to her library. They discussed which questions they wanted to ask. They agreed to allow Denkins to control the interview.

With nothing on besides her thong, Jordan pulled her arms above her head. He reached for chest, caressing, before he went down on his knees. He began to lightly bite her ass, first the left cheek, then the right. She decided to take over, forcing him to the edge of the bed. She started a strip tease dance. Before too long she forced him to lean back and she took him in her mouth. Stroking and sucking him, almost to completion, she would stop before he came. Getting on top of him, she came four times before he finished. They fell asleep not long after.

Chapter 54

Jordan arrived in Baton Rouge before 9 a.m. He stopped off at a coffee shop, meeting his dad. The Lewis case, the topic of discussion, and the recent arrests. He segued into the Southern Belle case.

Working with the FBI, providing an insight into a couple of their suspects, and Koi's theories. Jordan addressed concerns with his dad over Koi's theories. His dad sat and listened intently, before forming an opinion.

Interrupting his son, Charlie said, "Koi sounds like she might be working a couple of leads outside the box. I'll say this, her intuition, from talking with some of my contacts, should never be underestimated."

"Let me ask you something. Did you ever suspect Dr. Denkins in your missing person case?"

"I made a mistake, the one with Denkins. They found the girl a couple weeks later. The victim, they found drugs in her system. She could not recall the two weeks prior to finding her," said Charlie.

"Is she still around or do you know where she lives?"

"I'll look into it for you, kid." Both Jordan and Charlie left the coffee shop with questions for each other.

Before driving off, Charlie said, "Trust Koi."

The interview with Dr. Denkins took forty minutes. Predetermined questions, offered a non-accusatory interview. Looking for eye and body language, which might show dishonest behavior. Dr. Denkins, stoic with her replies. Nothing struck Jordan or implicated the doctor.

Looking at the books on the shelves Koi asked, "What is your expertise on mind-alternating drugs?" Moving to a different subject.

Denkins shuffled in her chair, looking uncomfortable. "The Russians engineered a combination of drugs that controls the mind in a zombie state."

"What do you mean?"

"Well, they have not shared their cocktail, but the person who is drugged continues to live a normal life, but under a constant state of control. The drug alters one's memory."

"How did you come about this information?" quizzed Jordan, reflecting on the story his dad shared earlier.

"Met a couple of their psychologists at a conference, and over dinner one night they talked about the drug. They called the drug Rapture."

Jordan sat in silence, unsure of what direction to take. He made eye contact. "Thank you for your candid responses, Dr. Denkins," said Jordan.

Denkins asked, "Does the FBI have any real leads in the case?"

"No real progress with a suspect, but finding some answers to questions," answered Jordan before walking out the door, puzzled by the doctors' responses. Koi might be onto something, but Jordan still didn't believe she was involved.

Next stop for Jordan, Olivia Downs. After receiving her name from his dad, Jordan wanted to interview her. Living in Lafayette and working for the high school as an English teacher, Olivia had moved on from the incident, with help from therapists.

Lafayette was about a half-hour drive from Baton Rouge. During the drive, a call came in. The feds had take Bernard into protective custody.

Arriving at three o'clock, Jordan entered Lafayette High School. He approached the office area, introducing himself. "I'm looking for Olivia Downs; heard she works here?"

"She is in room 204. I can take you to her. We don't allow anyone to roam the halls without supervision," answered the young secretary behind the counter.

The secretary escorted Jordan. Inside, Olivia, looking over papers from the day's classes. Room 204, not unlike most teachers' rooms across America. The American flag, with posters of sayings from presidents, adorned the classroom.

Over the years had she tried to remember what had happened to her. Using different techniques, including being hypnotized, all of them proved useless in jogging her memory.

Introducing himself, Jordan said, "Olivia I'm Detective Matthews with the New Orleans police department. I'm here helping the FBI, and wanted to see if you wouldn't mind answering some questions."

"Yes, Detective Matthews, how can I help you?"

She told Jordan, at the time of her ordeal, she was attending junior college and living at home. Her memory, lost after receiving numerous shots of a mind-controlling drug. Three weeks later they found her, clothed, walking along Mahoney Road.

One memory she did recall, a house deep in the woods. A therapist later believed Olivia might be recalling a house from her youth.

Professor Calkins met Tiffany at his place after a long day of teaching and meetings with students. Students fretted with the end of semesters, grades being the factor. Tiffany got out of her car after the professor pulled into the driveway. She walked over to him, putting her arms around him, and forcibly kissing him.

He took the hint, lifting her dress before tossing her on the hood of his car. After undoing his pants, he penetrated her deeply. She loved being dominated. Calkins squeezed her neck. She begged him to stop, worrying it may get out of hand. He relinquished his grip but turned her around. Ten minutes later, he made her bend over, pulling her hair with one hand, while slapping her ass with the other. She screamed for more.

The next morning, Tiffany asked about the aggressive nature from the evening before. Thinking for a moment before answering, "I took your cue, thought you wanted it rough?"

"I love rough, but no more choking, okay? I could not breathe," replied Tiffany.

"I won't choke again, I promise."

After completing his duties for NOPD, Jordan headed over to the FBI office. The subject of the drug cocktail became a topic, with Koi asking an agent to research more about the drug. Liz, walked in unexpectedly with some data on recent communications for all of the suspects including Brandon Mince from Texas. His involvement less likely by the day with recent knowledge he was out of the country when Elena disappeared.

"Is this the boyfriend?" as Liz checked out Jordan, going up and down with her eyes.

"Jordan, this is Liz; Liz, this is Jordan. She is a crackerjack hacker," said Koi. Liz sat down next to Jordan and she handed a file folder with the data in it.

"Hello, Liz, you are as Koi described you," with both Koi and Jordan laughing about their private joke.

"Really? So she described me as hot!"

"Liz, dial down the hormones. Let's stay focused on the case," said Koi, hoping Liz would respect her demands.

The FBI allowed Jordan to be a part of the investigation. He mentioned Olivia, and where they found her, Mahoney Road.

"Did you say Mahoney Road?" asked Liz.

"Yes, why do you ask?" answered Jordan.

"Well, one of Elena's last pings on her phone was around St. Francisville. The phone was wiped clean of all messages."

"This is no coincidence. Believe me, there are lots of estates or properties that are very hidden," expressed Koi.

Another puzzle piece found, but how did the piece fit?

Chapter 55

Spotted off the western coast of Jamaica near Montego Bay, Raul's yacht, at an exclusive club. The Jamaican authorities left Raul alone. He paid the government for protection.

Destiny and Raul, spent the day shopping, sightseeing, visiting the Old Fort, and having a leisurely late lunch. They returned to his estate around 6, with news about Bernard

"I want him killed, everyone, his entire family." She stewed for a second before adding, "After all I have done for him and his family."

"Love, we will get him, don't worry. We do, however, need to be cautious," requested Raul, as he grabbed her hands and squeezed tightly to illuminate the previous mistake made with Jaron.

"I'll let you handle it, Raul. Make sure it is messy. I want everyone to understand who they are dealing with."

Jordan received a call from Agent Batcker. They were following Raul's yacht, showing it docked in Jamaica. With Destiny, on the yacht, making an arrest far too risky. The FBI wanted NOPD to stay the course, keep things quiet in the hopes Destiny would let her guard down, and they would spring into action, arresting her and possibly her family at the same time. What the agent didn't tell Jordan, the meeting with Gabriela in two days in LA.

One of the lieutenants working for Emesto called Gabriela. She refused protection for her upcoming trip to LA. Her celebrity status, an ex-national soccer player, offered some protection, but Raul demanded she be guarded at all times, fearing a brave desperado might take a shot at his wife.

He informed his lieutenant to follow her at all times, covertly. The intrigue about Gabriela alarming. *Why would she refuse protection? What did she have to hide?*

Finalizing her travel plans to LA, Gabriela called Emesto to chat about her itinerary. She made arrangements for the servants to take care of the kids.

Wanting the whole thing to be over, she reminisced about the first time she met Raul. A chance meeting at a dance club. At the time, Raul worked for Juan Perez. Handsome, charismatic, and plenty of money. They dated for a couple of months before Raul asked her to marry him. She knew nothing of his illegal activities. She became pregnant six months after the marriage, which forced her to leave the national team for a bit. After the birth of her daughter, she went back to the national team until getting pregnant with her son, at age thirty. With two kids, she decided to retire from the national team.

Entering a large living room on the east side of the mansion, looking at one of Emesto's lieutenants, Rafael. "Rafael, will you make sure that Raul Jr. does his riding lesson tomorrow?"

"Yes, Mrs. Garza. I will make sure he rides tomorrow. I talked with Emesto, and he is disappointed you are forsaking protection," said Rafael, expressing the displeasure Emesto communicated over the phone.

"Rafael, you and Emesto do not need to worry about me. I plan on meeting with some old friends from my playing days to discuss how Daniella could train in the States over the summer."

"But..."

Gabriela raised her hand in a stop motion, "Rafael, I have this. There is no need for any more discussion—are we clear?"

"Yes, ma'am."

After speaking with the kids, Raul called.

"Gabby, love, I'm meeting with Cabera, talking business. How are the kids?" asked Raul, trying to switch the conversation.

Destiny continued to work on Raul's shaft with her mouth. He tried to remain silent, but occasionally moaned.

She replied, "Everything is set—the staff knows what to do. I'll be fine."

"Good, good. Maybe we should take a vacation somewhere over Christmas, maybe Hawaii?" questioned Raul.

"Sounds nice. Love you."

"Love you to, Gabby."

About to hang up the phone, something told Gabriela to continue listening. Raul set his phone down, thinking he'd ended the call.

She overheard, "Don't stop…. I'm coming, don't stop." Gabriela ran off, not allowing anyone to see her crying.

Landing at LAX airport, she took a cab to her hotel. The meeting with Agent Batcker set for 1 p.m.

Sensing someone might be following her, Gabriela decided to go through with the meeting and find a way to alert him. Inside the restaurant, Agent Batcker, sitting alone. An experienced agent, he figured someone might follow her. He asked Agent Jessica Ostrander to appear with him, acting as Gabriela's friend. Jessica came over after washing her hands in the bathroom. She walked over and hugged Gabriela, looking like long-lost friends.

Before sitting down, Jessica whispered in Gabby's ear. "You have followers—this is our cover."

Across the street, two men in a Mercedes, taking pictures. Both worked for Emesto, but lived in the States.

"Gabriela, I figured we would be watched. We are going to meet someplace else, but first I need to get your tails off of us," explained Agent Batcker. "When we meet again, I will provide you with a different phone and surveillance equipment, which will allow us to track your every move."

"When are we going to be able to meet again?"

"Tomorrow morning. I want you to go buy new clothes. Leave your purse at the hotel, leave your phone, and anything you brought with you from Mexico," requested the agent, explaining trade-craft secrets.

He handed Gabriela a file folder. Inside the folder, a thin phone they would use to communicate with each other.

Chapter 56

A recent missing person's case came across Koi's desk. The missing person, Tiffany Cook. The team started to work the case, with a warrant issued for Professor Calkin's arrest.

Koi sent a text to Jordan to tell him they planned on arresting Calkins. He was incredulous; could not believe the turn of events.

With Calkins in custody, and being escorted back to New Orleans, Koi ordered agents to go through his house and his other property. Cadaver dogs would also search the plantation property.

Nothing showed up at the Baton Rouge residence. The FBI confiscated both his computer and laptop. All of his computers at his office were confiscated. The FBI tore apart both houses, finding nothing that would link the professor to the disappearances.

They did find plenty of sex toys, including a sex swing, at the plantation. The FBI ran DNA testing, hoping to find traces of any of the missing women.

After talking with the agents, Koi called Jordan. "Hi, love. Looks like I'm going to have a late night."

"I figured. Don't worry about the kids—your parents and I will take care of them. You handle your business with Heath," answered Jordan.

"Be ready for me when I get home, if you know what I mean, I need a release."

"You may need to wake me."

"Don't worry, I'll wake you. We may go outside somewhere because I may be a little louder tonight," said Koi.

By late afternoon, back down I-10 and the FBI offices in New Orleans, Koi arrived and requested Professor Calkins be brought into the interview room. He looked disheveled; his world turned upside down.

Sitting across from Koi, he looked scared, before asking, "Agent Blackthorn, can you please tell me what this is about? No one said a word to me except reading me my rights."

"Well, as you know we are looking into the disappearances of young women all over the South."

"What does that have to do with me?"

"Do you know Tiffany Cook?"

"Yes, I do. Why, did something happen to her?" One thing Professor Calkins understood was interrogation techniques. He answered a question with a question.

"We aren't sure. She is missing and we know you have spent time with her."

"What do you mean by spending time with her?"

"Romantically, she stayed the night at the plantation house a couple nights ago," as Koi slid pictures of Tiffany walking into the residence.

"How long have you been following me?"

"Your concern should be her whereabouts."

"I have no clue. She sent me a text, be home on Monday. I didn't ask her where she might be."

The banter between the two would continue for another two hours. Questions about the professor's travel habits and communicating with the missing girls. His mood changed from annoyance to outright fury. He asked for an attorney.

The lab technicians came in around 10 p.m. describing what they found at both houses. Nothing connecting the professor to the Southern Belle case. DNA testing would require more time before receiving results. Koi's intuition told her, *something is not right.*

The next morning, Friday, the professor's attorney made a motion in front of the judge to release his client. Becoming agitated with the motion, Koi assumed the attorney did not understand the seriousness of the crimes. The lab technicians found sexual flirtations between two of the missing women and the professor. The prosecuting attorney presented the data to the judge. The judge would ultimately agree with Koi, and continued to hold Professor Calkins.

After the proceedings, Koi, Professor Calkins, and his attorney met in an interview room. The professor offered information about his relationships with students, and the two missing women. He affirmed the relationships with the two missing women, but emphasized everything was consensual and he had never harmed any of them. The professor offered a compelling argument, and Koi listened intently.

One piece of evidence in the professor's corner: he had left Atlanta early in the morning, driving to Orlando, for a meeting with an old college friend. Cell phone pings collaborated this, and also showed Veronica used her phone the same morning. Koi called the professor's friend, who concurred with the professor's timeline.

Chapter 57

On an island away from the stress of school, Tiffany decided to take a few days off, traveling to Turks and Caicos. The FBI reached her, after learning from a friend about her whereabouts. She apologized for the inconvenience she'd caused. Dionte asked her about the relationship with Professor Calkins, informing her about his arrest. She informed the agent that indeed they currently had a sexual relationship, but it was consensual.

An hour later the professor was released. Angry, he told Koi, "You have violated constitutional rights. My attorney will be in touch."

Heading back to Baton Rouge to decompress, Tiffany called. "I'm so sorry you got arrested on my behalf—please forgive me," said a sullen Tiffany.

"Don't worry about it. I'm glad you are safe. Where did you go?"

"Turks and Caicos. I needed some time alone. I told the truth about our relationship," explained Tiffany.

The professor and Tiffany talked for another few minutes before she asked about coming over later in the night, after taking an early flight home. He told her to show up around midnight; he needed to do a couple of errands.

After things settled down, Koi called Dionte back to talk more about the details regarding Tiffany's departure. Koi was confused as to why a twenty-year-old girl would disappear and not tell her family about why or where. Going alone, in this day and age, made the excursion even more dangerous.

She wanted to talk to the young woman, but Dionte relented on the idea, expressing, "Allow the girl some time."

The case, now unsolved again, began to weigh on Koi. Jordan tried to console, with little effect. She cried on his shoulder, thinking she'd failed, with the weight on her shoulders. *These women are counting on her.*

The next day, quiet for Koi, Jordan, and the girls. On Sunday, void of practices and games, they went for a hike at Bogue Chitto National Wildlife Refuge. The 36,000-acre refuge allowed you to hike, canoe, or participate in other activities. Koi expressed she needed some time away from the case. Sensing some distance between them, Jordan decided against asking lots of questions. Instead he allowed Koi to enjoy the moment, the moment away from being an FBI agent.

One mile into the hike Jordan said, "Koi, don't be so hard on yourself; it wasn't a mistake to arrest Heath. You based your decision on the facts."

"I know you are trying to make me feel better, but right now, I think I failed."

"You didn't. Listen, Heath was a prime suspect, but now you need to move on. The fact is someone is out there kidnapping young women, and your job is to stop it."

"You sound like my old coach: 'You need to do this, you need to do that,'" snickered Koi, explaining her college coach's motivational speeches.

"Been there. My college coach once said, 'Failure is a great motivator.'" Jordan paused, allowing his words to sink in before adding, "Only if you act on it in a positive way. If you continue with self-doubt, failure will become the norm instead of success."

He twisted Koi around while grabbing her ass and gave her a long, passionate kiss.

Unexpected but perfect timing. "Wow, your coach didn't motivate you with kisses, did he?"

"No, this is my motivational tool. Until you get out of your funk, no more kisses or anything else."

"Oh, please, all I need to do is wink at you and you will give in," as they laughed, knowing the statement to be true.

"Maybe. Sarg told me the other day, it's a woman's world, and we are along for the ride."

"Very true. Let's save the rest of this for later tonight," as Koi winked at Jordan, who cracked a huge grin, acknowledging her innuendo. They walked for a couple more miles, talking about the upcoming events, and whether or not Jordan would be able to attend Osika's games.

He asked Koi if he thought it would be a good idea to sell his house. "You haven't asked me to marry you," said Koi in a joking manner. Jordan knelt down on his knee and took both of Koi's hands with his.

He pulled a ring from his back pocket. "Koi, would you marry me?"

Shaking, she said, "Yes, Jordan Matthews, yes," as Koi continued to shiver.

At home they brought the girls and her parents into the library. They made the announcement about the engagement. Koi's mom hugged her, sharing tears of joy. Felton got up, shook Jordan's hand, and hugged his daughter.

Not to be outdone, Osika wisecracked, "It's about time."

"Hey, you knew ahead of time because I asked you and Kitna," bellowed Jordan.

"Hold on a minute. You two kept a secret from me?" questioned Koi.

"Yeah, on a need-to-know basis, and you didn't need to know," replied Kitna.

Chapter 58

LSU President Mallory Youngstone summoned Professor Calkins into her office. She came to LSU by way of Oklahoma State University. In her three years on the job, she performed admirably while instituting numerous policies; both the students and the faculty applauded.

With the university attorney's present, President Youngstone asked a point-blank question, "Are the rumors true about you and students?"

The professor answered that all the relationships happened after the students graduated, a lie of course. The dialogue, all one-sided, continued. The president made the decision to suspend the professor with pay until a formal investigation could be conducted. A news conference scheduled for later in the day by the president informed LSU students, staff, and the general public about the professor's confinement by the FBI. Later in the evening a large group of students protested outside the president's home, to voice support for the professor.

The media requested the FBI answer questions about the case, by badgering Koi with question after question about the Southern Belle case, and her reasoning for arresting the professor. She defended every move. The press conference became tense at times, but Koi answered all of the media's questions.

Highlighting aspects of the case, she made a plea to the media. "This is about missing young women." Her attitude toward the media standoffish, she felt they were overstepping their journalistic bounds. The impromptu news conference ended when someone asked Koi about her relationship with Jordan.

The news conference over, Jordan called Koi. He thought she did an outstanding job handling the media, and their relationship none of their concern.

"Don't sweat the media. They are looking for something to sell," offered Jordan, trying to console Koi.

"I know. They could hamper the case if they dig in the wrong direction," said Koi, expressing her disapproval of media interference.

"Will you still be able to go on vacation if the case isn't finalized?"

"Yes, most likely, the only fly in the ointment. If we are close to nabbing someone I need to stay in town."

"I think you are close—keep pressing. One of Sarg's rules: 'The answer sometimes is right in front of you.'"

"A good rule to live by."

Koi finally spoke with Tiffany. They talked about the relationship with Professor Calkins, how it started, and if they were still together. Also, did he hurt her in any way? Tiffany, forthright with some of the information, but vague on other aspects. She did say, "He can be a freak, but nothing that caused pain."

The next question: Why did Tiffany use someone else's identity to leave the country? Her response, "I needed some time away. Think things over. My friend and I look like sisters."

Before hanging up, Koi said, "End your relationship with Professor Calkins. He offers nothing except a physical relationship."

"Are you still following him?"

"Not at this time," said Koi as they hung up the phone. The next couple of days went on without any new leads or hitches in the investigation. The media still hounded Koi, but she brushed them off at every turn, except one young lady reporter from Knoxville. A crime reporter who followed the case, Cassidy Ellis, she worked for the *Knoxville News Sentinel*. She became obsessed with the case of Kennedy Beacon, who had disappeared from Nashville, her interest stemming from Kennedy being a friend of a friend.

Cassidy searched disappearances all over the South and came up with a list of girls with similar MOs in their disappearances. Koi, not keen on the idea of an amateur sleuth, a reporter who might give out information that might destroy the case against any suspect. She called the reporter after receiving a message, with details of the missing girls' names.

"I'm looking for Cassidy Ellis. This is Special Agent Koi Blackthorn," said Koi.

"I'm Cassidy. Thank you for calling, Special Agent Blackthorn," replied Cassidy. She expressed her interest in the Kennedy Beacon case. After taking a moment before answering, Koi said Kennedy's disappearance is a part of the Southern Belle case.

An important detail, Kennedy's recent dating habits. "My friend tells me Kennedy is bi. The thing my friend said, she believed Kennedy had not dated a man in over five years."

"Did she say whether or not she was dating anyone at the time?"

"My friend offered nothing concrete, only she believed Kennedy began dating an older woman. She overheard a call, with Kennedy acting giddy, as my friend puts it. They planned a romantic getaway that weekend."

"No idea where exactly?"

"No. Please, Agent Blackthorn, find her, please." Koi could sense the hurt through the phone.

"Listen, I don't like to share details with reporters. If I share something, and ask for you to keep it off the record, you must give me your solemn promise you will. This is a one-way street. I want you to share with me anything you find out. I can't have you contaminating the case when we catch this person. By the way, call me Koi and this is my cell number."

"I don't like the idea of a one-way street, but I want you to find Kennedy."

Since the surveillance ceased, Professor Calkins felt comfortable inviting Tiffany over for the night. After a few drinks, the professor started to give Tiffany a shoulder rub, moving his hands down her back and squeezing her ass. He lifted her shirt, cupping her breasts from behind. The sensation was overwhelming; she wanted more. He picked her up and slid her pants off, leaving only her thong on. He placed his hand between her legs. She reached behind her back, undoing the professor's pants. As they dropped to the floor, he bent Tiffany over the back side of the couch, and pushed himself deep inside her. The pleasure mesmerizing for Tiffany. She role-played in her mind, about being taken by a serial killer. They would move to two other rooms, performing in different positions, finishing in the TV room.

Chapter 59

The killer approached from the wooded area behind Professor Calkins' plantation. The doors unlocked. By coming from a swampy area, using an ATV, and stopping a mile from the house, this provided the needed cover of silence. Sliding open a door in the back, both Tiffany and Calkins asleep, never noticed the killer.

Sneaking quietly to the edge of the bed, the killer used chloroform, knocking her unconscious. Next, making Tiffany incapacitated, after dragging the body outside, she was given a lethal dose of potassium chloride, with the killer watching her take her final breaths.

The next morning Professor Calkins felt groggy, before opening his eyes and gazing at the clock. With no Tiffany in sight, he figured she left sometime in the early morning.

A knock at the front door forced the professor to get out of bed. Standing by the front door, the Baton Rouge police department.

The professor opened the door, and the officer asked, "Health Calkins?"

"Yes, I am, what is this about?"

"Step inside, sir," demanded Officer Wallace.

"Yeah, yeah, what is this about?"

"We are looking for Tiffany. Do you have any idea where she might be?"

"Not this again. She left early this morning," replied the professor.

The officer informed him of his legal rights before showing the text, a picture of Tiffany in a shallow grave.

"Is this a joke? Come on," said a pissed-off Professor Calkins.

Officer Wallace placed the professor under arrest and escorted him to his vehicle. Wallace later called Koi, informing her about the arrest and finding Tiffany dead.

Koi showed up as the Baton Rouge tech teams were sifting through the crime scene. She asked for Officer Wallace, who took her to the body.

Glancing down, while putting her gloves on, "Any idea how she died?" asked Koi.

"Nothing definite, but I see bruising on the left arm, from a needle," offered the medical examiner.

"How long has she been dead?"

"About twelve to fourteen hours."

Koi asked Officer Wallace if they could have a private moment. The two of them walked about thirty yards from the body before Koi spoke.

"Did the professor say anything?"

"Nothing much. He seemed very surprised she was dead."

"Do me a favor and take bloodwork from the professor. I want all kinds of tissue samples, and want to know anything detectable in their bodies."

"The ME smelled some substance, but we will definitely get blood samples for a toxicology report," said Officer Wallace before continuing, "To me it makes sense the doctor knocked her out and killed her."

"I'm sorry, this is staged. Why would the professor send a text showing Tiffany after he killed her?"

"Guilt, who knows. I thought you were looking at this guy as a serial kidnapper anyways."

"I'm telling you this murder has been staged for our benefit." Koi went back over to the body and spoke with the ME. Walking further to the west she noticed raking; someone had tried to hide their tracks. She summoned the techs to take pictures and investigate the raking and possible tracks. Her next request, the chance to interview Calkins. Wallace relented at first but agreed. The FBI teams showed up an hour later, to gather evidence for a forensics analyst.

Chapter 60

Toxicology reports came back showing both Professor Calkins and Tiffany with traces of the Russian drug Raptor in their system. Welcoming news to Koi. She believed the professor's innocence; this set her theory in motion.

In interview room No. 2, Koi snickered. "Looks like we meet again, Professor Calkins. Tell me all the details about last night."

"I didn't kill Tiffany; I promise you," the professor said in a stern voice. He answered each question, with permission from his attorney. They covered all the details, from the time Tiffany arrived until they both fell asleep.

Begging for his recollection, Calkins said, "Agent Blackthorn, if I could remember, I would tell you. I remember falling asleep, and when I woke, she was not in bed."

"Can you see my dilemma here?" asked Koi, sitting back in her chair before adding additional comments. "You both fell asleep, yet the only evidence, a dead girl in your backyard."

"Why would I send a text of the murder scene?"

"I can't answer."

Koi told the professor they would be holding him for now until some other toxicology reports came in. She went back to New Orleans after the interview, believing the murder had been staged.

She called Jordan.

Scratching his head, Jordan said, "This is odd, Koi. The professor's phone was wiped clean of prints, according to my confidant inside the department."

"That does not make sense," replied a puzzled Koi.

"Exactly. You are going to send out a text showing a girl you murdered. Then you wipe the phone clean."

The FBI continued searching for clues, with Koi instructing all agents to set aside the Southern Belle case for the time being. By 3 a.m. they decided it was time to put things away for the night.

Jordan received a call; he had caught a case. Before he left, Koi hugged him.

"Text me when you get a chance."

"Don't worry—lots of coffee will get me through, and thoughts of you," said a smiling and exhausted Jordan as he left the house.

Another murder in New Orleans. TV crews and neighbors started to congregate with family members watching outside the ropes.

With Jordan as the lead detective, the murder revolved around a nineteen-year-old male walking home from his girlfriend's house around 2 a.m. He fell asleep, and after waking up, decided to head home. With his first class scheduled for 8, he wanted to be closer to school; he attended the University New Orleans. A young man with no gang affiliation, killed by a drive-by shooting. A Computer Science major, Antonio, the murdered victim, worked at a computer store to help pay for his college expenses.

The task of calling the victim's mom fell upon Sarg, who said he would make the call.

"Mom is coming over. I don't want her to see her son lying on the ground. Put him in the wagon now, please," demanded Sarg.

Jordan looked around, noticing a camera on the side of a house. He said, "That house has a security camera facing the road. I will find out if it is operational." Jordan walked over and knocked on the house. A couple minutes later an older gentleman answered the door and told Jordan the camera worked. The footage would be retrieved by the IT department.

After getting back to the office, Jordan found that the camera footage showed a license plate number. The car, registered to Janece Williams, with her address five blocks from the murder scene. Jordan and Sarg decided it was time to pay the young lady a visit.

Before they left, Jordan called Koi, telling her about the murder, a senseless murder. They talked about meeting up for lunch later.

"Kitna has regionals on Saturday," said Koi, switching gears to the weekend's events.

"Yes, I have to work early, but I believe I will be there."

"The house is on the right," said Sarg, with Jordan pulling up to the front of the house. The neighborhood, typical as any other, hardworking families, loved BBQ, jazz music, and their city.

Jordan knocked on the door; a young lady answered. "Good afternoon, I'm Detective Matthews and this is my partner Detective Jacobs. We are looking for Janece Williams."

"I am Janece. What is this about?" questioned the young lady as her mom approached the door.

"What is going on, baby?" said her mother.

"We are looking into a shooting a couple blocks over early this morning. Would you mind if we come in?"

"Yeah, I mind," replied the young woman, as she tried to slam the door in the officer's face before her mom stopped her from doing so.

"You stop, this instant," demanded her mother as she pushed her away, and proceeded to take over the conversation.

"Officers, what is this about?"

"We have a few questions, ma'am. Would you and your daughter be able to come with us to the station?" questioned Jordan.

"Can you tell me what this is about, first of all?"

"Janece's car was used in a drive-by shooting this morning, and we need to find out who was driving the car."

At that moment, the mother turned to her and began to demand answers, her fury pointed directly at her daughter for allowing her boyfriend to use the car.

"Shut up, Mom, you don't know what you're talking about," yelled back the angered daughter.

"Ma'am, step aside, please, we are going to place her under arrest and take her to the station. You can follow us if you would like," as Sarg walked in and told Janece to turn around while reading her rights and placing her in handcuffs.

"I want a lawyer," screamed the young lady, before being placed in the squad car.

Two hours later, with angered feelings, she sat across from the detectives. Her mother earlier explained how her boyfriend had used the car. She went on to tell the detectives that her daughter's boyfriend possessed a long rap sheet.

The detectives decided to bring the mother into the interview room. "Mom, get out of here! This doesn't concern you," yelled Janece, with spit coming from her mouth.

"You aren't going down for this. You listen real well, girl. I will make sure these officers find that loser," said her mother, pointing a finger at her daughter.

Janece was still uncooperative for the next hour, but the detectives were able to piece together evidence, including the fact that her boyfriend was driving the car at the time of the murder. A BOLO went out for the boyfriend and his friend.

The next day both of them were picked up after Janece contacted them with her cell phone. The officers triangulate his position, with the SWAT team arresting both men before they left town. The case, mistaken identity, three lives changed forever.

Chapter 61

The Baton Rouge police department received a call from the FBI, they provided the necessary evidence, Calkins could not have committed the murders. The Superintendent of the department called back with blistering comments. He did not plan on releasing the Calkins.

Koi, listening in on the call, spoke up, "If you do not release him, I will be on tv, explaining how you are holding an innocent man."

A little while longer Latrell Davis, from the Baton Rouge police department, called Jordan, to tell him how the FBI turned the entire department on its head, angered by the FBI requesting the release of Calkins. Wallace, according to Davis, wanted Koi to stay in her lane.

They laughed. "Let them know that if they ever come across her again, she will ask for an explanation, which lane should she stay in," said Jordan.

BOPD made a statement. They would be releasing the professor, per the FBI's request, with no other suspects under suspicion.

Watching the press conference, BOPD laid the blame on the FBI. The superintendent tried to tie the professor to the Southern Belle case, after the media learned what the FBI was calling the case. The department continued putting the blame on the FBI, for requesting the release of a murder suspect.

Wondering if she made the wrong call, Liz knocked on Koi's office door. Dr. Denkins' cell phone pinged in the same area as Elena's phone did before being shut off. This meant both of them were in the same vicinity.

'You can now place them in the same area, but not kidnapping, no matter the coincidence.' Koi requested the FBI start following every move of Dr. Denkins.

"Mom, can you pack a bag for me? I will be a part of one of the surveillance teams watching a suspect," asked Koi.

With the events of the day, after the FBI had been accused of letting a killer loose, Koi relaxed with a glass of wine, her mother sitting with her.

"You are angry; this is not good. Anger turned outward leads to destruction," said Catori.

"Mom, I feel like all these men are keeping me from arresting my suspect. First Jordan, now Baton Rouge police, and the deputy director called today. He thinks I need to be taken off the case."

"What did you say to him?" said Catori.

"Latrell spoke with him. He defended me and my work. He told the director if he steps in again, he would resign."

"You have people in your corner, including Jordan," Catori said. "The great spirit says: open your mind, your heart, and listen, and you will find the answer."

"Mom, others need to listen to *me*."

"What the spirit meant, think of those who are suffering. You need to think of the women, not the men putting up roadblocks," offered Catori.

"I understand now. Thanks, Mom."

"Your arrow is a weapon. Make sure your arrow hits the target." Catori reached for her daughter, pulling her close. "This moment needs calm leadership. You are here at this time, with this case, for a reason. You have been chosen by the spirit."

Planting devices all over the estate, Gabriela felt anxiety setting in. She pondered if this was the right move. The only place void of devices: the Intel Room, off-limits to everyone except a few trusted confidantes of her husbands.

Hoping to pick up conversations between Raul and others, the FBI handed Gabriela a new device, which could not be detected by the latest detection equipment. She found a secluded place outside, and called Paige. Using a coded messaging system, devised by Paige and Agent Powers, by means of soccer language.

"I set soccer balls out in the drill you suggested," explained Gabriela with one of her coded messages.

"Look forward to our competition in two weeks. Can't wait to see the kids," replied Paige on one occasion.

The FBI scrambled, putting together two operations, one to apprehend Destiny and the other to keep Gabriela safe. With the deputy director fearing the operation might spook Raul, and in retaliation, he would kill Gabriela and anyone else he deemed a threat. The operation would continue with a tight-knit group knowing the full apparatus.

As for protecting Gabriela, Agent Cattrell made sure only a handful of agents including the head of the FBI office in LA would know about the operation, and the reason for the meeting. He decided to only fill in some parts of the operation including the surveillance to Koi. The director feared that if Raul found out he may might a shot at Jordan or Koi.

The kidnapping case stalled, after the release of Calkins, Koi's intuition kept telling her that Bailey Denkins was her main suspect. Jordan pushed back at times, seeking evidence. They haggled over the coincidences, the ability for Denkins to carry out the kidnappings, and her resources.

Opening a folder, Jordan, found a possible missing piece. A bank account in Switzerland. The account belonged to Denkins, with $10 million in cash, bonds, and other securities being held inside. The account slipped the FBI until Liz found it. The doctor used an alias, one from her college days, Sophia Drakos, the name of her aunt who passed away during her freshman year in college. In college she opened two accounts using her aunt's name, both credit card accounts. She'd found the account by chance, and only after Liz interviewed a friend of Denkins in college, an old roommate.

The new evidence offered the financial means, but still nothing that showed Denkins did the kidnappings.

Chapter 62

By 8:30 a.m., Koi was on her second cup of coffee, when Agent Yukolvich knocked. "Yes, Brett, you have something?" questioned Koi.

Tasked with looking deeper into Denkins' background, he proceeded to offer his opinion. "She is clean. Nothing out of the ordinary, outside of her travels to different states. No tie-ins to the missing women."

"My gut is telling me she is involved, and we are missing something. Liz found the account in Switzerland. I believe there is a property here in Louisiana. She won't use her real name for the property. Find it, and we will find evidence of the missing women."

"Do you know of any other aliases she may be using?"

"Not at this time," replied Koi. Before Brett left, Koi added, "She may not be doing the kidnapping, but somehow…somehow she is a part of this."

Dionte came into Koi's office and closed the door. "I have something for you. Top secret. You cannot tell anyone, including Jordan. According to the NSA, they believe Raul's organization is following Jordan, listening to his calls and reading his texts," said Dionte.

"What the hell are you talking about?" demanded Koi.

"NSA believes Raul has agents following Jordan, and somehow, they have tapped his phone. This all pertains to the murder case, not you."

"Are my kids in danger, and what about my parents? Do I need protection?" questioned an angered Koi.

"No, it is a covert activity. They want to know what NOPD is up to, nothing more."

"So, what am I supposed to do?"

"Nothing. Act as if you don't know anything, and that is a direct order handed down from the top."

"Okay, I'll keep it to myself, but I need to know if my family is in any sort of danger. If I find out, or something happens, I will be the most unpleasant person on this God's given earth," relented Koi, explaining her position that family came first, not the FBI.

In a private conversation, Dionte shared the NSA intel with Sarg. He wanted the department on alert. One suggestion, allow NOPD to drive by Koi's place every three hours.

Going about her day, with her mind in overdrive after the revelation from Dionte, Koi thought about warning her parents without causing a panic. The other question? How to share the information with Jordan.

Outside alone on a picnic table with her thoughts, Koi looked down at her engagement ring. She wondered, *Are things moving too fast?* She loved Jordan, but his recent behavior brought second thoughts

Rubbing her eyes from lack of sleep, Liz stepped outside and noticed Koi sitting alone. "If you don't want to talk, I'm okay with not speaking. Sometimes you need to meditate."

"We can chat if you want," said Koi.

The women talked about life, their parents, and upbringing. Liz told Koi that her parents were not involved in her life much. Mom is a drug addict, and dad an alcoholic. She escaped her home life by staying in her room on the computer. If things became rough, she would head to the library, and on some occasions, sleep inside overnight.

"What city did you grow up in?"

"Burrillville, Rhode Island. Ever heard of it?'

"No."

"Small eastern town. Uppity people who believe they are better than everyone else," said Liz.

"Why did you leave?"

"Boyfriend wanted to move to New Orleans, job opportunity. Men, useless," explained Liz.

Koi could not agree more about the man comment. She transitioned, "How did we catch you?"

"I made a dumb move; one of your hackers was an agent. Two hours later the FBI is at my door."

"I'm happy you are on our team," said Koi.

The women went back inside. They needed each other, and after talking, would become friends for life.

The next couple of days produced no new leads. The FBI case became a surveillance case, watching Denkins every move, while other agents took her life apart.

Gabriela, through Paige, sent a coded message. "Team Capitan is planning a trip to America." The FBI did not know which airport Destiny would land at. They staked out Raul's airport, and planned on tracking the flight with radar. They needed resources on the ground to apprehend Destiny once she landed. They figured she would land somewhere in Louisiana. With Malisa's phone being tapped, the FBI knew Destiny had planned a meeting with her sister.

The FBI called Jordan around 3 a.m. They wanted NOPD to provide three teams, watching smaller airports.

Two day later radar showed the plane landing in fifteen minutes. The airport, in Lake Charles. With the sister staying the night in Lake Charles, the FBI and NOPD believed they were about to make a major arrest. As the plane approached, Agent Jackson told everyone to be ready. The plane taxied and came to a stop. When a car drove near the plane, the agents with four SUVs sprang into action.

By the time Destiny reached the third step down, the FBI agents surrounded the plane with four cars.

As Agent Nixon approached Destiny, he had a huge smile on his face, "Good morning, Destiny. He read Destiny her rights. "Do you understand these rights? Have I read them to you?"

"What is this about?" demanded Destiny, her anger evident.

"The NOPD is going to be here and tell you about their charges, which include murder," Agent Nixon continued with federal charges including drug trafficking. Defiant, abusive, and uncooperative, Destiny demanded to be let go. Sarg and Jordan showed up and explained the charges, including the murder of Jaron. She spat at them and started yelling about police brutality.

"Miss, you are making this difficult on yourself," said a calm Sarg.

Unwilling to cooperate, she continued kicking and screaming, while being loaded in the car.

"Well, young lady, you are going to have to answer for a lot of charges, starting with the murder of your cousin!"

"I don't know what you are talking about." She paused for a moment before adding, "I'm not going to be spending any time in jail and you can bank on it."

"We have you, and soon the FBI will bring down your boyfriend's organization," said Sarg in a sarcastic manner.

"Whatever, you got nothing. I want to call my lawyer!" demanded Destiny.

"You will get your chance to call your lawyer after we process you. This may take a couple of days. We are busy recording all of your co-conspirator's statements, implicating you," chuckled Sarg.

"I'm done with this—you can kiss my ass!"

The detectives processed Destiny. She called her lawyer, who called Raul. He became enraged. After telling Emesto of the arrest, he yelled, "Find the mole!" Problem, the mole had left the day before for LA.

Destiny's lawyer showed up and requested his client be released at once. Sarg told the lawyer, "Your client has been arrested for first-degree murder. She will be spending the rest of her life in prison. See you at the arraignment tomorrow," said Sarg, leaving the lawyer to scream at other officers at the front desk.

Singing out loud, "I feel good, da, da, oh so good," Sarg retreated to his office.

The officers laughed, realizing who the lyrics were meant for.

Chapter 63

Sitting together watching the late-night news, Koi and Jordan enjoyed the coverage. National news outlets along with websites covered the arrests.

"I love you," said Koi.

"I love you. I am sorry about not believing you on Denkins. Can I help in any way?"

"No, don't worry, we will do this together."

Little did she know, they would work together on future cases.

With her phone on vibrate, Koi looked at her phone after the news ended. All the calls from the same number, Liz. She called her back. After learning about disposable phones, Liz tracked the phones, with one of them pinging west of St. Francisville, and being used by Denkins.

"Keep tracking the phone," said Koi.

The next day Koi informed Dionte about the phone, and Liz tracking it.

"How did she find out about this phone?" asked Agent Cattrell.

"Liz learned about phones coming from Jamaica. She tracked this particular phone to Dr. Denkins. The phone contacted our last kidnapped victim, Elena," offered Koi.

"Are you sure this phone belongs to her? This shows the phones being delivered to Jeff Peterson," questioned the agent. He did not want the repeat of the Calkins arrest.

"Give me a couple of agents and allow Liz to keep tracking. Plus, allow me to do some covert observation," demanded Koi.

"I won't give you any agents, but you can follow her, and Liz can keep digging, okay?" as Dionte continued to explain his position. She thanked him for giving her some leeway, with the understanding this would not be a long-term situation, and she needed to come up with evidence soon.

The next day, Koi headed to St. Francisville, with Liz back at the office tracking Denkins every move. They figured she would not be able to lose them.

The local police station provided services for the surrounding area. Koi called ahead to speak with one of the detectives. She asked about any secluded homes or old mansions. The officers offered no recollection of such a place. They did tell her about an abandoned cemetery, with reports of strange happenings; some of the locals passed it off as folklore. They provided directions, since a GPS would be useless. She made the decision to drive to the cemetery.

Area residents knew about the cemetery, but never visited. Two hours later, still unable to find the cemetery, Koi thought about giving up. After another mile, she found a trail, one with no access for her car. She decided to walk the path, and soon found a gate, locked. Behind the gate, a mausoleum, which looked decrepit. Hopping the fence, she peered around the mausoleum, taken aback by the site of a new gravestone. As she approached, the name on the tombstone, Kennedy. Her mind racing, she walked around and found sixteen burial plots from more recent times, the earliest, 1998.

Unable to get a signal, she left the area.

"Dionte, I've found it. I've found the spot. All of my kidnapped victims are buried here," said a stunned Koi.

"What the hell are you talking about?" followed a perplexed Dionte.

"I'm at an abandoned cemetery, and it is full of graves with names of my kidnapped victims on them. I'm telling you this is it—you need to send the lab people up here now," demanded Koi.

"Okay, okay, calm down. Listen, I need you to leave now. Take a couple of pics, but get your ass out of there now, and that is an order," said Dionte.

"What the hell are you talking about?" questioned a peeved Koi.

"Listen, you don't know who or what is around there, and I don't need you disappearing as well. I need you to get out of there and contact me as soon as you get to the nearest town."

"All right, I understand. We need to put together a group to take charge of this place and make sure whomever comes here is arrested on the spot," said an unrelenting Koi.

"I will, but we need to keep this low-key. We still don't have the suspect, only the burial site," said Dionte, challenging Koi to listen to him.

"Okay, I'm leaving. I'll call in about forty minutes," said Koi as she assured Dionte she would be careful.

Chapter 64

On the way back to New Orleans, Koi called Liz to check on Denkins. After receiving direct orders not to share her findings with anyone, she needed to be vague about her questions.

"On campus all day," offered Liz.

"Do we have someone keeping tabs on her all night?"

"Yes. We will know if she travels anywhere."

"I'm driving home now. Call me if she leaves Baton Rouge."

A group call, which included superiors in DC as well as Dionte. They made the decision to send some help. Walking into the office, Dionte asked Koi to come to his office. "Can you sit down, please?"

"We need to stay on top of this!" said Koi.

"The director wants to monitor the cemetery; they do not want to move on it or arrest Denkins."

"Are you freaking kidding me? They want us to monitor the cemetery?" screamed Koi as she felt like this might be a repeat of the Jamaican case.

"This is a direct order and you will be fired if you don't comply," said Dionte as he continued, "They are sending Special Agent Forsome from DC. His experience and ability to stay covert, they feel this is necessary."

"Bullshit. They are going to let some asshole receive the credit, or worse, screw up the investigation. I am a capable agent," yelled Koi.

"Koi, please sit down and calm down," as Dionte moved his hand in a gesture toward the chair in front of his desk. "I am on your side, and believe me no one is going to screw this up or take credit," responded Dionte.

"They don't believe in me. They want a man, not a woman, to collar the perp," said a sullen Koi.

With past experience an indicator, Koi believed the men running the FBI became disillusioned when women become lead investigators. The director showed little empathy toward women agents.

"You are the one in charge. Any arrests will be yours," suggested Dionte. "I know Agent Forsome. He is low-key and not looking for recognition." Dionte paused for a moment before continuing, "He will be here in the morning, and we are to brief him on everything with the case."

"Dionte, you have never done me wrong, but I swear to you if this goes wrong, I will bring everyone down, and I don't care if it costs me my job," said an irate Koi as she walked out.

Koi ran into Liz before leaving the office. "Koi, I'm glad I caught you. Got a minute?" asked Liz.

"What's up, and understand I'm not in the mood for games," asked Koi.

"The transmitter for Dr. Denkins' car shows the car moving, but her phone is at home."

"Can you track her from your house?" questioned Koi.

"I can track her from my home. I have my laptop hooked up, so I will know exactly where she is located at all times," replied Liz.

"Contact me if she heads toward St. Francisville," said Koi.

Dr. Denkins parked her car at a parking garage near campus. She walked over to RightWay rental car company, and picked up the car she rented for the next couple of days. She drove to her hidden house. With the heat coming down, time to eliminate the latest kidnapped victim.

Chapter 65

Agent Murphy arrived at the office by 5 a.m., with Koi arriving not much later. They used Dionte's office to go over the case. They were forced to inform the agents about the tracking device. Dionte, furious at first, but let it go as he was trying to stay focused on the task at hand. They all agreed, Koi needed to stay as the lead investigator.

Shuffling through papers, Murphy offered, "This is outstanding detective work. If they take you off the case, I will walk away. There are no other agents who would have suspected Denkins for the kidnappings."

Koi emphasized the FBI needed to make a move on Dr. Denkins within the next couple of days. She left the meeting extremely agitated. With Fordsome believing in her, she paused with the idea of calling the director.

"I got something for you," expressed Liz, adding, "I think she is holding someone hostage. I cannot find her right now," revealed Liz. Laying out a map on Koi's desk, the women looked for a secluded area; problem, the state offered numerous secluded areas, case in point the cemetery.

By triangulating the phone and areas, Liz figured the best place to start, south of Spillman.

"Let's look at this from a logical standpoint. I know the cemetery is here," said Koi, providing Liz with information about the gravesites.

"This is a starter, but she may be killing them someplace else, and transferring the bodies to the cemetery," replied Liz.

"I think I need to follow her for the next couple of days. The problem is the higher-ups don't want me to be close to her," countered Koi as she looked at Liz shaking her head.

"This is such bullshit. Let me guess, some righteous man or men made this decision," sarcastically said Liz.

She sat down to think for a moment. "I could really use Jordan's help on this one," she blurted out loud.

"Think he can get a couple days off?" questioned Liz. The problem involving Jordan would be a big no-no with FBI protocol.

Her mother's words now more than ever played in her head.

The Choctaw heritage came to the surface. *Women are strong and should never back down in the face of danger.*

"I'm going to ask him—I need him with me," said a determined and defiant Koi.

"Where do you think we should start?" asked Liz.

"Well, you keep digging up what you can. I'm going to call Jordan and ask him if he can help." She walked outside, making sure her conversation remained secret. Twenty minutes later she walked back in with a smile on her face. Jordan had agreed to help.

Chapter 66

Following Denkins, a covert operation. By keeping Koi from the surveillance detail, this allowed Jordan to ride with her. She received permission to walk through the cemetery, while others followed Denkins.

About ten minutes outside of Baton Rouge, Koi's phone rang. Dionte on the other end. "Hello, Dionte, what's up?"

"Dr. Denkins knows we are following her." Knowing full well that Koi would blow up, he braced himself for the eventual verbal abuse.

"What happened?" questioned Koi.

"Murphy got too close, and she confronted him." For Koi, this was her fear. DC had made the decision; now the possibility of blowing the case became real.

"I told…," said Koi in a low tone. "Listen, I'm almost to Baton Rouge. I'm going to check into the hotel. I'll call you back."

"I don't believe this crap. Things got harder for us. We need to make sure we stay out of sight. Denkins knows we are onto her," blurted out Koi before sighing.

"What happened, did she make someone?" said a confused Jordan.

"She made our agent, the so-called experienced agent," responded Koi.

"I don't understand why they didn't allow you to finish this case," said Jordan. The next few hours were spent on the phone with Dionte and Liz, trying to rekindle the surveillance.

"Hi, Liz." Before she could say another word, Liz hysterically said, "She is on the move."

"Where?"

"Not sure yet—looks like downtown," said Liz, providing what she knew of Dr. Denkins' current movements. Koi told Liz to keep monitoring her movements. They planned to follow her the rest of the day. Before they left the room, Koi called Agent Murphy—no answer. *Guess he checked out after Denkins confronted him.*

Keeping their distance, with help from Liz, they followed Denkins. The possibility of an accomplice disposing of the bodies, or the doctor stopping, became prevalent. Later in the day, Dionte replied to a message. The judge would not allow warrants until ironclad evidence was submitted. With the previous cover blown, Denkins would be cautious.

Around 8 p.m. Denkins left her school office. Something strange, however; tracking her phone showed the device still at the office, with her route, not heading home.

"Where the hell is she going?" asked Koi out loud. The detectives, fifteen minutes from Denkins' current location, feared losing her.

"Take a left on Market," said Koi. Jordan knew Baton Rouge like the back of his hand.

"Where is she now?" he questioned.

"Off Groom Road. Step on it—we can't lose her," demanded Koi.

"We won't lose her," replied Jordan. They tracked her as she made a right onto Hovey Avenue. The car stopped, which forced Jordan and Koi to cautiously turn down the road. They slowed down, noticing the rental car in a driveway.

The home looked abandoned. At a loss as to what to do, they decided to sit nearby. Liz called asking why they'd stopped. After learning the address of the house, Liz did some checking. The house was owned by a corporation, with Denkins as the corporate owner. Being discreet, Koi walked a hundred yards from the house, trying to get a closer look inside. A car drove from the backside of the garage, traveling toward a farmer's field.

Waving for Jordan to pick her up, he drove alongside with Koi getting in. "We need to follow her—she is using a different car."

He kept the lights off, which allowed him to follow her headlights. Denkins turned on Highway 61 and headed north. Following from a distance, Koi stayed on the phone with Liz. The map showed lots of wooded areas as they turned on Mahoney Road. Fifteen minutes later, the car turned down Mertz Road. With very few homes, the question of a setup came to light.

"I can't see the lights," yelled Jordan, fearing he'd lost the car.

"What? Catch, up damn it!" yelled back Koi.

"There is nothing there. I'm telling you she got off somewhere after the bend."

"Turn around. Let's backtrack to the point we last saw the car," requested Koi. Jordan turned the car around and they went slowly searching for a trail or hidden drive.

"Go slower, maybe we can see some tire tracks," as Koi rolled down her window while setting her laptop aside. Two miles down the road she yelled for Jordan to stop. She got out of the car and walked over to tire tracks heading into the woods. The tracks ended in the woods. She walked into the woods, and noticed a gate covered with brush to make it look like it was natural.

Walking back to the car, "Time to park the car. There is a secret gate, covered with brush."

Opening the trunk, they retrieved a shotgun, two other weapons, and backpacks. Before they set off on their trek, they called Dionte, letting him know their location. He replied that other FBI teams with dogs would be an hour away.

Koi and Jordan used hand signals as they walked down a two-tire road. The phones showed no reception; they would be alone. Jordan wondered if the road led them to a drug or moonshine operation. They continued for another hour, in the dark. Koi held her hand, wanting Jordan to stop. He was twenty yards behind her, watching her six.

She waved him forward; in the distance the outline of a structure. They needed to cross a bridge, with a house four hundred yards beyond the bridge. After they crossed the bridge, they both carefully approached the house. Koi noticed a figure walking inside the house, but could not make out if it was Denkins or not.

Approaching the house, Denkins walked outside. The detectives stayed still, fearing booby traps.

While retrieving a medical bag, Koi jumped up and yelled, "Freeze, Dr. Denkins!"

She froze for the moment, then hurried inside.

"Freeze," screamed Koi before she fired two shots, missing the target. Jordan ran toward the house, with Denkins slamming the door behind her. Both Jordan and Koi carefully closed in. They motioned to each other, with Jordan kicking the door in, with Koi as backup.

He jumped inside to one knee; she followed, looking to her left. They cleared the rooms together, first the kitchen area, a living room, before heading to a bedroom. They found Elena in the bedroom, alive, breathing erratically. Believing Elena was no longer in danger, they searched for Denkins. She disappeared, using a four-wheeler.

The FBI showed up and sealed off the entire area. A medical doctor checked on Elena; she could not recall the last two days.

A worldwide manhunt began, with all federal and state agencies on the lookout for Denkins. Koi later learned that Denkins had flown out of the country, last known destination, Cuba. They lost track of her after she landed in Havana. Her accounts all closed with the money transferred to unknown overseas accounts. The two houses now belonged to a brother, who had no idea about his sister's current location. Denkins disappeared, with no trace.

In a private meeting with the director, Koi, punctuated her feelings. "You BASTARDS F'd this up! I should go to the papers, but I am going to be a team player—this time. You almost cost a young woman her life, and I will never forgive you for it."

The director confronted her with a stern warning. She paused. and landed a right cross to his chin, knocking him unconscious. The president intervened, forgiving Koi, with no reprimand, but asked for her to never hit the director again. The director, embarrassed, did his best to keep the altercation, or ass-kicking, under wraps.

Once the FBI processed the cemetery, they found sixteen graves. All the bodies returned to their families, with Elena reunited with hers. Congressional hearings laid blame on the FBI, but no agents faced discipline as Congress didn't want to make a sizable reprimand for the fear of the press looking deeper into the competency of the FBI. Questions from the press and the families only produced half answers or more questions. Koi believed that she would cross paths with Dr. Denkins again.

In mid-December, Koi and Jordan, along with the girls, enjoyed a great time on the beaches in the Cayman Islands. From a distance, watching Dr. Denkins.

CPSIA information can be obtained
at www.ICGtesting.com
Printed in the USA
JSHW031603050223
37168JS00003B/18

9 781958 878149